Murder with Reservations

····································

A DEAD-END JOB MYSTERY

Elaine Viets

OBSIDIAN
Published by New American Library, a division of
Penguin Group (USA) Inc., 375 Hudson Street,
New York, New York 10014, USA

Penguin Group (Canada), 90 Eglinton Avenue East, Suite 700, Toronto,
Ontario M4P 2Y3, Canada (a division of Pearson Penguin Canada Inc.)
Penguin Books Ltd., 80 Strand, London WC2R 0RL, England
Penguin Ireland, 25 St. Stephen's Green, Dublin 2,
Ireland (a division of Penguin Books Ltd.)
Penguin Group (Australia), 250 Camberwell Road, Camberwell, Victoria 3124,
Australia (a division of Pearson Australia Group Pty. Ltd.)
Penguin Books India Pvt. Ltd., 11 Community Centre, Panchsheel Park,
New Delhi – 110 017, India
Penguin Group (NZ), 67 Apollo Drive, Rosedale, North Shore 0632,
New Zealand (a division of Pearson New Zealand Ltd.)
Penguin Books (South Africa) (Pty.) Ltd., 24 Sturdee Avenue,
Rosebank, Johannesburg 2196, South Africa

Penguin Books Ltd., Registered Offices:
80 Strand, London WC2R 0RL, England

Published by Obsidian, an imprint of New American Library, a division of
Penguin Group (USA) Inc. Previously published in a New American Library
hardcover edition.

First Obsidian Printing, May 2008
10 9 8 7 6 5 4 3 2

Copyright © Elaine Viets, 2007
All rights reserved

OBSIDIAN and logo are trademarks of Penguin Group (USA) Inc.

Printed in the United States of America

For the hotel maids—
the people we don't see but do need

ACKNOWLEDGMENTS

Special thanks to the staff at the Holiday Inn Express in Highland, Illinois. This hotel has earned its reputation for excellence. Manager Lori Huelsebusch, Julie Genteman and Justin Gibbons at the front desk, and the housekeeping staff of Jan Bryant, Ronie Hanson, Sharon Smith, Cindy Ford, and LeAnne Shoot gave me excellent advice and careful instructions in the arts of dusting, vacuuming, and bed making.

Their hotel in no way resembles the Full Moon, an imaginary hotel in another place and time.

Thanks also to Nancy Genteman, who drove me around Highland and took me to dinner at Farmers Restaurant & Bakery, which has fried chicken and green beans almost as good as my grandmother's.

I wish I could thank all the booksellers who helped with my books, but there isn't room. Please know that I am grateful for your help and handselling. Books are sold with love and recommendations, and you've given me lots of both.

Thanks to my husband, Don Crinklaw, who uses his English-teacher abilities when he reads the manuscript, and his acting abilities when he says it's the best yet.

Thanks to my agent, David Hendin, who always takes my calls.

Special thanks to Kara Cesare, one of the last of the real editors. I really appreciate her careful readings and editing. Thanks also to her assistant, Lindsay Nouis, to the NAL copy editor and production staff, and to the folks who do the terrific covers.

Many people helped with this book. I hope I didn't leave anyone out.

Particular thanks to Detective R. C. White, Fort Lauderdale Police Department (retired), and to ATF Special Agent Rick McMahan. Any mistakes are mine, not theirs.

Thanks also to Susan Carlson, Valerie Cannata, Colby Cox, Jinny Gender, Karen Grace, Kay Gordy, Jack Klobnak, Bob Levine, and Janet Smith, and to Carole Wantz, who could sell air conditioners in the Arctic.

Once again, thanks to the librarians at the Broward County Library and the St. Louis Public Library who helped with my research. I couldn't write this without your help.

Special thanks to librarian Anne Watts, who let me borrow her six-toed cat, Thumbs, for this series. Check out his picture on my Web site at www.elaineviets.com.

CHAPTER 1

The young couple looked like inept burglars sneaking through the lobby of Sybil's Full Moon Hotel in Fort Lauderdale. They were both dressed in black, which made them stand out against the white marble. At their wedding two days ago, they'd been slim, golden and graceful, trailing ribbons and rose petals through the hotel.

Now they moved with the awkward stiffness of amateur actors trying to look natural. The bride's black crop top exposed a midsection sliding from sexy to sloppy fat. The groom's black T-shirt and Bermudas failed the test for cool. They were boxy rather than baggy. He looked like a Grand Rapids priest on vacation.

The honeymooners avoided the brown plastic grocery bag swinging between them, carefully ignoring it as it bumped and scraped their legs. That screamed, "Look at me." They stashed the bag behind a potted palm while they waited for the elevator.

"Red alert," Sondra at the front desk said into her walkie-talkie. She was calling Denise, the head housekeeper. "The honeymoon couple just passed with a suspicious grocery bag. They're getting out on the third floor."

"I'll check them out," Denise said. She was stocking

her cleaning cart with sheets and towels in the housekeeping room.

Denise turned to her coworker Helen Hawthorne. "We've caught the honeymooners red-handed. I'm going to investigate. You stand by as a witness. I'm rolling."

Rhonda, the third hotel maid, squawked almost as loud as the walkie-talkie. "I'm coming, too. This affects my life." Rhonda, stick-thin and excitable, ran around the cart like a dog yapping at a car.

"Quiet, please," Denise said.

Rhonda shut up at this stately squashing.

A woman of substance, Denise and her cart rolled down the hall with slow deliberation. Helen followed. Rhonda skittered at the rear, skinny body rigid with rage, red hair flying. She looked like an electric floor mop.

As the bridal couple stepped out of the elevator, Denise moved majestically past them, bumping the groom with her massive cart. The grocery bag slipped to the floor. Cans and bottles clattered on the carpet. The young woman flushed scarlet. The young man stuttered apologies, even though the accident was Denise's fault.

"Here, let me help," Denise said, reaching for a bouncing bottle.

"And me." Helen corralled a rolling can and stuffed it back in the grocery bag. Rhonda folded her skinny frame to pick up a brown plastic container.

Once everything was back in the bag, the young couple ran for their room. Denise waited for the slam of their dead bolt. Then her cart rumbled solemnly back to the housekeeping room.

Rhonda and Helen crowded inside the room. Rhonda's pale face was set with furious determination. "If you think I'm—" she said.

"Shush," Denise said. "I have to make my report to the front desk."

The walkie-talkie squawked like an angry parrot. Denise talked through the static. "Sondra, I saw two cans of whipped cream, two squeeze bottles of Hershey's syrup and no evidence of ice cream."

"Suspicions confirmed," Sondra said through the electric crackle.

Rhonda started wailing like a storm siren. "Oh, no. I'm not cleaning whipped cream *and* chocolate out of their Jacuzzi." Angry brown freckles stood out on her pasty face. "The whipped cream alone took me a solid hour. I had to climb inside the tub to clean it. I'm calling in sick tomorrow."

"The honey on the sheets was bad enough," Helen said. "Sticky stuff put me off my breakfast toast. How many more nights are the food lovers here?"

"A whole week," Denise said. "Maybe now that they know we know, they won't use the whipped cream and chocolate."

"They'll use it," Rhonda said. "Once a couple gets on the sauce, they won't stop."

"At least they've stayed clear of the produce," Denise said. She reminded Helen of a vegetable goddess. Her broad bosom was twin cabbages, her tight white hair was a cauliflower, and her powerful arms were blue-ribbon zucchini.

"Maybe they'll have a fight," Helen said hopefully.

"Hah," Rhonda said. "Those types never do. They just bring in weirder and grosser stuff, and we have to clean it up. And they never tip."

"If you want your job, you'll be here tomorrow at eight thirty," Denise said.

The head housekeeper silenced any further discussion with a glare. Her massive arms maneuvered the cart out the door. "Helen and Rhonda, take the third floor. Cheryl will work the second floor, and I'll do one."

"I hate three," Rhonda said, when Denise had trundled out of earshot. "It's the hottest and dirtiest floor in the hotel."

"And we're the newest workers," Helen said.

"After two years, I'm entitled to some consideration,"

Rhonda said. She yanked their cleaning cart so hard it smacked the door frame. "Denise saves the best jobs for herself. She cleans the lobby and the free breakfast room. They're easy."

"I don't think mashed bananas in the carpet are any easier to clean up than whipped cream in the Jacuzzi," Helen said. "The lobby's white marble and glass show every scuff and fingerprint, and people leave disgusting things in the fountain. They're supposed to make a wish and throw in money, not half-eaten candy bars."

"You missed the kid who threw in his baby brother and wished he'd drown. Sondra had to leap the front desk and do a lifeguard rescue in the lobby. Ruined her good blouse."

The memory of Sondra's loss cheered Rhonda. The woman ran on resentment. She was an odd creature with a round white face like a cocktail onion. Her vibrant red hair seemed to suck the color out of the rest of her. Helen thought she was plain, but she saw men stare at Rhonda. They found something about her bony body compelling.

"We're not going to get anything done standing around yammering," Rhonda said. "Might as well get started."

"What's the room count today?" Helen said.

"Full house," Rhonda said, checking her sheet. "All twenty rooms on this floor are occupied: seventeen queens, two kings, and the honeymoon suite." Thirty-seven beds and a foldout couch, twenty refrigerators, twenty-one toilets, twenty tubs, and the dreaded Jacuzzi. Sixty-five mirrors and sixty wastebaskets. Twenty carpets to vacuum and twenty-one bathroom floors to mop.

"Checkouts versus stay-overs?" Helen asked.

That was the crucial question. After the guests checked out, the rooms required a deep cleaning. Even the insides of the drawers were dusted. For stay-overs, the maids scrubbed the bathrooms, made the beds, and emptied the wastebaskets. If they were lucky, guests piled suitcases, clothes and papers on all the furniture, and it couldn't be dusted. More stay-overs meant a shorter cleaning day.

"Six stay-overs," Rhonda said.

Fourteen checkouts. A long day. More sore muscles. Helen had worked at the hotel one week and she was just beginning to get over the back pain and muscle aches. She still winced when she had to kneel at the tub or reach for a mop. Cleaning hotel rooms required back-breaking amounts of bending, stooping and lifting. After her first day Helen went home at three thirty in the afternoon and curled up with a heating pad and a bottle of Motrin. She woke up at seven the next morning, feeling like she'd been stomped in an alley.

Helen figured she was combining work with working out. She wouldn't have to waste time exercising when she got home. She'd have more time to sit by the pool and drink.

"Our first room is a stay-over," Rhonda said. She maneuvered the cart so it blocked the door, then knocked. "Hello? Anyone home?" Rhonda pounded and shouted until Helen thought she overdid it.

"I'm not taking any chances," Rhonda said between shouts. "Not since I surprised that naked geezer getting out of the shower. He was too deaf to hear me knock."

"Ever see any flashers?" Helen asked.

"All the time," Rhonda said. "It's always the guys with the little weenies. A man with something worth seeing never shows it."

Satisfied that the room was empty, Rhonda opened the door with her passkey card. The room looked like an explosion at a rummage sale. Dirty clothes and smelly shoes littered the floor. Shirts and shorts spilled out of suitcases. Hamburger bags and drink cups cluttered the dresser. Something crunched under Helen's foot.

"What's that?" Helen asked. She was afraid to look.

"Cheerios," Rhonda said. "Usually means there's a baby in the room. People with little kids are big slobs."

"Is that a diaper on the bedspread?" Helen said.

"Yep. A dirty one. People use those spreads for diaper-changing stations, among other things." Rhonda pulled off the bedspread and piled it with the clean pillows on a chair.

"Yuck," Helen said. "Shouldn't we throw the spread in the wash?"

"No. Our bedspreads get cleaned every two weeks."

Helen's stomach lurched.

"Hey, we're better than most hotels," Rhonda said. "But I'd sooner sleep in a Dumpster than on a hotel spread."

"Why didn't they put the diaper in the wastebasket?" Helen said.

"That's on top of the TV to keep it away from the baby."

"Well, I'm glad this room is a mess," Helen said. "There's less for us to clean. We can't dust around all that junk. How do you want to divide the work?"

"I'll make the beds. You take the bathroom."

Rats. Helen hated cleaning bathrooms. Half the human race wasn't housebroken, and people shed worse than long-haired dogs. This bathtub was a hairy horror. Wet towels turned the floor into a swamp. Helen picked them up by the corners and prayed the brown stains were makeup. She didn't have much time to brood. Helen and Rhonda had exactly eighteen minutes to finish each room.

The next room was a checkout. The smell of sweat and smoke slugged them when they walked in the door. Cigarette-butt mountains overflowed the ashtrays. Helen counted eighteen beer cans tossed near the wastebasket. Two made it into the can.

"A male smoker," Rhonda said. "The worst kind of slob."

"How do you know it's a guy?" Helen said.

"Look at the john. I swear I'm going to paint targets on the toilets. Oh, man. This is so disgusting."

"What?" Helen asked.

"The guy ate peanuts and threw the shells on the floor. Peanut shells take forever to vacuum out of the carpet. You know, I can understand people thinking, 'I'm on vacation and I'm going to enjoy myself.' So they behave like total slobs and wreck the room. But if they're going to indulge, at least tip. Some women leave a couple of bucks for the privilege of throwing their towels on the floor. But men expect to be picked up after. Men are pigs."

"The men in this hotel are," Helen said. She didn't think Phil was a pig, but this was no time to praise her nearly perfect boyfriend. Rhonda wanted to rant. Helen didn't mind. A raging Rhonda cleaned faster. The two women had the room done in eighteen minutes flat, peanut shells and all.

They spent the next two hours companionably cleaning and complaining, until they were in the zone. That was when they moved through the rooms, swift and wordless, creating their own tidy ballet. Rhonda did the beds. Helen did the bathrooms. Rhonda dusted. Helen cleaned the mirrors. Rhonda vacuumed. Helen mopped. The room was done and they were on to the next one.

By two o'clock they had three rooms to go. One was a checkout. One was occupied. The last was 323, the hotel's most notorious room. Whenever anything went wrong, it was always in 323. This was the room with the loud parties. Wives caught unfaithful husbands and started bitch-slapping battles in 323. People did drugs and threesomes in that room. One man killed himself with pain pills.

Some staffers thought the room was jinxed. Others believed the problem was the location. Room 323 was near the back exit to the parking lot, so guests thought they could sneak in and out. But the security cameras caught them lugging in giant coolers or hiding little Baggies, smuggling in old hookers or underage girls. The guests in 323 were drunk, loud, rude—or all three.

Room 323 was a smoking room, and even on a quiet day it was the dirtiest of all.

"Wonder what's waiting for us today," Rhonda said.

"It can't be any worse than the dirty diaper on the bedspread," Helen said.

"Trust me, it can," Rhonda said.

Before they could find out, there was a walkie-talkie squawk from Sondra at the front desk. "The woman in 223 says there's water running down her walls," she said.

"Did you say water on the walls?" Rhonda shook the walkie-talkie, in case it had garbled the words.

"You heard right," Sondra said. "She thinks it's coming from the room upstairs."

"That would be 323," Rhonda said.

"Of course it would," Sondra said.

"I'll look into it," Rhonda said, with a martyred sigh.

She knocked and pounded louder than ever on room 323, but the only response was silence. This wasn't a peaceful quiet. It felt ominous. But Helen knew the room's deadly reputation.

Rhonda snicked open the door with her key card. They heard the running water the same time as it sloshed over their shoes in an icy wave. Cold water was roaring into the bathtub full force and rushing over the tub's sides in a man-made Niagra. The bathroom floor was flooded.

Rhonda waded into the bathroom. "Look at this," she moaned as she turned off the faucet. "We'll be in here till midnight."

Helen sloshed past the disaster area into the dimly lit bedroom. At first she wondered why someone had left a pile of pillows and a Persian lamb stole on the unmade bed. Then she realized she was looking at acres of white, doughy skin. A broad back and broader bottom were carpeted with curly black hair. The hair wandered down the backs of the meaty thighs and across the upper arms. There were little hairy outbreaks on the fingers and toes.

A naked man was lying facedown on the bed.

"Not another suicide!" Rhonda shrieked like a lost soul. "I can't take it."

Rhonda's screeches jabbed at Helen like a rusty knife. The maid had turned into a creature from a horror movie. Her pale face was corpse white and her long red hair looked like a curtain of blood.

Rhonda couldn't stop screaming, but her frantic shrieks did not wake this man. Helen didn't think anything would.

CHAPTER 2

....

"Helen, call 911," Denise said. "Tell them we need an ambulance."

Helen's supervisor seemed to materialize in the sopping chaos of room 323. Rhonda's shrieks were hitting Helen like hatchet blows. She couldn't think. She couldn't move, but she wanted to run. The same two sentences chased each other inside her head: I've found another body. The cops will find me and so will my ex-husband.

A drop of sweat landed on Helen's arm with a tiny plop. Soon it was rolling off her in the steamy room. The air conditioner was off, the window was sealed, and the temperature had to be ninety. Helen could almost hear the mold growing in the warm, swampy carpet. The air smelled foul, like something had d—

Helen put the brakes on that train of thought. She tried to avoid the monstrous sluglike body on the bed, but it seemed to glow and pulse in the dim light like an alien creature.

Denise put a motherly arm around the shrieking maid. "Rhonda, honey, it's OK. Go downstairs to the breakfast room and get yourself some hot tea with lots of sugar." Denise pushed Rhonda toward the door. The maid moved like an extra in *Day of the Dead*, but at least she'd quit screaming.

Helen was slightly dazed by the sudden silence.

"Don't stand there, Helen," Denise said. "Call 911 and get that ambulance. It's hot in here." She mopped her face with a wad of tissues, then turned on the room's air conditioner.

She's disturbing the crime scene, Helen thought. "We want homicide, right?" she said.

"What for?" Denise said.

"For the dead man," Helen said.

Denise laughed, loud and hard. The barroom laugh sounded strange coming from this maternal white-haired woman. "He's not dead. He's dead drunk."

Denise reached under the bedspread and fished out two empty fifths of Jack Daniel's. "His pal Jack here knocked him out. I'm sending him to the hospital to protect our hotel from liability, in case he's in an alcoholic coma or had a heart attack. Personally, I think he's healthy as a horse. But Rhonda's screaming could wake the dead, and it didn't make him twitch, so we gotta have him checked. Besides, I want to make sure he's well enough to cough up the money to repair this room and 223. I hope we got his credit card imprint. Big Boy here will pay for your overtime."

There was a ripping sound, as if a giant had torn the bedspread in two. The reek in the room grew worse.

"You'll probably want to call from downstairs," Denise said. "Hurry, before I kill this gasbag myself."

Helen left. She would have laughed if she hadn't been so scared. She would have danced down the hall if her knees weren't so wobbly. The body on the bed wasn't dead. The cops wouldn't find her. Her ex wouldn't know where she was. She was safe and snug in South Florida, where everyone was from somewhere else.

She'd still ask Sondra to call 911 from the front desk, in case the police showed up anyway. The Full Moon was in Seafield Village, a little community that fit into Fort Lauderdale like a puzzle piece. Helen figured the Seafield police must talk to the Lauderdale cops. She didn't want them comparing notes about her.

The paramedics turned up twelve minutes later in a shiny red ambulance. No police cars were in its wake. Helen felt her heart flutter when three tanned hunks rolled a stretcher into the lobby.

"Where is he?" the hunk with the broadest shoulders said.

"Up on three," Helen said, leading the hotties to the elevator. It was a tight fit with the strapping men and the stretcher. That was fine with Helen.

"Naturally," the hunk with the wavy blond hair said. "They're always on the top floor. I bet he's overweight, too."

"And naked," Helen said.

"How come the good-looking guys are never naked?" the third hunk with the sapphire eyes said. The other two paramedics nodded. Helen's fantasies were DOA before the elevator doors opened.

By the time the corpulent, crepitant occupant of room 323 was loaded up and wheeled out, Rhonda had recovered from the shock of seeing his undead body. She was back in the room, pale as old paper and bristling with resentment.

Denise bustled in with two portable fans. "Run these to dry the carpet around the bathroom door," she said. "Wipe down all the surfaces, strip the bed to the mattress, send the spread to the laundry, and mop up as much water as you can in the bathroom. At least you won't have to clean the tub."

Denise grinned. Rhonda didn't laugh. She waited till Denise left, then wielded the mop with vicious swings, slopping more water on the already wet carpet. "This is the last straw," she said. "If she thinks I'm going to clean that nasty Jacuzzi tomorrow, she's got another thought coming. She can go ahead and fire me. I don't care. Where's she going to find another hotel maid in South Florida who speaks English?"

Helen threw the room towels on the bathroom floor, hoping to absorb the water before Rhonda flung it on the carpet. "The Full Moon has to be the only hotel around here where the staff speaks English." Helen was eager to change the subject.

"That's Sybil's doing," Rhonda said. "You met the owner yet?"

"Just when I was hired." Helen picked up the dripping towels and carried them to the dirty laundry sack. The water wasn't sloshing around on the floor quite so much.

"They don't make 'em like Sybil anymore," Rhonda said. "She and her husband, Carl, built this hotel in 1953. They found all those seashells in the lobby on the Lauderdale beach. Carl died years ago and she runs the place by herself. Sybil doesn't want a lot of scared illegals working for slave wages. She only hires people who speak English well enough to answer her guests' questions. That costs her more. You have to admire that."

"I do," Helen said. She knew the three little words whispered most often in South Florida hotel rooms were, "No speak English." Cowed and confused maids scuttled out, avoiding guests' desperate pleas for towels and lightbulbs.

Helen had to admit Sybil had a knack for hiring people. Her employees stayed, another unusual phenomenon in rootless Florida. Denise had worked at the Full Moon eight years. Cheryl had been there six. Sondra had run the front desk for three years, and Rhonda had cleaned rooms for two. Helen got her job only because Naomi, a sixty-six-year-old maid, tore her rotator cuff making beds. They met on Helen's first day, which was Naomi's retirement party. "I'm just like that baseball player, Ozzie Smith," Naomi had declared. "We got the same work-related injury."

"Sybil seems like a good person," Helen said. "I'm lucky to be working for her. But I have to say, room 323 outdid itself today."

Damn. She could kick herself. She'd brought Rhonda back to the topic Helen wanted to avoid. She braced herself for another tirade. But cleaning seemed to drain the anger out of Rhonda. Her skinny body was electric with energy as she mopped the floor, then ripped the linens from the bed. She pulled and pounded the new sheets and pillows into place.

Helen was dusting when Rhonda went back to finish the now-dry bathroom. In the dresser mirror, she saw Rhonda wipe the toilet seat, then use the same rag to clean the in-room coffeepot. Helen's stomach lurched. She'd be drinking tea for a while.

Finally the room smelled fresh and looked clean, though the carpet still squished. The maids closed the door to the quiet whir of the drying fans and carried the dirty linens downstairs to the laundry room.

"I'll be back in a minute," Rhonda said.

It was more like fifteen. Rhonda returned with dust bunnies in her hair and a black, oily smudge on her right cheek.

"What happened to you?" Helen said. "I thought this hotel was too new for a coal chute."

Rhonda laughed, but didn't answer. She stood in front of the mirror by the time clock and scrubbed at the smudge on her cheek with a wet paper towel. Then she combed out the dust that grayed her fiery hair and started changing into her street clothes behind the rack of clean smocks.

Helen threw her soiled smock in the wash pile. She'd walk home in her jeans and T-shirt.

"Glad this day is done," she said.

"Do you want to go out for something to eat?" Rhonda called from behind the rack. Helen saw a flash of bright red hair, like an exotic bird darting by.

"Sorry, I'm broke," Helen said. "I had a root canal

and it took a big bite out of my savings, excuse the pun."
Twenty-five hundred dollars was a nasty hit, more than
a third of her stash.

Rhonda didn't ask if Helen had dental insurance. No
one did at the Full Moon.

"My treat." Rhonda held up a crisp fifty. Helen
blinked. This was major money where maids hoped for
two-dollar tips.

"Wow. Some big spender really tipped you," Helen
said.

"Are you kidding—at this place? It's from my boyfriend." Rhonda's shrill voice softened. "He gives me
walking-around money. He's so considerate. He's going
to take me away from all this."

Helen was glad Rhonda couldn't see her face. Pale,
skinny Rhonda did not seem like the kind of woman
men took away from anything. She was born to wield a
mop, a surly Cinderella without a fairy godmother.

"He sounds wonderful. I'd like to meet him," Helen
said.

Rhonda's face appeared over the top of the rack. She
looked foxy-sly. "He's very shy," she said. "But he's so
handsome. He listens to me. What man does that? He's
working on this plan. I can't say anything yet. But when
he makes his big score, I can tell everyone about us. I'll
have a diamond ring and everything."

Rhonda held up her empty left hand, the nails dry
and chipped from cleaning solvents. She saw the doubt
on Helen's face.

"He doesn't have a wife," she said quickly, though
Helen had never mentioned one. "He's single for sure.
He'll be real rich, real soon. He's going to take me away,
and we'll live on the water and have a big house with a
boat, like all the rich people in Florida."

Her plain face lit up and turned a lovely pink. Her
strange red hair glowed. For a moment Rhonda was almost beautiful.

She's in love, Helen thought. She's so far gone, she's

afraid to say his name, as if that ordinary act would destroy her dreams.

"Thanks," Helen said. "I appreciate the offer. But I have to meet Phil."

Rhonda shrugged. "It's OK. I'll eat alone. I'm meeting my boyfriend in an hour. Until he shows, it will be nice to sit in a booth and have someone wait on me for a change."

"Amen, sister," Helen said.

"Here, let me show you what else he's done for me." Rhonda dug into her shapeless black leather purse and brought out a plane ticket. "It's to Mexico City. My mama's wanted to go to Mexico all her life. She's never been out of the country. My boyfriend said I could buy anything I wanted with his money. I saw these cheap fares in the paper and I thought, I can send my mama on her dream trip. All because of my boyfriend."

"Sounds like you've got a good man," Helen said. She caught a glimpse of herself in the mirror and winced. "I'd better get home and clean up before I scare my guy."

She poked her head around the corner to say good night to Sondra at the front desk. Sondra was on her hands and knees, using a screwdriver to remove the cover on a large air vent. It was a dirty job, and Helen wondered why the elegant African-American clerk was doing it herself.

"Sondra, you're going to ruin your pretty outfit," Helen said. "Why don't you call maintenance?"

Sondra looked strangely guilty. Helen could see the flush under her milk-chocolate skin. Her neck and shoulders were suddenly rigid. "Uh, they're busy," she said. "They're checking for water damage in 223. This vent isn't working right. Sometimes paper scraps get sucked into it. Thought I'd take a look."

Helen stared at her. "You're wearing a white blouse. Why mess it up?"

"Think I don't know how to fix things because I'm a girl?" Sondra said. There was an edge to her voice.

"Of course not." Helen backed off. It wasn't her business. "You don't have school tonight, do you?"

Sondra was getting her degree in business administration. Her job at the Full Moon paid for her tuition.

"Nope. I'm here till midnight." She smiled, her temporary snappishness gone. "What was Rhonda carrying on about?"

"She got upset over the guy passed out in 323. She was already unhappy about the whipped-cream Jacuzzi in the honeymoon suite."

"Work here long enough and you'll learn that girl is always moaning about something." Sondra quit poking in the vent with the screwdriver, stood up, and wiped her long, slender hands on a paper towel. "She was born unhappy. You can't please her. Cheryl's got real problems with her child, but you'll never hear her complain. She loves that little Angel to death. Thinks God gave her a gift instead of a burden. Rhonda's not happy unless she's miserable. That's just the way she is. Now if you'll excuse me, I have to get back to work. If Sybil sees me talking to the help, we're both in trouble."

Long purple shadows were falling when Helen walked out the front door of the Full Moon. She saw Rhonda slip out the side entrance. Helen waved, but didn't stop. She was headed in the other direction, toward home. Cold wine and a hot man, that's what she needed. The other maid glided toward the harsh lights of the highway.

Rhonda had combed out her long red hair and changed. Helen thought she wore an odd outfit to meet a lover. Rhonda was twenty-eight, but her clothes were suitable for a woman of seventy. Her shapeless navy skirt hung below her knees. Her pale blue blouse had long sleeves and a high lace collar. In Florida, young and old shamelessly—even mercilessly—bared their skin.

Helen shrugged. Maybe Rhonda's mystery man liked old-fashioned women. As the night closed in, Rhonda looked like someone from another time. Helen watched as she disappeared into the shadows.

Later, Helen would regret that she didn't call out to Rhonda and say she'd changed her mind. Her refusal set off a chain reaction that ended in three deaths. Helen would always wonder if she'd let Rhonda buy her that dinner, would at least one victim have survived?

But Helen said no and started the events that would create a new widow and a world of sorrow.

CHAPTER 3

Helen grew up in St. Louis, where houses were redbrick boxes with forest green shutters. To her, the Coronado Tropic Apartments were wrapped in romance. The Art Deco building was painted a wildly impractical white and trimmed an exotic turquoise. The Coronado had sensuous curves. Palm trees whispered to purple waterfalls of bougainvillea. The pool was a misty oasis.

In the hard daylight, Helen knew the building showed its fifty-eight years. The hot sun beat down on cracked sidewalks and cruelly revealed the rusty air conditioners sticking out of the windows like rude tongues. But on this November night they were concealed by the softening darkness, and their rattling brought soothing memories of long-ago vacations.

Margery, Peggy and a freshly showered Helen sat around the pool, sipping wine and swatting slow-moving mosquitoes. Margery presided over the box of white wine like a society matron at her teapot, pouring until everyone was mildly looped.

The Coronado's landlady was seventy-six. Margery's face was brown and wrinkled as a cured tobacco leaf, but her long tanned legs belonged to someone thirty years younger. She liked to show them off with sexy shoes. Tonight she wore a pair of geometric ankle-wrap sandals. Helen wondered how Margery walked in them without strangling her feet. And where did she get those cool clam diggers? When Helen wore that style, she looked like her pants were too short. Of course, the pants and shoes were purple. Margery loved purple. She also liked Marlboros. She was surrounded by a perpetual cloud of smoke, like an ancient soothsayer.

"Where's your policeman, Peggy?" Margery said. "I haven't seen him lately."

Her upstairs neighbor was stretched out on the chaise longue with a wineglass in one hand. Pete, her green Quaker parrot, walked back and forth on her shoulder like a sentry on duty.

"You won't," Peggy said. "We're finished."

"Awwk!" Pete said.

So much for Margery's ability to predict the future, Helen thought.

"Life can be tiring with a cop," Margery said. "You're always wondering if he's going to come home or if you're going to get that call."

Peggy sighed. She looked weary in an interesting way, like a forties actress. She wore black, as if mourning her dead romance. It made her skin milky white in the dusk. Her dramatic nose gave her face unexpected elegance.

"You could say I got tired of the danger, if you consider drinking with his cop buddies life threatening," Peggy said. "His pals wouldn't take away his car keys when he was drunk. Every time the phone rang I expected to hear he'd wrapped his car around a tree. Sometimes he didn't see me for several nights. He said he was working late on a stakeout. He was staking out a strip joint on the Dixie Highway. I was afraid he'd bring home something nastier than a stripper's phone number on a cocktail napkin. I told him to straighten up and fly right."

Pete stretched and flapped his wings, as if demonstrating.

"What did your cop say?" Margery asked.

"He swore he was done with strippers. Then I found a red satin G-string in his pocket."

"How did he explain that?" Margery said.

"He said he found it."

"You were right to dump him," Margery said. "A man who can't bother to make up a good lie doesn't care anymore."

"Pete's the only man for me." Peggy stroked the little bird's head with one finger.

Pete nuzzled her neck, but wisely stayed silent. So did Helen. Even Margery shut up. The three women stared at their wineglasses, lost in their own thoughts. Helen could say plenty about the treachery of men, but she didn't dare. She was on the run in South Florida because of her ex-husband, Rob.

"I'm sticking to the lottery," Peggy said. "It's the only way I'll get lucky."

Helen didn't know what to say. Peggy spent some thirty dollars a week on her "retirement plan," but she never won a nickel.

The cell phone by Margery's chair rang and the land-lady snapped it open. "Hello?" she said. "Kathy? You want to speak to your sister? What's the matter? OK, calm down. Helen's right here."

"What's wrong, Kathy?" Helen was so frightened she could hardly say those three words. Kathy was the only person from her old life who knew how to reach her at the Coronado. This was an emergency.

Suddenly, all her fears poured out in a flood of questions. "Are Tom and the kids all right? Was there an accident? Is something wrong with Mom?"

"Everyone's fine," Kathy said. "I'm worried about you. Rob is on your trail. I found out from Mom. She still talks to him."

"That makes me furious," Helen said. "That snake thinks he can charm information out of her."

"This time it worked the other way," Kathy said. "Rob told Mom he tracked you to South Florida."

Helen's heart turned to ice. "How? I've been so careful."

"I have no idea," Kathy said. "But he's smart. I'll give him that. He even found out the name you're using now. Rob is desperate. He's been dropped by his latest lady friend. She kicked him out of her apartment. He can't make his car payment. He told Mom he's on the verge of bankruptcy. If he can't get his court settlement money from you, he'll have to get a job."

"A day's work would kill him," Helen said.

"It's not funny, Helen," Kathy said. "He pawned the Rolex you bought him to buy his plane ticket."

"He won't starve," Helen said. "He's still got the Cartier tank watch."

"Will you listen to me?" Kathy said, and Helen heard her exasperation crackling in the atmosphere. "Rob is flying into Fort Lauderdale tomorrow. He says he knows where you work."

"Is he coming to the Full Moon?" Helen's voice shook, and she felt sick. Am I going to have to quit this job, too? she thought. Please, God, don't let Rob find me at the hotel. The only thing harder than working is looking for a job.

"I don't know which job he found out about," Kathy said. "He didn't tell Mom. I can't keep track of them all. How many has it been now: five, six?"

"Seven, including the Greek diner," Helen said. "Eight if you count the time Margery roped me into working on a cruise ship. Where is that worthless bum staying in Lauderdale? Did Rob get a hotel or is he sponging off some woman?"

"He didn't say. I've told you all I know. I called right away, so you could take precautions."

Sensible Kathy, Helen thought. She's identified the problem and expects me to fix it. But this can't be fixed.

"Precautions?" Helen said. "What precautions? Can I get an anti-Rob vaccine? Can I board up my windows and hope he blows out to sea? What the hell am I going to do?"

Margery and Peggy had been frankly eavesdropping. Now Margery spoke up. "You're going to quit badgering your sister, Helen. It's not Kathy's fault that jerk is coming to town. You're going to thank her for caring enough to make this call. You're going to tell her you'll be fine and your Florida friends will watch out for you. Here, give me that."

Margery grabbed the phone from Helen. "Kathy, did you hear me?" she asked. "You have enough to worry about with a house, a husband and kids. I'll handle Helen."

Margery listened and nodded, then said, "Rob's nothing! A minor-league lowlife. Don't you worry, Kathy. There isn't a man alive who can get past me."

She snapped the phone shut, then turned to Helen. The landlady's hair was wreathed in smoke and she blew more out her nostrils, like an irritated old dragon. "Now, Helen Hawthorne, you're going to tell me the truth for a change. It's the only way I can help you."

"I—" Helen said.

"No, I'm not giving you time to make up another lie. Start talking or start packing."

Margery's face was hard as New Hampshire granite and just as weathered. Helen knew her suitcases would be on the sidewalk if she didn't talk. She stalled. "What about Peggy?"

"What about her?" Margery said. "If Rob is looking for you, then he'll come here. You've dragged Peggy into this mess. She has a right to know. Why is your ex really after you? Did he beat you? That's what you told me. That's why I was supposed to watch out for him. Is Rob violent?"

"No," Helen said. "I attacked him."

"Awk," Pete said.

Peggy dropped her wineglass. Helen heard it shatter on the concrete. No one moved to clean it up.

"Well, well. This is interesting. I thought you were a victim," Margery said.

"I am," Helen said, suddenly angry, although she didn't know if it was at Margery or herself. "But I did it to myself. For seventeen years I was Mrs. Perfect Yuppie. I worked my rear end off in a corporate job. I had this brand-new mansion in a St. Louis suburb. I was the director of pensions and employee benefits for a big company."

Scenes from Helen's old life flashed before her: the beige suits, the bland conversations, the dull meetings and endless memos. And the money. She'd made mountains of money then, compared to her current job. Helen had earned a hundred thousand dollars a year. It was all gone, most of it blown on things that bored her. The rest went to Rob, her lawyer and bad investments.

"Go on," Margery said. "You've just started."

"Rob was a top salesman. He made a good living. We'd been married ten years when he was fired. Then he couldn't find the right job."

"How long did he look?" Margery said.

"Seven years," Helen said.

Peggy made a small choking sound. Margery blew out a cloud of smoke. "What did he live on all that time?" she said.

"Me," Helen said. She hung her head. She'd been as gullible as a schoolgirl. "He strung me along with excuses. Sometimes I'd get angry and tell Rob to find a job, any job, even bagging groceries. Rob would sweet-talk me with flowers and candlelight dinners that turned up later on my credit card. I was dumb enough to believe him when he said he was looking for work that used his abilities."

Helen couldn't say the rest out loud. It was too painful. She'd really thought Rob had loved her. She still remembered him holding her hand in the restaurant and saying, "Please believe in me, Helen. There's no one like you."

He was right, Helen thought bitterly. No other woman was quite as stupid as I was.

"So what happened?" Margery said.

"I went around with my eyes wide shut for seven years. I knew things weren't right, but they weren't wrong enough for me to do anything. Then one summer afternoon I was on my lunch hour at work reading this women's-magazine article called, 'Ten Ways to Turn Your Marriage from Ho-Hum to Hot.' Number six said, 'Be impulsive. Surprise your husband with a romantic interlude in the afternoon. Your life will never be the same.'

"So I did. I canceled another boring meeting and went home. I surprised Rob on the back deck with our next-door neighbor, Sandy. They were boffing like bunnies."

"Awk!" Pete said.

"My feeling exactly," Helen said. "Rob had been working on the deck before he started nailing Sandy. I saw this crowbar right at my feet."

"So you beat the living daylights out of him." Margery's smile was ferocious.

"No, I beat up his SUV. Reduced it to rubble."

"You really know how to hurt a man," Margery said.

"Oh, I hurt him, all right. He cried when they towed it away. He never drove anything as nice again. I paid for that car, and I was glad I'd wrecked it. It felt good. You want to hear the ironic part? He always said he didn't like Sandy."

"You don't have to like a woman to screw her," Margery said. She gave that scary smile again. Pete huddled against Peggy's neck. Helen didn't blame him.

"Did Rob press charges for assault?" Peggy asked.

"He was too embarrassed. When the cops showed up he was cowering inside the battered SUV, naked as a jaybird."

"Awk!" Pete said.

"I don't understand," Peggy said. "If you didn't beat him up, why are you on the run?"

"His lawyer got me. When I divorced the unfaithful creep, his lawyer showed photos of the wrecked SUV in court. The idiot judge decided Rob wasn't a layabout for seven years. His Dis-Honor said Rob was a house husband who'd worked hard to control his hysterical wife and helped her be a productive earner. He awarded Rob half my income. He actually wanted me to give that worthless SOB fifty thousand dollars a year. I went crazy. I stood up in court and swore on the Bible that Rob would never see a nickel of my money."

"That must have been dramatic," Margery said.

"It was," Helen said. "Even after I realized I'd sworn on a copy of the *Missouri Revised Statutes.* It looked like a Bible. Anyway, I took off in the middle of the night and ended up here in South Florida, where I work low-profile jobs for cash under the table.

"I thought I had it figured out. I wasn't in any company computer. I didn't have a phone, a credit card, a bank account, or a Florida driver's license. I was sure Rob couldn't find me. But he did."

"He's after your measly income?" Margery said. "What do you make? Two hundred fifty dollars a week?"

"Two sixty-eight," Helen said. It sounded pathetic when she said it. A month's pay as a hotel maid wouldn't cover her American Express bill from the old days.

"Hardly seems worth his effort," Margery said.

"No handout is too small for Rob to accept. But it's more than money. I'm in contempt of court," Helen said. "He could have me dragged back to St. Louis. I could wind up in jail for running out on him. Or I might have to go back to a corporate job to avoid jail—and that would be almost as bad as prison."

"Why?" Peggy said. "What's wrong with making six figures?"

"I hated every day of that job," Helen said. "I had no life outside the office. All I did was work. I sentenced myself to seventeen years of hard labor. In Fort Lauderdale, I set myself free. I don't have as much money, but I can come home and toast the sunset. I can sit out by the pool with my friends. I have a good man like Phil."

"He's sexy, too," Margery said. "Don't forget that."

Peggy winced, and Helen thought the subject of sexy men might still be painful. "What about your family and friends back home?" she said.

"What friends?" Helen said. "I didn't have any real friends—not like you two. I had business contacts and lunch partners. I love my sister, Kathy, but she's so perfect I don't know what to say to her. I love Mom, but she's hopeless. She thinks Rob and I should get back together. That's why she still talks with him. She didn't take my side in the divorce. She said marriage is forever."

"It just seems that way," Margery said. "Listen, Phil's a private detective and a smart guy. Why don't you get him to help you? I gather Rob had more than one squeeze. Phil can find witnesses to your ex's constant cheating. He can dig up people who will swear Rob spent seven years loafing on your money. You can go back to court with better ammunition."

"No, thanks," Helen said. "Rob knows how to talk to the old boys on the bench. He'd charm a woman judge right out of her robes. You don't know him. He'll win again, and I'll wind up in jail. I'm not risking my life and my freedom in a system that's already messed up once. I don't trust it."

"Can't say I blame you," Margery said.

"Me, either," Peggy said. She'd had her own problems with the law. That's where she met her policeman.

"Besides," Helen said, "I want to keep Phil out of this. It's my problem, not his."

"Maybe I can find a solution that doesn't require a lawyer," Margery said. She stared into the smoke.

"You know any hit men?" Helen asked.

CHAPTER 4

Y*ou know any hit men?*

Helen's question hung in the air like a curse. She was surprised she'd said it. Then a red rage surged through her and she wanted Rob dead. Helen would have given anything—her money, her freedom, her life. She hated her ex-husband, hated how she'd believed in him, hated how she'd run from him. How could that twisted judge give Helen's hard-earned money to the man who'd used her?

God or the devil handed me a crowbar when I walked in on that cheating scum, she thought. She could feel its sun-warm heft in her hand and its heavy, destructive strength. *If I had it again, I wouldn't slaughter an innocent SUV. I'd smash Rob.*

Peggy went rigid, watching her face. She knew Helen was serious.

The taut silence stretched into the black night, as the three women sat there. Helen nursed her hate, Peggy held her fear, and Margery stayed a silent sorceress in sexy shoes.

Then Margery laughed and blew smoke, and the red demon eye of her cigarette winked. "Helen, I'm an old lady living in Lauderdale. All I know are other old women. All they'd do is love Rob to death."

The spell was broken. Helen's brutal anger fled like a mugger who'd heard a police siren. She could barely hide her relief. Margery hadn't taken her seriously. She'd saved Helen from her own murderous impulse by pretending she didn't mean it. Helen felt weak with relief. How many of the divorced wished their exes dead, just for a moment? How many gave in to that temptation?

Helen looked up and saw a man with ice-white hair shimmering in the moonlight. It was Phil. How long had he been standing there? What did he hear? Did he know Rob was looking for her? Did he know she'd wanted to kill her ex-husband? Could he love a woman with her ugly desires?

Phil gave his crooked grin, the one that made the corners of his eyes crinkle, and said, "Hi, Helen. I'm cooking dinner for you tonight."

He sounded so ordinary, so good, Helen was sure he couldn't have heard their conversation. A normal man would have run from her unnatural rage.

"Sexy, and he cooks," Margery said. "Why didn't they make men like Phil when I was young? Helen, get out of here. Go have some fun." She made shooing motions with her glowing cigarette.

"Have a good night, you two," Peggy said. She rose from her chaise as if from a trance, and began picking up the wineglass shards. Pete stayed silent, but he watched Helen with beady eyes.

Helen was eager to get away from the scene of her temptation. She hurried Phil to her little apartment at the Coronado. He'd left an ice chest full of food and a pitcher of margaritas on her doorstep. As she reached in her pocket for her keys, Phil put his arm around Helen and drew her to him. They were hidden in the shadows of a bougainvillea. Something sweet bloomed in the night air. Helen wondered how she'd been so lucky to find this man. For a while it seemed like she'd dated every druggie, drunk, and deadbeat in South Florida—after seventeen disappointing years with Rob.

"Damn, you look good," he said.

"I do?" Helen was always surprised that Phil found her sexy. She was forty-two, with long chestnut hair, longer legs, and good skin. Her eyes were an interesting hazel, and her mouth was generous, or just plain big. She felt the years of unhappiness were etched in her face.

"Mmm. You smell nice, too," he said, as he kissed her hair. "How about dinner?"

Helen liked everything about Phil: the soft skin on the back of his neck, his long silver ponytail, his hard chest and freshly ironed shirt. She wanted him, right now.

"How about dessert first?" Helen said, opening her door. They dumped the cooler of food in the kitchen and kissed their way toward her bedroom, leaving a trail of clothes. Helen wondered if her evil impulse stirred up some primal hunger, and then she didn't care. She just wanted him.

At her bedroom door, Phil tripped over her cat. Thumbs let out a startled yelp, and stalked away with offended dignity. Helen and Phil were too wrapped up in each other to worry about the cat's wounded feelings. Somehow they were on her bed, under the sheets. Helen reached for him, and Phil groaned.

"Oh God, you're good," he said.

"No, I'm bad," Helen said.

"But in a good way," he said, and that was the last coherent exchange for some time.

It was nearly an hour before Helen and Phil were back in the kitchen, barefoot, slightly woozy, and wrapped in matching terry robes. Phil was at the kitchen counter, carefully dipping the rim of her margarita glass in bar salt.

"Quit fussing and serve it," Helen said. "I'm thirsty."

"Some things are worth fussing over," he said, finishing her drink with a perfectly cut lime slice. "A well-built drink is one of them. Now, stand aside and let me concentrate on my shrimp fajitas." He smiled at her, and Helen got another close-up of those sexy eye crinkles. Her heart, and something else, gave an interesting flutter.

Helen leaned against the counter and watched Phil mash avocados into fresh guacamole with a fork. He seemed to have at least four hands, because he also sautéed the onions and red and green peppers, then added the shrimp. His long, shapely fingers worked with quick, precise movements.

Thumbs twined around Phil's legs, purring loudly. The cat stopped to pat Phil's bare feet with his huge six-toed paws, then went back to winding himself around Phil's ankles.

"He's forgiven me for falling over him," Phil said. "He's a good guy. He doesn't hold a grudge."

"Especially when you're holding a shrimp."

Phil dropped the fat shrimp on the floor. "Oops," he said. "I really am clumsy. Thumbs, will you pick that up, old buddy?"

The big gray-and-white cat pounced and chomped the shrimp. Phil gave him another.

"Phil!" Helen said. "Not a whole shrimp. Just the tail. You'll spoil him."

"I spoil everyone I love," he said. "Sit down, so I can bring you dinner. The tortillas are warm."

Helen purred nearly as loudly as her cat when Phil set the fragrant, colorful plates on the table. She carefully constructed her fajita, adding the salsa, sour cream, and guacamole in measured spoonfuls, then folding the tortilla like an origami sculpture.

"Now who's fussing?" Phil asked, and gave that crooked smile again. His nose was crooked, too. Helen thought it saved his face from bland handsomeness.

"Fajitas taste better if the sour cream and guacamole are not running down my arm," Helen said. "This is delicious. Did I thank you for dinner? I hate to cook but I love good food. Most nights I settle for scrambled eggs or tuna out of the can."

"Life is too short for bad food," Phil said. "I could teach you to cook."

"I'm hopeless," Helen said.

"How come women who can't cook are proud of it?" Phil said.

"Because we've escaped a drudgery men never have to face. Some men think cooking is creative. Women like me think it's a trap. We're afraid we'll have to waste our time making meals instead of doing what we really want."

"Which is?" Phil took a thoughtful bite of his fajita. Helen saw guacamole squirt out on his fingers, but said nothing.

"For a long time, I thought it was my corporate job with the big salary," Helen said. "But now, I think it's living here. I enjoy working jobs with no responsibility, toasting the sunset by the pool, and loving you."

"So tell me about your low-stress day at the hotel," Phil said, with a wicked gleam in his eyes.

He knows, Helen thought. Somehow, he found out what happened at the hotel today. She decided to play it for laughs. "We had a flood in a bathroom and I found a body in a bed."

"Sounds relaxing," Phil said. "And worry free."

"The guy wasn't dead, just drunk," Helen said. "He was in room 323, of course. Rhonda got hysterical. She'd already had a hissy fit about the whipped cream in the Jacuzzi."

"Which reminds me," Phil said, "dessert is ready. Keep talking."

She did, while he cleared the plates and served vanilla-bean ice cream with warm cinnamon sauce.

"Let me get this straight," Phil said, when he sat down again with his dessert. "You'd rather clean rooms at this nuthouse than have a real job that uses your training and education?"

Helen knew where this conversation was heading, and tried to stop it. "It's entertaining," she said. "I used to crunch numbers and go to meetings. What I do now seems real and useful."

Phil looked at her with those startling blue eyes. "Helen, I heard your conversation with Margery."

Her heart seemed to stop. This was it. This was good-bye. He was letting her down easy, with love and food, but he couldn't keep seeing someone like her.

"Then you know I wanted to kill Rob," Helen said, carefully choosing each word. "It was only for a moment, but I really meant it when I said it."

"He's still breathing, isn't he?" Phil said. "Too bad Margery didn't know any hit men."

"You're saying that to make me feel better."

"Do you know how many times I've thought about murdering my ex-wife?" Phil said. "I never acted on those thoughts, any more than you did. But I'd be worried if you didn't have them, after the way he treated you."

He reached across her tiny turquoise table and took her hand. "Helen, I know you're on the run from Rob. I heard he'll be in town. You know he'll find you in a few days. Lauderdale isn't that big. Margery's right: I can help you. I can set you free. I know the top lawyers, the good cops and the best investigators. If you let me, I'll get Rob out of your life forever."

"You have your own work to do," Helen said. Phil was a private detective who did government contract work. He'd been testifying in a big case that they hoped would send a lot of crooks to federal prison.

"The trial is winding down," Phil said. "My work is nearly finished. I'll have time to help you."

Helen felt suddenly weary. Rob had stolen her money and her life, but she wasn't going to give him this night. It still belonged to her.

"I don't want to talk about Rob anymore," she said. "Forget about him. We're divorced. He's my past. You're my future."

"But what about—" Phil began.

"Not now," Helen said. "Not tonight." She settled into Phil's lap and kissed him, long, slow kisses with the cold, sweet taste of cinnamon. She kissed away his questions, but not her fears.

Later that night, as she lay in Phil's arms, Helen realized she was not alone. Rob was in her room. Not physically. Not yet. She'd run a thousand miles to get away from him, but it wasn't enough. Her ex-husband had found her again, and he had the power to take her away from her seedy little paradise.

Helen stared into the dark and knew this sad truth: Divorce bound her to Rob more than marriage ever did.

CHAPTER 5

....

"**R**honda didn't show up for work this morning," Denise said. She slammed down a stack of towels so hard the housekeeping cart bounced.

"It's only nine o'clock," Helen said. "She could be late."

"She's not late," Denise said. "She doesn't want to clean that Jacuzzi." She heaved a pile of queen sheets with a heavy thud. The cart jumped again.

"Maybe she's sick," Helen said.

"She's sick of work. And I'm sick of her." Denise smacked a tower of washcloths on top of the towels. Helen jumped.

"We could call her house and check," Helen said.

"I've called her cell and her home four times already," Denise said. "She always answers one or the other. She's not picking up the phone."

She crossed her powerful arms over her ample bosom. Her face looked like thunder under her cloud of white hair, and her eyes flashed lightning. "You heard her yesterday. Rhonda said she was going to do this. I warned her. I told her to report or she'd lose her job. I've had it. This is insubordination."

"But—" Helen said.

"But, my ass," Denise said. "She's fired."

"But she's a hard worker," Helen said. When Rhonda got a grudge going, she cleaned with record speed. Helen decided not to say that. It might give Denise more ammunition. It was true Rhonda had wiped the coffeepot with the toilet rag, but since people made coffee with boiling water, Helen figured it didn't make much difference.

Denise didn't want to hear pro-Rhonda remarks. "If she worked as hard as she complained, she'd be a wonder. She's a whiner and a slacker."

Helen remembered Rhonda flashing that fifty-dollar bill and talking about her handsome boyfriend scoring big soon. Was that why he wanted to see her last night? Did he make his money and take her away from a life of drudgery? Helen couldn't blame Rhonda if she didn't call to quit. She was rich now. But how did her man make his money? In Florida, most reasons for sudden wealth were illegal: drugs, gunrunning, illegal-immigrant smuggling.

Denise was still ranting. "I told her to show up or else," she said. "I'm not backing down. I'd better let Sybil know. She's not going to be happy. You want to come with me?"

"But Sybil's the owner," Helen said. "I'm not management."

"Didn't say you were," Denise said. "But I might need you as backup. You can tell Sybil what you heard Rhonda say."

Helen didn't like that. She felt like she was snitching. But she didn't know how to say no.

Denise moved at a stately pace to Sybil's office, her anger giving way once more to her innate dignity. By the time she knocked on Sybil's door, Denise was calm and collected.

"Come in," Sybil called.

The office air was thick with chilled smoke, and the blinds were yellow with nicotine. Sybil's puff of white hair was barely visible behind the paper piles on her desk. She had an ashtray the size of a turkey platter heaped with lipsticked butts.

Sybil was seventy-five, but seemed older. She was small and stooped, with skin the color of an old lemon. Her face was crisscrossed with so many wrinkles it looked like a street map.

"What is it now?" she said, looking up from an account book. A cigarette dangled from her red lips.

"Rhonda didn't show up for work," Denise said. "I warned her, but she didn't come in."

Sybil stubbed out the cigarette and said, "That girl's always been trouble. I hire 'em reliable. It's my one talent, but it failed me this time."

"We have to fire her," Denise said.

"She's gone, and good riddance," Sybil said. "I'll get the ad in tomorrow's paper. You realize it's not going to be easy to find qualified help. You, Cheryl and Helen are going to have to take up the slack till somebody else turns up, and we've got a full house."

"Full? Did you rent 323 already?" Denise said.

"Sure did," Sybil said. "Carpet was a little damp, but the guy paid cash and didn't care. Watched him on the security camera, sneaking two women up the back stairs to his room. He thought I didn't know. I don't care what they do as long as they're quiet and don't break the bed."

Helen giggled.

"I'm not joking, young lady," Sybil said, pointing her cigarette at Helen. "They crack my mattresses and ruin my bedposts doing God knows what."

Denise looked anxious, as if she sensed an impending tirade. "What happened to the guy who was hauled off in an ambulance?" she said.

"Nothing wrong with him but a hangover," Sybil said. "He flew home to Minneapolis late last night. Wished I could have been there when his wife met him at the airport. When she called here and found out he was in the hospital, she knew he'd been on a bender. Sounded mad as a wet cat."

Denise shrugged. "She's welcome to him, smelly old drunk. I'd rather sleep with a pound of Limburger. Helen, we need to start cleaning. I'll start on the first floor. You and Cheryl can take three, and we'll meet somewhere in the middle."

It was hot up on the third floor. Air-conditioning couldn't keep the hall and rooms completely cool when the Florida sun pounded on the Full Moon's flat roof. The dirty, bitter odor of cigarettes lingered everywhere upstairs, even in the nonsmoking rooms.

Cheryl met Helen at the elevator with a stocked cart. She was about thirty, with dark brown hair turning gray and tired brown eyes. Worry lines were etched into her forehead and some forty extra pounds cushioned her frame. Comfort weight, Helen thought. She bet Cheryl secretly soothed herself with sweets.

"Shall we begin?" Cheryl gave a dazzling smile. "I like to clean bathrooms. What about you?"

"Beds," Helen said. "I like making beds. We're going to get along just fine."

They made an excellent team, and were soon in the zone, that mindless place where they cleaned automatically, heaving heavy blankets, hauling vacuums, and wiping surfaces smoothly and efficiently.

"People think this is like cleaning house," Cheryl said. "It's like cleaning fifteen houses in one day. The only thing worse than hotel work is cleaning houses."

"Did you do that?" Helen asked.

"Yes, after my daughter was born," Cheryl said. "I hated it. I had to please ten different people, and they were impossible. I like this job: regular hours, regular pay, no excuses on payday and no bounced checks."

Cheryl sprayed the bathroom mirrors with rubbing alcohol. There were no wasted movements as she wiped the glass.

"I learned a lot from Sybil," Cheryl said. "Like her trick of using alcohol to clean glass and mirrors. Works better than glass cleaners, and it's cheaper. Sybil knows how to squeeze a dollar, but she's smart."

Helen was surprised when Cheryl said, "Break time. I'll be outside at our place." The morning had gone faster than she realized.

The staff used the bench in the side garden as their rest spot. The maids didn't eat lunch. Food made them sleepy in the afternoon. But they'd stop for a smoke or a snack. In the laundry room, Cheryl pulled a Hershey bar the size of a license plate off a shelf. Helen searched for the bag she'd brought that morning.

"I can't find my pretzels," she said. "Maybe Denise knows what happened to them."

Denise's cart was parked in front of room 119, but there was no sign of her. Helen walked the length of the hall, then turned the corner to the elevator alcove. The head housekeeper was standing by the plant urns. She'd pulled a small palm out of a pot and was running her fingers through the dirt at the bottom.

"What are you doing?" Helen said.

Denise dropped the plant and it landed crookedly in the pot. "I'm checking for root rot."

"I thought we had a plant-care service," Helen said.

"We do," Denise said. "But they're not very good. That palm tree is in bad shape."

She mopped her forehead with the wad of tissues she kept in her pocket.

The plant looked OK to Helen, but she couldn't tell a palm from a petunia. "Have you seen my pretzels?"

"I moved them over by the time clock when I was folding sheets," Denise said. She stood awkwardly by the crooked palm until Helen left the floor.

Helen enjoyed her ten remaining minutes of peace. Cheryl silently nibbled her candy bar. Neither woman spoke. Helen wondered what Denise had really been doing with that plant.

Last night, Rhonda had disappeared somewhere and

returned with a head full of dust bunnies. Sondra, their ambitious African-American clerk, had been rooting around in an air-conditioning vent, ruining her clothes. Now Denise was pulling up palm trees. What was going on at this hotel? Helen could think of no explanation for their odd behavior.

At eleven fifteen, Cheryl said, "Now that we're rested, we can clean room 323 if the occupants are out. The *Do Not Disturb* sign was still on the door when I checked."

"It can't be worse than yesterday," Helen said.

"Don't bet on it," Cheryl said.

When they rolled their cart down the hall, they saw a huge man closing the door to room 323. His beer gut flopped over his low-hanging jeans, and he had a Seminole Sam tattoo on his wrist. His dirty brown hair and gray beard were in biker braids. A lush blonde with brassy hair and bad skin was hanging on his arm. Beside her, drinking Busch out of a can, was a woman so skinny her tube top didn't bulge in front. The biker nodded to the two maids and said, "It's all yours, ladies. We're outta here." His grin showed a missing eyetooth.

Beer cans rolled across the floor when Cheryl opened the door. They were hit with the odor of cigarettes and the feral, meaty smell of sex.

"Glad you're making the bed," Cheryl said. She flipped on the bathroom light and groaned.

"What is it?" Helen said.

"Someone peed in the coffeepot," Cheryl said.

Helen gingerly gathered up the twisted bedsheets. She felt something odd and hard buried in the sheets. She shook them and out fell a longish green object with straps. It took Helen a few seconds to realize she was looking at a strap-on dildo.

"Ohmigod," she said.

"Holy cow," Cheryl said, peeking around the corner. "That thing's big."

"Should it go to the hotel's lost and found?" Helen said.

"Can you imagine anyone going to the front desk and asking, 'Did I leave my dildo in room 323?'" Cheryl said.

"Yeah. Those three characters who just left here," Helen said.

"Throw it out," Cheryl said. "Sondra is a nice girl. She shouldn't see something like that."

Helen used a pillowcase to carry the object to the trash. She threw the case away, too.

"Ugh," she said. "Let me wash my hands."

"Use a fresh bar of soap and a clean towel," Cheryl said. "Don't touch anything they used."

While Helen washed her hands, Cheryl reached in her pocket for a plastic holder. "Here," she said. "You need to see something nice." It was a photo of a little girl with long dark hair and soft brown eyes with an upward slant. She wore a pink party dress iced with white ruffles, and smiled happily for the camera.

"She's beautiful," Helen said.

"Yes, she is," her mother said. "My daughter, Angel. She has Down syndrome."

Of course, Helen thought. That explained the upward-slanting eyes and slightly flat face.

"How old is she?" Helen said.

"Six. I'm really lucky. She doesn't have a lot of the symptoms. No heart defects, thank goodness. The retardation is mild. She goes to regular school, and she's proud of that. She wears thick glasses, but not for pictures, and she has a hearing aid, but you can't see it with her long hair. Someday I'm going to get her an operation and she won't need those glasses anymore, not the Coke-bottle-thick ones, anyway."

How was Cheryl going to afford an operation on her salary? Helen wondered. "She looks happy," she said.

"She is," Cheryl said. "People think children with Down syndrome are naturally happy, but that's not true. They have moods like everyone else. There's a little boy at the clinic who's mean as a rattlesnake and in trouble all the time. But Angel is just like her name. I'm so lucky."

Lucky. How many women would feel that way in her circumstances? Cheryl was as special as her daughter.

"My mother wants me to put Angel in a home," Cheryl said. "She says if I lost forty pounds and didn't have Angel, I could marry. She even offered to pay for the home, but I told her no. Children with Down syndrome do better when they're mixed in with the community. I can't convince Mom. She's got old ideas. She still slips sometimes and calls Angel 'the retard.' Her own granddaughter. Why can't she see how beautiful Angel is?"

"She's too busy being ugly," Helen said.

"My mother says Angel is the punishment for my sin," Cheryl said.

"What sin?" Helen was too shocked to say more.

"I wasn't married when I got pregnant, and her daddy abandoned me. Mom says Angel's Down syndrome is my punishment."

"You don't really believe that, do you?" Helen said.

"No! She's a gift," Cheryl said fiercely. "She's the only good thing that ever happened to me. My Angel is going to graduate from school and get a job and even marry, if she wants to." Helen got the feeling that Cheryl had repeated that last sentence to herself many times. She put the plastic-covered photo back in her smock pocket.

After that outburst, they worked in silence for the rest of the afternoon. They finished the hot third floor and started cleaning on two. The feeling was companionable, not embarrassed. When they closed the door on their last room a little after three o'clock, Cheryl said formally, "Thank you, Helen. You're a hard worker."

That was the highest compliment one maid could give another.

"We made good time, even shorthanded," Helen said.

"I'm afraid Rhonda won't be missed," Cheryl said. "All her whining made me tired. I'm glad she's gone."

Helen was, too, but she didn't say so.

They pushed their cleaning cart toward the house-keeping room on the second floor. When they reached the balconied section overlooking the lobby, Helen saw a man checking in at the front desk. Something about him seemed familiar. She leaned over the railing for a closer look.

Helen nearly overturned the cart. It was her ex-husband, Rob.

CHAPTER 6

Cheryl saw Helen's pale face. "Are you going to faint?" she asked.

"No," Helen said, as everything went dark.

She woke up in the housekeeping room with a mean headache. She was stretched out on two chairs with her legs propped on a box of toilet tissue. Helen tried to sit up, but the chairs wobbled ominously, and she remembered why they'd been retired.

"Easy there," Cheryl said. She held an open bottle of ammonia under Helen's nose. Helen breathed in and choked.

"I think she's awake now," Denise said. "You can put that away." The head housekeeper draped a cool washcloth on Helen's forehead.

Her head pounded. She felt foolish and angry at herself. Helen hadn't seen her ex-husband in years. She'd spent hours imagining what she would do if she ever ran into Rob. Chain saws, crowbars and knockout punches were at the top of her list. Fainting was not.

"Are you OK?" Cheryl said.

"Sure," she said. "I didn't eat anything, that's all."

"Nonsense," Denise said in a voice that sounded like "liar." When the head housekeeper folded her arms and frowned, she looked like Sister Mary Justine, one of

Helen's high school teachers. Helen felt sixteen again, explaining that she hadn't gone drag racing with Tommy McIntyre on her lunch hour.

"You saw that man in the lobby and passed out," Denise said. "What did he do to you?"

"Uh," Helen stalled. For years she'd kept quiet about Rob. It was her protection. Now silence couldn't save her, but talking might. Helen decided to trust the two women with some information. She had no choice.

"He's my ex-husband," she said. "Rob flew here from St. Louis, where I used to live. He's looking for me. He wants my money."

"Don't they all?" Denise said.

Helen noticed for the first time that the head housekeeper wasn't wearing a wedding ring.

"It's always money with men," Cheryl said. "Either they want yours or they won't give you theirs."

Helen studied their faces. No one looked away. They believed her. Of course, she was telling the truth, which made convincing them easier.

"I've been hiding from him," Helen said. "I need to know something: Did he check into this hotel by accident or does he know I work here?"

"I can find out," Denise said. "Let me ask Sondra. She's working the front desk this afternoon. I'll be back in five minutes. Don't try to get up. You've had a nasty shock."

Cheryl slid a stack of sheets under Helen's head for a pillow. "Close your eyes and relax until Denise returns," she said.

But Helen couldn't. Denise was gone too long. The time stretched into ten and then fifteen minutes. Where was she? What was wrong? Helen saw Rob pounding on the front desk, demanding to see her, searching the staff rooms, calling for Sybil, the owner.

Twenty minutes later, Denise arrived with a can of 7UP and a pack of graham crackers. "Here," she said. "Drink this and eat a cracker to settle your stomach."

Helen pressed the cold soda against her temple. It helped her headache. Then she popped the top and drank. The sugar rush revived her. The graham cracker helped, too. Its homey taste was comforting.

"What happened?" Helen said. "You were gone so long, I was worried."

"Your ex was hanging around the lobby, picking up a free *USA Today* and getting a Coke out of the machine," Denise said. "If he'd stayed any longer, I swear I would have him arrested for loitering. Finally he went to get his luggage out of his rental car and I had a chance to talk to Sondra. She says he paid by credit card and didn't ask about you by name.

"He didn't say he was looking for anyone, either," Denise said. "He didn't seem curious about our staff at all." Like Sister Mary Justine, she seemed to see through Helen. "Sondra said he acted like a normal guest. No odd questions or unusual requests. He also hit on her."

"That's Rob," Helen said. "I'm sure Sondra had too much sense to say yes."

"Sondra isn't going to throw herself away on some old white guy," Denise said, then looked embarrassed. "I mean—"

"I know what you mean," Helen said. But they knew she'd thrown herself away on him.

"When I left he was back in the lobby, asking for the ice machine," Denise said. "Sondra will call me when he goes up to his room. He's staying in 210."

"That's on this floor," Helen said, panic clawing at her insides. Suddenly the housekeeping room seemed small and suffocating. She wanted to rabbit down the stairs and out into the fresh air. The past and all her mistakes were too close. "I have to get out of here. I can't come back to the hotel until he checks out, and he won't leave until he finds me. What am I going to do? I'll have to quit this job. I like it here." That last sentence was said with a slight tremble. Helen realized it was true.

"You don't have to leave," Denise said. "We'll protect you."

"How am I going to get out of here without Rob seeing me?"

"We'll sneak you out while he's in his room. There's no reason for you to quit work. We'll bring you up the back stairs and you can clean on three. He won't go up there."

"But he'll see me when I leave," Helen said.

"Not if you take the stairs. Only the health nuts use them. Most guests take the elevator. We can get you safely in and out."

"Don't forget you're a maid," Cheryl said. "No one notices us. That smock is your cloak of invisibility."

There was a squawk on Denise's walkie-talkie. "Subject heading for his room," Sondra reported.

Denise waited a few minutes, then grabbed a stack of towels. "Reconnaissance," she said. "I'll be back."

She returned shortly, without the towels. "Your ex has the *Do Not Disturb* sign on his door. It's safe to leave."

"What happened to your towels?" Helen said.

"Guy letting himself into 212 wanted extras," Denise said.

Helen stood up, surprised at how good she suddenly felt. She wasn't afraid anymore. The other maids would protect her. She would survive.

"Let's get you out of here," Denise said. She opened the door and studied the hall. "We'll make a run for the stairs on the count of three. One. Two. Three."

Denise and Cheryl surrounded Helen like trained bodyguards. They briskly crossed the hall to the stairs and threw open the door without stopping. Helen ran down to the parking lot. Once outside, she breathed in the humid air. She was free.

"I'll drive you home," Cheryl said.

"I'd rather walk," Helen said. "Thank you both for your help. I appreciate it."

"Any woman would do it," Denise said.

But Helen knew her own mother wouldn't help her. She'd send Helen back to Rob's lying arms. She'd say it was Helen's wifely duty to put up with his infidelity. She'd endured her own husband's tomcatting, and she expected her daughter to do the same.

Helen found a pay phone two blocks from the hotel and called Margery. "Rob's staying at my hotel," she said.

"On purpose?" Margery asked.

"By accident."

"He hasn't come to the Coronado," Margery said. "Come home and relax. We can see any cars that pull into the parking lot. There's no way he's getting by me."

On the walk home, Helen was acutely aware of small, odd scenes: A bright burst of red flowers. A brown lizard with a throbbing orange throat. A dignified old woman in a motorized wheelchair, her Boston terrier riding at the helm. Could Rob take her away from this rich, colorful life? Then she remembered Rhonda, whose lover promised to take her away to something better. She hoped the troubled maid was enjoying the lush life.

Margery met her by the gate to the pool. Her landlady was wearing purple espadrilles and ruffled shorts the color of an old bruise. "There's no sign of that buzzard," she said. "I've been on the lookout for him. Peggy's on the alert, too. Even Pete's watching. We're all out by the pool. There's someone I wanted you to meet."

"Please don't tell me Cal's back. I can't face him right now." Helen had had an embarrassing romantic interlude with the long-term Coronado tenant. He still owed her money.

"No, Cal's in Canada through December."

Helen looked at Margery. "You've rented 2C."

"Yes," Margery said too cheerfully. "I have a nice older woman in there."

"What's she do? Cheat orphans? Rip off widows? Steal from dead men?" Helen said.

"There's no need to be sarcastic. I admit we've had a few problems with the tenants in 2C." Margery picked at her nail polish, which was an improbable tangerine.

"A few? One's in jail, one runs ads on late-night TV, and the rest skipped town, usually with your towels. Age is no guarantee of honesty. The old ones are as slippery as the young ones."

"Arlene's different," Margery said. Her mouth was set in a stubborn line.

"That means she hasn't been caught yet," Helen said.

"Shush," Margery said. "Don't let her hear you. Arlene is very normal."

Helen caught a flash of red and black, and realized Margery meant normal for South Florida. In Helen's hometown of St. Louis, Arlene would make jaws drop. She was about sixty-five, with spiky gray hair and a short, sturdy build. Her bright red muumuu made her look like a fireplug. Swinging red earrings and flowered flip-flops completed the ensemble.

Arlene was talking to Peggy, and the parrot lady looked like she might be enjoying the conversation. Pete was perched on Peggy's shoulder, watching Arlene with alert eyes.

"Arlene, meet another neighbor, Helen Hawthorne," Margery said.

Arlene stood up, which didn't make her much taller than when she was sitting down, and held out her hand. "Pleased to meet you. Have some onion dip and chips. It's my special recipe, with olives and pimento. Can I pour you a drink?"

Helen had to admit Arlene was a pleasant change from some 2C tenants, who disapproved of drinking. Her olive-and-onion dip was good, too.

"Can you believe this weather?" she said, throwing out her stubby arms. "Back home in Michigan I'd be shoveling a path to my car. Here I'm sitting by the pool. This is paradise."

For thirty minutes, Arlene talked about the fine weather, the rotten move down here, and the impossible traffic, all polite Florida topics. Then she said, "Nice meeting you. Think I'll turn in." She gathered up her empty chip dish and flip-flopped to her apartment.

"What do you think she really does?" Helen asked Peggy after Arlene closed her door.

"It could be anything," Peggy said. "Murder, arson and armed robbery. She has the gift of looking innocent."

"Awk!" Pete said.

"Stop it, you two," Margery said. Her cigarette looked red and irritated. "Don't make Arlene pay for my mistakes. She's not a crook. I checked her out. She has references. She worked at an insurance company for twenty-eight years. She's retired now. I saw her pension check stub."

"And getting a pension proves she's innocent," Helen said.

"It shows she held a steady job for a lot of years," Margery said. "She is what she says she is." But her voice lacked conviction. She knew her track record for 2C was not good.

"Time will tell," Peggy said. "I'd love to talk, ladies, but I have to go."

Helen looked closer at her friend. "Is that a new green blouse? And a very classy makeup job, including a subtle touch of eye shadow? You've got a date. I thought Pete was the only man for you."

"Awk!" Pete said.

Peggy's pale complexion was highlighted with the faintest pink. "He is. I'm meeting a guy for coffee on Las Olas. It's not a date. It's only a grande latte."

" 'This could be the start of something big,' " Helen sang off-key.

Peggy glared at her.

"So who is he?" Margery said.

"What is this, high school?" Peggy said. She rose out of her chaise longue so fast Pete flapped his wings to stay on her shoulder. "I'm going to be late. I have to take Pete home."

"Coward," Margery said. "You don't want to talk."

Peggy giggled and ran toward her apartment.

"I'd better say good night, too," Helen said.

"Don't worry about Rob," Margery said. "I'm a light sleeper. He can't go sneaking past me."

Helen heard Peggy's door slam again and watched her friend run lightly across the lawn, the full silk sleeves of her blouse fluttering like butterfly wings. Where did Peggy get the courage to date again, after her last man betrayed her with a stripper? She seemed happy, hopeful and touchingly brave.

Helen walked to her own apartment, and bolted the door against the man she'd once loved.

CHAPTER 7
....

The next morning Helen sneaked into the hotel while her ex was in bed.

Years ago, she'd dreamed of slipping up some sleazy back stairs and having an affair with her own husband. She'd wanted hot honeymoon sex, with the headboard thumping against the wall.

Then she found out Rob was already having hot sex, just not with her. Now she was sneaking into a hotel, hoping to avoid her ex-husband so she could rendezvous with a dust rag.

Helen's plans had never included hiding behind a smelly Dumpster. But Denise told her to be at the back door by the Dumpsters at eight thirty. The big rusty green containers were hidden by a stockade fence, but it couldn't hold in the powerful stink of sun-roasted garbage. Guests never used this door unless they were up to no good.

Denise was waiting at the entrance. "Hurry," she whispered, though there was no need to lower her voice. "Your ex is still in his room." Helen could swear the head housekeeper was enjoying this covert operation.

As she sidled past the Dumpsters, Helen caught some odd top notes to the garbage bouquet. "What's that perfumey smell?" she said. It was somewhere between her grandmother's dusting powder and a flowery room deodorizer.

"It's the latest thing—trash perfume," Denise said, leading the way up the stairs. "All the big hotels and high-class condos use it. You put this perfume on the trash and it doesn't smell so bad. Keeps the kids away, too. Some boys were playing in the Dumpsters, but they won't get near our trash if they come out smelling like girlie perfume."

Hmm. The Full Moon's owner enjoyed sneaking up on the little buggers in the Dumpsters and scaring them to death. And the rank garbage didn't bother the guests. Most never even knew about this door. Sybil certainly wasn't sensitive to odors. Her office reeked of refrigerated smoke.

"Are you sure there isn't another reason?" Helen asked.

Denise stopped on the second floor to mop her forehead with her perpetual wad of tissues. Helen could see the big woman's sides were heaving and her face was red. Climbing three flights was not easy for her, and she welcomed a chance to rest.

"Sybil thought she could cut back on trash pickup one day a week if she doused the Dumpsters with perfume," Denise said. "It's not supposed to be used that way, but Sybil is always looking for a way to save money."

"Now, that makes sense," Helen said. She thought honest trash smelled better. She'd caught an unpleasant whiff of decay under the perfume. But she didn't say anything. Denise seemed proud of this pungent cost-cutting innovation.

"We had a stroke of luck this morning," Denise said. "A new cleaner showed up at eight o'clock. That's a minor miracle right there, someone in South Florida looking for work so early in the morning. He saw our ad in the paper. Sybil and I had him clean room 112. He did a good job. We hired him on the spot."

"He?" Helen said. "Rhonda's replacement is a man?"

"A cute one, too," Denise said.

"Cute?" Helen said. Sister Mary Justine never said *cute*. Denise no longer looked like the stern nun. She was smiling like a love-struck teen. "How old is this guy?"

"He's twenty-four," Denise said. "They were very good years."

"Why is a guy that age cleaning rooms?" Helen said. "He could make real money in construction. If he's that cute, he could park cars on South Beach for big tips."

"Maybe he likes it," Denise said. "His grandma cleaned houses. She taught him well. A man can clean as well as a woman. I'm not prejudiced."

"Especially against cute guys," Helen said, but she grinned, and Denise knew she was kidding. "Hey, I've nothing against scenic coworkers."

"You won't see him until after break today. You're working the third floor again with Cheryl, until your ex leaves the hotel. We figured you'd be safest up there. Sondra and I will keep an eye out for your ex. Here's your smock."

Helen put on her cloak of invisibility, but she was jumpy and distracted all morning. There was no reason for Rob to come upstairs, but that didn't mean he wouldn't.

The cleaning did not go well. Some of it was the guests' fault. The rest of the blame went to Helen. The couple in room 308 left two used condoms on the floor. Room 310 was a checkout, which required a deep cleaning. It didn't seem especially difficult until Helen opened the nightstand drawer to dust the inside.

"What's this stuff?" she said. "Looks like mulch."

"Don't touch it. Let me see." Cheryl pulled a red bag out of the trash. "I thought so. Sunflower seeds. The guy spit the hulls into the drawer."

Helen's stomach flopped like a fresh-caught fish. "What's wrong with the waste can?" she said.

"He doesn't have to use it. He's not at home," Cheryl said. "People go to hotel rooms so they can indulge their fantasies. For some it's sex, drugs or booze. But others enjoy being slobs. Women who have to pick up after their families love to throw towels on the floor. Men whose wives nag them for being sloppy Joes leave nasty surprises like this."

Cheryl found a shirt cardboard in the trash and scooped the damp sunflower hulls out of the drawer.

"Doesn't that make you mad?" Helen asked.

"No," she said. "I just wish they'd tip when they go on a slob bender."

"Did Mr. Sunflower leave anything besides those hulls?" Helen asked.

"Seventeen cents."

"Bringing our tip total for today up to a dollar twenty-three," Helen said.

"I've fought to stay off welfare, because I want my daughter to be proud of me," Cheryl said. "But it's a struggle. If everybody tipped a dollar a room, my life would be much easier."

"Twenty rooms. Ten bucks a day for each of us," Helen said. "If I was making an extra fifty a week, my uninsured root canal wouldn't have been so painful. A bellman carries the bags thirty feet across the lobby and gets tipped two bucks. We're up here lifting mattresses and cleaning spit seeds out of drawers, and people won't tip us." She flipped the spread off the bed so hard she knocked the lamp shade crooked.

"Helen, don't waste your energy getting angry over what you can't change," Cheryl said. "It will wear you down." She scraped out the rest of the drawer and sprayed the inside with cleaner.

Suddenly Helen understood why Rhonda refused to clean the whipped-cream Jacuzzi. After years of dirty diapers on the bedspreads and wet towels on the floor, something had snapped. Rhonda was tired of being used and angry at the inhumane expectation that she'd clean up anything, no matter how disgusting. She felt wiped out, invisible. No wonder she ran off with a man who gave her fifty-dollar bills. It beat dollar-twenty-three tips.

Cheryl didn't seem to be afflicted with that same anger. She serenely vacuumed the carpet. Helen straightened the lamp shade and turned out the lights. They closed the door on another clean room.

"Let's see what delights 314 has for us," Cheryl said. She started to open the door when she heard a low feral growl, and slammed it shut.

"Is that a guest?" Helen said. It sounded like the room was rented to a werewolf.

"It's an illegal dog," Cheryl said. "Probably a little ankle biter, but I'm not going in there. I'm a maid, not a postal worker. I'll tell the front desk. The guests sneaked in that animal to avoid the twenty-five-dollar pet fee."

Any other day, Helen would have laughed. But the growling dog made her more jittery. It was something else she didn't expect when she wanted no surprises. Helen was so rattled, she pulled the sheets off a bed she'd already made.

Every time Cheryl's walkie-talkie squawked, Helen jumped or dropped something. Denise, the head housekeeper, kept her alerted to Rob's progress. She called Cheryl's walkie-talkie every half hour. Rob was in his room at nine, nine thirty and ten that morning. Ditto for ten, ten thirty and eleven. At noon he finally emerged from 210, looking freshly showered and shaved. Denise called upstairs, and Helen hid in an empty guest room until she gave the all-clear.

When Rob's car was gone for twenty minutes, Denise searched his room. She came upstairs to deliver her report. "Your ex wears expensive clothes, throws his socks on the floor, leaves beer cans by the bed and has a woman's phone number on the dresser."

"Nothing has changed," Helen said. "He's still skirt chasing. At least he's single now."

"He's taking Rogaine, too. He's losing his hair."

"Good." Helen felt a small, secret satisfaction. Rob was proud of his thick blond hair.

"What's the unlucky woman's name?" Helen said.

"Juliana," Denise said. "I wrote down her phone number."

That was the dress shop where Helen used to work. She felt dizzy with relief. The former boutique was now a coal-fired-pizza place. "Thank God," Helen said. "Juliana isn't a woman. It's where I worked four or five jobs ago. There's no way Rob can trace me from that number. The dress shop is out of business."

"Oh, *that* Juliana," Denise said. "I remember reading about it in the newspapers. Or maybe I saw it on TV. Wasn't there a murder there?"

A murder. And a trial. Helen's testimony didn't make the paper, but some of her coworkers' did. Her ex could find the details in the old newspapers at the library. He could track down the shop's staff and find Helen. She frantically ran through her mental files. Who had testified? The owner was in Canada. One coworker was dead. But there was Tara. Right. Helen had to call Tara and warn her. She would be an easy target for Rob's greasy charm.

"Quick! I need to use the pay phone in the lobby," Helen said. "Will you stand guard for me? There's someone I have to warn, a woman from my old job. Rob may be able to find her."

"Use my cell," Cheryl said.

Helen looked up Tara's home number in a guest room phone book and punched it in with fear-clumsy fingers. There was no answer. Good, she thought. If I can't reach her, neither can Rob.

She didn't leave Tara a message. Helen didn't want the former saleswoman to know her current job. Rob might be a flirtatious old white guy, but Tara was susceptible to old white guys, especially if they looked rich. Rob would look rich even when he was down to his last dime.

"No luck," Helen said, and handed the phone back to Cheryl.

She tried to work, but she was useless. In room 317 Helen knocked over a half-full can of Pepsi. The sticky liquid ran over the edge of the dresser and dripped onto the carpet. Helen tried to wipe it up, and smeared it further.

"Good thing this room is a checkout," Cheryl said, scrubbing the stained carpet. "There would be hell to pay if you spilled soda on a guest's belongings."

When she finished rescuing the dresser and the carpet, Cheryl gave Helen her cell phone. "Try again," she said. "You won't be any good until you reach that woman."

Helen called. Still no answer. She didn't have Tara's cell phone number. She imagined a hundred disastrous scenarios, each one a horror movie starring Rob. In *The Great Giveaway*, she saw Tara handing Helen's home address to Rob. In *My Little Runaway*, Helen saw Tara abandoning her current boyfriend for Rob. Helen knew that last movie would never be made. Paulie might be crude as a bus-station toilet stall, but he was filthy rich. Exotic-looking Tara, with her size-two figure and long dark curtain of hair, had an adding machine for a heart. She'd figure out Rob didn't have any money the first time he hit her up for the dinner check.

Still, the movies didn't stop. Helen continued to torment herself. She dropped a room phone and hopelessly tangled the cord. She tripped over a wastebasket full of cigarette ashes.

Cheryl slapped her cell phone into Helen's hand for the third time. "Call again." She sounded out of patience. Her daughter might be named Angel, but Cheryl wasn't a saint yet.

Helen hit redial, the only button on the phone she could manage, and prayed.

Tara picked up on the third ring. "Helen," she said.

Helen heard the pleasure in Tara's voice. After a rocky start, they'd genuinely liked each other.

"I haven't heard from you in ages," Tara said. "I guess you're calling to thank me. Congratulations. No one deserves good luck more than you."

"What good luck?" Helen said, knowing she didn't have any.

"The St. Louis lawyer who's trying to track you down, silly," Tara said. "That's why you're calling me, isn't it? He said you'd inherited almost a million dollars. He wanted to get in touch with you. I didn't know your phone number—oh, wait, you don't have one, do you? I couldn't remember your address, but I said you lived in that cute little place near the old shop, the Cranford."

"The Cranford?" Helen said, relief flooding her voice.

"Yes. That's the name of your apartment house, isn't it?"

"Right," Helen lied. "The Cranford Apartments. I just called to say thank-you. It was a complete surprise. How is Paulie these days?" She played a brief game of catch-up. As they talked, Helen wondered if Tara still flipped her waist-length hair. It had seemed to be in constant motion at the store.

When Helen hung up the phone, she sank down with relief on a freshly made bed.

She was safe. At least for now. Tara had accidentally sent Rob to a dead end.

CHAPTER 8

$\mathbf{H}$elen spent her break staring at the rain. This was a Florida frog strangler, a lashing rain that turned the long lobby windows into tropical waterfalls. Even through the gray veil of water, Helen could see the Full Moon's lawn was a lake and the parking lot was flooded. She watched the headlights of the cars trying to negotiate the hubcap-deep water.

A storm so fierce would be over soon, but so would Helen's break. She morosely munched her pretzels, gone soggy in the humidity. She might as well eat salted sawdust. Nothing was going right today.

"Helen!" Cheryl said. "Get away from those windows. What if your ex-husband sees you?" Her dark curls were crinkled with concern.

"He won't be out in this weather," Helen said. "Rob is holed up in a bar somewhere."

"You're taking an unnecessary risk," she said. "Let's go upstairs. Ready to tackle room 323?"

"Do we have a choice?" Helen tossed the rest of her limp pretzels in the trash and brushed the salt off her smock.

"There's always a choice," Cheryl said. "But we may not like it."

Helen was in no mood for philosophy. Even a stoic would have trouble facing room 323.

She nearly gagged when Cheryl unlocked the door. The greasy odor of old pizza and stale cigarette smoke smacked her in the face.

"No doubt about it," Helen said. "A smoker slept here."

"Slept badly, too," Cheryl said. "You can tell a lot looking at a bed someone's slept in. You can see if he was alone or with someone. When you see the sheets all tumbled and twisted, you know he had a night full of worries."

Helen hoped she didn't have many nights like this guest. The sheets were tortured into knots and the pillows were punched into unyielding lumps. She pulled off the bedding and put on new sheets, the king-size expanse of linen flapping like a ship's sails. As she raised her arms, lightning strikes of pain threaded down her shoulders and stabbed her neck and back. Her body still wasn't used to hard labor.

"Doesn't this job wear you down?" Helen said, rubbing her sore shoulder. She had another date with the Motrin bottle tonight.

"Working at the convenience store was worse," Cheryl said, carefully dumping a butt-filled wastebasket into the trash bag. That was supposed to be Helen's job, but Cheryl wasn't taking any chances today. "I worked the late shift and lived in constant fear I would be gunned down by a robber. Drunk guys yelled at me. Women screamed when I didn't move fast enough. After two weeks I quit to clean homes, but I burned out on that, too. You can't please some people. When this job opened up, I took it and was glad. I do my work. No one breathes down my neck. When I'm done, I go home."

A good attitude, Helen thought, though she wasn't sure that 323 would ever get done. The room had more ash than Pompeii. Helen sprayed the furniture with lemon wax, but the cigarette ash floated into the air and settled somewhere else. She sprayed the dresser so much, the ash stuck in the lemon muck.

Enough, Helen decided. Smokers sleep here. They're not going to mind a little ash. She started dusting inside the drawers. At least this guest didn't spit sunflower seeds in them.

Helen wiped out the top drawer in the long dark dresser. It wouldn't shut. She pulled it out a little more and shoved it back in. The drawer was stuck. She yanked it harder, and pulled it out completely. Helen tried to force it back into the dresser. No luck. Helen felt like a befuddled baby trying to shove a square puzzle piece into a round hole.

"What's wrong with this drawer?" Helen asked, trying to slam it into the dresser.

Cheryl popped out of the bathroom. "Another problem?" she said.

"This drawer won't go back in," Helen said, sounding like a petulant child.

Cheryl put down her bathroom spray and got on her knees before the dresser, as if bowing to a dark beast. She expertly jiggled the drawer, while making soft, soothing sounds. It slid smoothly into place.

"I'm sorry I'm so much trouble today," Helen said.

"That drawer is not your fault," Cheryl said. "It's left over from the bank robber."

"You had a bank robber stay here?"

"I thought everyone knew about Donnie Duane Herkins. Robbed the Seafield Bank and Trust six months ago. It was all over TV."

"I don't follow the news as well as I should," Helen said. "I guess I missed that story."

"Donnie Duane didn't actually rob the bank," Cheryl said. "He carjacked a depositor on her way to the bank in broad daylight. She was an office manager delivering the cash deposits for a telemarketing company. The owners were too cheap to hire an armored car service.

They made their office manager take the money to the bank. Donnie Duane pistol-whipped the woman and stole a hundred thousand dollars in cash."

Helen whistled.

"That's a lot of cash. What were they selling?"

"Septic tank cleaner," Denise said. "The cops thought it was way too much cash, too. Once they started poking around, the telemarketing company suddenly pulled the plug. They're out of business—at least under that name.

"Donnie Duane got all their dirty money, then took a room at our hotel, two miles from the bank."

"That was dumb," Helen said. "Why would he do that?"

Cheryl shrugged. "Didn't make the slightest sense to me. The FBI believed he had an accomplice in the area and was waiting for the guy to show up when he got caught."

"Did the robber go to prison?"

"He wasn't that lucky," Cheryl said. "His picture was on TV every ten seconds. An anonymous caller spotted him at our hotel and told the police. They surrounded the place and evacuated everybody so he couldn't take hostages. Donnie Duane was asleep in this very room— 323. He didn't realize what was going on until it was too late. He tried to climb out the window."

"I thought the windows were sealed," Helen said.

"They are. He threw a chair through the glass and tried to escape. He didn't make it. They shot him right out of the window. Donnie Duane died in the parking lot. He looked so young lying there on the blacktop. I don't think I'll ever forget that sight."

Helen stared at the ordinary square hotel window with its plain blue curtain. It was hard to believe a man died there. Cheryl leaned against the bathroom door, her chores forgotten. Her voice was sad, but her eyes were bright and her face was pink. Donnie Duane's death was the most exciting thing that ever happened at the Full Moon.

"The FBI took this room apart looking for the money," Cheryl said. "They never found the hundred thousand dollars. They think he may have been setting up a drug buy, and that's why he stayed here, waiting for his contact."

"Do you think his accomplice made off with the hundred thousand?"

"No," Cheryl said. "If the deal went through, Donnie Duane would have cleared out. There was no other reason for him to stay. It was plain foolish with a manhunt going on. The loot was never found. That cash just vanished.

"The FBI searched the hotel for days. The dresser drawers have never been right since they worked the room over. You never saw such a mess, but the feds didn't find a dollar. Rhonda and I used to joke that we were gonna find that money ourselves and disappear."

"Do you think it's still here in the hotel?" Helen said.

"I don't think so," Cheryl said, "or we would have found it." But her eyes shifted and she studied her sturdy shoes. Helen saw a dark flush steal across Cheryl's cheeks.

She's a terrible liar, Helen thought. The staff thinks the cash is still hidden here. That's why Denise was pulling up palm trees, Rhonda had a head full of dust bunnies and Sondra was taking apart air vents.

"What would you do if you found the money?" Helen asked.

Cheryl didn't hesitate, and Helen knew she'd given this question a lot of thought. "I'd take my Angel and move to Ohio."

"Why Ohio?" Helen said.

"Because I'm sick of the Florida heat. Because my mother treats my daughter like a second-class citizen. Because my Aunt Claire lives in Ohio and she loves Angel. There's another little girl like her in Aunt Claire's neighborhood. She's the same age as Angel. They could go to school together, and Angel wouldn't be so alone."

"Are the kids mean to her?" Helen said. "They used to call me Four Eyes because I wore glasses."

"It's nothing that obvious," Cheryl said. "The teachers watch for that kind of thing. Only her grandmother calls her a retard." The bitterness in those words made Helen wince. "The other children are nice and polite, but they don't invite Angel to their birthday parties, and she sits by herself in the cafeteria. Don't get me wrong. I'm in favor of inclusion. I'd just like Angel to be in a school where she'd be more included.

"But I can't afford the move, so I'm stuck here. It's another dream that will never come true. I looked for that money. We all did. The most I ever found was a five-dollar bill on the hall floor—and that was before the robber checked in."

Rhonda had been waving fifty-dollar bills before she took off. Did she stumble across the bank money? She'd told Helen what she'd do if she found it. She'd disappear, same as Cheryl.

Now Rhonda was gone.

Then Helen was struck by another thought. Maybe Donnie Duane's accomplice wasn't a man. Maybe it was a woman. A woman who worked at the hotel. That's why he checked into the Full Moon. She put him in touch with the drug dealer. And she knew where the money was. She tipped off the police and got Donnie Duane killed. Then she waited six months, dug around in some dusty hiding place, and disappeared with her boyfriend and the hundred grand from the holdup.

Nah, that had to be a complete fairy tale. Rhonda dressed like an old woman. She wouldn't date drug dealers. But she was definitely gone.

"Has anyone heard from Rhonda?" Helen said.

"Not a word," Cheryl said. "I never liked that girl. Leaving us in the lurch is so typical. I'm glad she's gone."

Helen bet Rhonda was happy to be out of here, too.

Cheryl seemed strangely eager to end the conversation. They finished their rooms early, at two thirty. Helen's ex-husband still wasn't back at the hotel. At least the sun was shining for Helen's walk home. Cheryl sneaked her out by the smelly Dumpsters and Helen promptly stepped in an ankle-deep puddle. She squished down to a pay phone hidden behind a dripping ficus tree and called Margery.

"Is Rob there?" she asked.

"Haven't seen a tail feather on that buzzard," her landlady said. "Come on home."

It was too wet to sit out by the pool, but Helen knocked on Margery's door. She was making homemade screwdrivers with a juicer she'd confiscated from one of the hightailed tenants in 2C. The juicer sounded like a buzz saw as it gleefully gutted the oranges. Margery held down the hapless orange halves, a maniacal grin on her wrinkled face. She looked cool in a tie-dyed purple top and lavender shorts. Slender thong sandals showed off her bold tangerine pedicure.

"Where's Peggy?" Helen said. "Still at work?"

"Out on a date with that guy from the other night," Margery said, fretting and measuring.

"That's good," Helen said.

"Is it?" Margery asked. She handed Helen a tall, frosted glass. "Vitamin C with a little anesthesia."

"I need it," Helen said. "I'd like to forget this whole day."

She told Margery how Rob had tricked her former coworker, Tara, into giving away her address. "He told her I had a big inheritance. The louse couldn't even give me an imaginary million dollars. He said 'almost a million.' What's wrong with a full seven figures?"

"He told Tara you inherited a fortune and she fell for it," Margery said. "Oldest trick in the book, but it still works."

"If Tara wasn't such a ditz about names, Rob would be here at the Coronado." Helen downed nearly half a drink at the thought.

"How good a detective is your ex?" Margery said, taking a healthy swig of her own drink. "Think he can find you?"

"He couldn't find a job," Helen said. "He looked for one for seven years."

"I'm serious," Margery said.

"I don't know," Helen said. "I thought I knew the man, but I didn't. He sponged off me. He strung me along with promises, borrowed money he never returned, let me buy him expensive presents, and all the time I felt sorry for him because he couldn't find work equal to his vast talents."

"He's a good con artist," Margery said. "He's highly motivated to find you. He needs money. He hates work. He's smart, and he knows how to use women."

Helen felt stupid. It was all true, and the woman he'd used most was her.

"It's not going to take him long to find out there are no Cranford Apartments in this neighborhood," Margery said. "Then he'll look at similar names within walking distance of your old dress shop. There's the Randell House, two blocks away. He might see the Crumley Arms, the Brandford—or the Coronado. He could be knocking on my door in a day or two."

"Unless he thinks Tara lied to him and starts looking somewhere else," Helen said. "I'm harder to track down than you think. I don't have a phone, a bank account, a credit card or a driver's license. I'm not in any employer's computers. I get paid cash under the table. I'm not traceable."

"Except you have this habit of getting mixed up with murder," Margery said.

"But so far, my name's stayed out of the paper," Helen said.

"Then you've been lucky."

"And I'll stay lucky," Helen said.

"Your luck ran out when Rob got on that plane for Fort Lauderdale," Margery said.

CHAPTER 9

....

This was Helen's second day of slipping into the hotel the back way. She paced by the rusty door for about a minute, but it seemed longer. The nearby Dumpsters made the wait longer. The cloying perfume didn't mask the decay. It made the reek worse.

Hiding never works, Helen thought. I ran from Rob and look what happened. He's here in this hotel, digging into my past and ruining my future. How am I going to get out of this? My mother was right: We're bound till death parts us. But will it be my death or his that sets me free?

She wanted to get away from the foul smell, but she had to stick close to the Dumpsters. Rob might look out his window and see her loitering.

Helen heard a creak and the door opened. The head housekeeper, soothing, motherly Denise, was smiling on the threshold. Helen felt calmer already.

"I'm glad you're here. I was about to gag on that trash perfume," Helen said. "It smells like someone poured cheap aftershave on spoiled meat."

Denise wrinkled her small, turned-up nose. "That trash does seem extra stinky," she said. "Too bad it won't be picked up until tomorrow. I'll tell Sybil we should go back to three pickups a week. While we're talking trash, your ex-husband was up and out early this morning."

"Rob is never awake before ten unless there's money involved," Helen said.

"I searched his room," Denise said. "This time he's got the name of a septic-tank cleaner on his dresser. Maybe he's full of shit."

Helen felt the blood drain from her face.

"What's the matter, hon? You're dead white," Denise said. "I'm sorry. I didn't mean to make a tasteless joke."

"He's getting closer," Helen said. "I used to be a tele-marketer. I sold septic-tank cleaner. The company is out of business now. The feds raided it. Most of my old bosses are in jail."

"Wish mine were," Denise said. "If the company's gone, there's no way he can track you down. Relax."

Helen still felt sick and scared. Rob could read the stories about the raid in the newspaper files at the library. He'd find her coworkers. Which one would talk to him? Taniqua? Maria? She didn't think they had her home address, but did they know where she worked now? Some thirty people were crammed into that telephone boiler room, but they didn't socialize like normal office workers. Did she even know their last names? What was Taniqua's—Johnson? Smith? Washington? She had one of those last names that went on for pages in the phone book. Maria was the same thing—Rodriguez. Or was it Gomez? She knew it was the Hispanic version of Smith. Rob wasn't going to find them. But he might find out her next job. She had to get in touch with Millicent's bridal salon. She'd call Millicent today.

"The other girls have been thinking about how to get rid of your ex-husband," Denise said, pulling Helen out of the past. "Cheryl has this free offer from a new Inter-net dating service. Your ex-husband has a laptop. She left the card in his room. Maybe he'll sign up for a free date."

"Thanks," Helen said. "But it's not fair to sic him on another woman."

"You never know. He could meet his match," Denise said.

"There you are." It was Sondra.

Helen jumped at her voice. She wasn't expecting Sondra in the stairwell. The slender clerk looked like a brown satin angel in a white linen sheath. No wonder Rob hit on her.

"I don't know if we should be worried about this or not," Sondra said. "Rhonda's mama called. Shirley hasn't heard from her daughter in a couple of days. She went to her apartment and Rhonda's cat, Snowball, was at the door. The poor animal acted like it hadn't eaten in days."

"My cat always acts like that," Helen said.

"The food dish was completely empty and Snowball didn't have any water," Sondra said. "It was drinking out of the toilet." She screwed up her face in disgust.

"You don't have cats, do you?" Helen said. "That's their favorite cocktail."

"All I know is Rhonda takes good care of that cat," Sondra said. "Her mama says she always leaves Snowball plenty of food and water. Shirley is worried. She doesn't think Rhonda's been home for two or three days, and she doesn't answer her cell phone."

If Rhonda found that hundred thousand dollars, would she tell her mother? Helen wondered. Would I tell mine? She knew that answer. Helen didn't trust her mother. She'd turn in her own daughter so Helen could be "reunited" with Rob. If Helen found a hundred thou, she'd do exactly what Rhonda did—take the money, leave the lid up on the emergency water supply for the cat, and figure her mother would check in a day or two and rescue Snowball.

Denise didn't seem worried, either. "She'll turn up," she said. "I'll bet she's shacked up with that biker boyfriend of hers."

"Rhonda has a biker boyfriend?" Helen said. That was a surprise.

"Sam. Fat guy with a beer gut and a beard braid. Rides a big old Harley. Knocks Rhonda around when he's had a few. I heard he was selling meth, but he can't be much of a drug dealer. He's always borrowing money from Rhonda and he never pays it back. Rhonda likes to sleep with trash."

"Our Rhonda?" Helen said. "The woman who dresses like a church lady?"

"That's the one," Denise said. "She may look sweet but she's got some bad ways."

"She told me her boyfriend was rich and handsome," Helen said. "He gave her fifty dollars. I saw the money."

"You saw the fifty," Denise said. "You didn't see him give it to her. I doubt any man would give her that much, even if she got on her knees for him."

"Denise!" Helen said. She wished the housekeeper didn't look so much like Sister Mary Justine.

"Denise is right," Sondra said. "Rhonda has a low-down streak when it comes to men. She showed up at work once with a black eye. Said she fell."

"She fell, all right," Denise said. "She fell into bed with that biker again."

"Sam sure doesn't sound like the handsome, generous man she told me about," Helen said. "Maybe Rhonda's got two boyfriends."

"Huh," Sondra said. "She's lucky to have Sam."

"We've wasted enough time on that woman," Denise said. "We have fifty-six rooms to clean. Cheryl is already upstairs on two. I'll take the first floor. Helen, you need a little eye candy. You work with the new guy, Craig, on three."

"I like working with Cheryl," Helen said.

"Don't get huffy. I'm not fixing you up on a blind date. Craig will cheer you up. Make you quit worrying so much. Your ex won't get past Sondra or me. Come on upstairs and I'll introduce you."

Denise puffed her way up to the third floor, despite Helen's protests that they could take the elevator if Rob was gone.

"You never know when he'll pop back." When Denise got to the third-floor landing, she stopped and put on light pink lipstick from a little tube with a mirror on the side.

She really likes this Craig, Helen thought. I wonder why she doesn't work with him. Because she wants to do me a favor. Besides, Denise is too sensible to make a fool of herself over a young man. A little lipstick is as silly as she'll get.

Craig was stocking the cart in the third-floor housekeeping room. He looked like the lead singer in a boy band. His blond hair was dyed dandelion yellow, but its fake color suited him. His eyes were hazel with a wicked sparkle. His chin was strong. Even the smock couldn't hide that surfer body. Underneath, he was wearing a plain white T-shirt and blue jeans—the sexiest and simplest of men's outfits. He was so naturally cute, Helen wanted to pet him.

"Do you want gloves?" Denise asked.

The question startled Helen, till she realized Denise was talking about latex cleaning gloves.

"I do," Craig said. When he slipped them on, Helen noticed a wide Band-Aid on his wrist.

"What about you?" Denise asked Helen.

"Can't stand the feel," she said. "They're hot and sticky."

"Amateur," Denise said. "When you've worked here long enough, you won't want to touch some of that stuff in those rooms. Craig already found that out. He cleaned the honeymoon Jacuzzi yesterday."

Craig grinned, showing even white teeth. "I don't think I'll eat a hot-fudge sundae anytime soon."

"He really cleaned in the corners," Denise said.

"The Jacuzzi has a round tub," Helen said, wondering why she was behaving like such a jerk.

"What I mean," Denise said, "is this man can clean. He knows his way around a scrub brush."

"That's a switch," Helen said. "You couldn't tell by the men who stay at this hotel."

"Hey, give me a break," Craig said. "I can see why you're down on guys after some of those rooms. But we can be neat and clean. I'll prove it."

"He's hardworking and shows up on time," Denise said. "That's rare in South Florida. Take good care of our new man. I have lots to do today."

"Do you want to dust and make beds or clean the bathrooms?" Helen said.

"I like to alternate," Craig said. "I don't like routines."

Helen hated to admit it, but Craig lived up to Denise's praise. He cleaned with a professional system, starting with the beds, then dusting his way around the room clockwise. He wiped inside the drawers, looked under the furniture, and checked around the beds for left-behind shoes and old condoms. He dusted the pictures bolted to the walls and checked to see if any were loose. He'd mastered the art of cleaning mirrors without smearing the glass. He used what Helen's grandmother called "elbow grease."

The day seemed to go better with Craig around. People picked their towels off the floor and left five-dollar tips.

"Hey, look at this," Craig said. "The stay-over guest in this room didn't put out the 'Please Change the Bed Linens' card. Not only that, she made her own bed."

"Bless her," Helen said.

"Does using the linens two days in a row really save our natural resources?" Craig said. "Or is that management bullshit?"

"It saves my natural resources," Helen said. "Less bending and lifting for me. I thank anyone who saves me a linen change. We've got more good news. Room 323 wasn't rented. We can bypass the hotel's nastiest room."

"I'm kind of disappointed," Craig said. "I've heard so much about it."

"You'll get your chance soon enough," Helen said. "We're making good time. It's two o'clock and only the honeymoon suite is left."

She unlocked the suite door. Craig entered first. "Hey, guess what's all over the floor and the bed?" He blocked her view with his broad shoulders. Helen noticed how his back tapered into firm buns.

"Hershey's syrup? Honey? Chocolate ice cream?" She'd found them all on honeymoon beds.

Craig shook his head.

"Not bananas again?" Helen said. "Those are worse than whipped cream."

"Use your imagination. It's the honeymoon suite," Craig said.

"If it was my marriage, it would be Rocky Road," Helen said.

Craig laughed and stepped aside. A trail of white rose petals led to the deliciously rumpled bed. The sheets were covered with the fragrant petals.

"This marriage is a bed of roses," Craig said.

"That's so sweet," Helen said. "I hope it's true."

"Some people do live happily ever after. Not all men are pigs." Craig looked sad, and Helen wondered if he'd been hurt, too. She wanted to hug him. No, she wanted to do a lot more than that. An uncomfortable silence stretched between them.

"Well, I'd better get to work," Helen said. "I'll take the two bathrooms." She closed the door behind her, hoping to shut out Craig's words. Not all men were pigs. Phil certainly wasn't. Why did she find Mr. Boy Band so attractive? She was worse than Rob, flirting with someone eighteen years younger.

I'm a slut, she thought, and scrubbed harder, as if she could wipe away her flirtatious thoughts.

She finished both bathrooms in record time. When she opened the door, the suite smelled of lemon polish.

Craig had made the enormous bed and was vacuuming up the last rose petals. She watched the long, strong muscles in his arms as he worked the heavy vacuum.

When Craig turned off the shrieking machine, she said, "That's it. We've finished early."

"I really enjoyed working with you today." Craig looked shyly at the freshly vacuumed floor. "Care to join me for a drink on Las Olas?"

Helen searched for the nicest way to say no.

"We could have coffee if you don't drink," he said.

"Thanks, Craig," Helen said, "but I'm meeting my boyfriend." How was that for subtle?

"The good ones are all taken," he said, and flashed that engaging grin. "I'd still like to have coffee with you sometime—as a friend. But I won't keep you. I'll go change."

Craig pulled off his smock, revealing the tight white T-shirt. Running a vacuum cleaner sure pumped his pecs. Then he was down the hall and gone.

Helen was flattered and flustered. She pushed the cart to the housekeeper's room, humming a little tune. Denise and Cheryl were inside, counting supplies.

"How was the new guy?" Denise said. She looked way too innocent.

"He's a good worker," Helen said.

"A fast one, too," Denise said.

"He ask you out?" Cheryl said.

Helen said nothing, but a blush gave her away.

"Hah. I thought so," Denise said.

"He asked me out, too," Cheryl said. Suddenly Helen saw how pretty she used to be, with her pink complexion and curly dark hair. "I told him no. I had to get home to Angel. But it felt good, anyway. It's been a long time since a hottie asked me out."

"How did you know I said no?" Helen said.

"You wouldn't be stupid enough to throw away a man like Phil," Cheryl said. "But I bet you enjoyed the invitation, same as me."

"Maybe the guy has a mother complex," Helen said. "I'm a lot older."

"I've got news for you, sweetie, you don't look like anyone's mother," Denise said.

"Anything I can help you with before I leave?" Helen said.

"For that subtle change of subject, you can help us haul the trash bags to the Dumpsters," Denise said. She called Sondra on the walkie-talkie.

"It's clear," Sondra said. "No sign of you-know-who. Come down the service elevator. I'll distract Helen's ex if he shows up."

"I bet you will," Denise said. She handed Helen and Cheryl each a huge, heavy industrial trash bag, then took two more in her muscular arms. Helen was pretty sure Sister Mary Justine didn't have muscles like that.

When Denise unlocked the fence around the Dumpsters, hordes of flies poured out. "Pew. Get a whiff of that," she said. "Something must have crawled inside and died, maybe a raccoon."

"That smell is strong for a raccoon. Must be something bigger. Maybe it's a dog," Helen said.

"How can a dog get into a tall Dumpster behind a locked fence?" Denise said.

"It's just rotten trash," Cheryl said. "Nothing's dead in there. The trash man's coming tomorrow. Let it go."

"I hope he comes early," Denise said. "By tomorrow we'll be able to smell it out front."

"It is powerful," Helen said. "You don't think some kid was playing around in the trash and fell in?"

"No!" Cheryl said. "That's a ridiculous idea."

"Sybil chases off any kids," Denise said. "That's one reason why we put that perfume all over the trash, to keep the kids out."

But the wind shifted and the sickly sweet odor was stronger. Helen's stomach turned. She smelled death.

"Let's go back inside," Cheryl said. She sounded frightened.

"I'd better check those Dumpsters," Helen said. "If some kid fell in, I'll never forgive myself."

"What are you doing?" Cheryl said as Helen dragged a small, sturdy recycling bin over to the tall Dumpster with the most flies.

"I'm going to take a look inside," Helen said.

"No, don't," Cheryl said. "There could be things in there. Snakes. Rats."

"They'll run at the first sign of humans," Helen said. She hoped that was true.

"Diseases," Cheryl said desperately. "There are diseases and bacteria in there. You'll catch something."

"I'll take a shower," Helen said.

"Please, don't! I've got a bad feeling," Cheryl said.

"All the more reason for me to look," Helen said. She hoisted herself up onto the bin. The Dumpster was sticky with unknown substances, and she wished she were wearing those gloves. An evil yellow liquid oozed down one corner.

She held her breath and pulled herself inside. The bags shifted and squished under her feet. The smell was overpowering. Flies buzzed frantically, bombing her face. She tried to shoo them away, but there were too many. Ouch! Did flies bite or were there mosquitoes in there, too? Helen slapped and fought the crazed insects as she pawed through the trash. A metal rod poked through a bag and scratched her leg. She hoped her tetanus shots were updated.

"There's nothing up here," Helen said. "I've shifted two layers."

"It could have crawled under those bags at the bottom and died," Denise said.

"No, it didn't," Cheryl said. "Get out of there now before you get hurt."

Helen kicked some bags aside. "Nope," she said. "I'm almost to the bottom. There's nothing. Wait! I see something orange, like cat fur. No, not orange. More like—"

Red. Long red hair and a stick-thin arm.

"Rhonda's sleeping with the trash," Helen said.

CHAPTER 10

···

I'm standing on a dead woman, Helen thought. She stepped back and her foot sank into something sticky. Her stomach made a sickening sideways shift. Please God, don't let it be Rhonda. Helen looked down and saw she'd squashed a carton of ice cream.

A fat fly stung her neck, and she slapped it. Maybe I can slap some sense into myself. Poor Rhonda's dead and I've insulted her. *Rhonda's sleeping with the trash.* How could I say something so stupid?

The parking lot was unnaturally quiet, except for a soft, steady weeping. She peered over the side of the Dumpster and saw Cheryl was making that mournful sound. Denise stood as if she'd been turned to stone. Even her curly white hair didn't move.

"I'm sorry, Cheryl," Helen said. "I should have never said that about Rhonda. I guess I was in shock, but that's no excuse."

Cheryl cried harder, a roller coaster of wails that raised the hair on Helen's neck. I've got to get out of here, she thought. Denise was still paralyzed, staring at the body with her mouth hanging open in surprise. Helen wondered if one of the buzzing flies would sail inside, and almost giggled. Do something, Denise. You got me into this mess.

Helen looked down again at the tangle of orange-red hair and the pale greenish arm lying across a clear plastic bag. She could see a red-and-white can through the plastic.

"Rhonda is hugging the honeymooners' whipped cream," Helen said. "She'd hate that." She almost giggled again, but managed to control herself. What's wrong with my mouth? Why are all these wretched things coming out of it?

Cheryl howled louder. The sound jarred loose a wild, hopeful thought in Helen. Maybe the woman in the Dumpster wasn't Rhonda. Maybe it was some stranger and she wasn't dead. She was a homeless person who'd crawled in there for a nap and fainted from the heat.

Helen moved the head gently to see the face. She heard a shriek of shock and horror, then realized she'd made that sound. She was screaming. The woman was definitely Rhonda, though Helen hardly recognized her. She was also definitely dead. Her face was a dreadful mix of dark reds, vile greens and purples. It was oddly lopsided. She's been beaten, Helen thought. Someone hit her so hard they broke the bones in her face.

Helen slowly lowered the battered head back on the trash bag, as if it were a pillow. Rhonda had had a hard life and a harder death.

Cheryl was making odd birdlike screeches. They finally broke Denise's trance. "Cheryl," she said. "Stop that." It was her stern-nun voice, and it worked, sort of. Cheryl subsided into soft weeping.

Denise issued her next order to Helen. "Get out of that Dumpster," she said. "You can't do anything more for Rhonda. You crawled in there to find her, and that was brave. You saved her from being buried in a landfill."

Helen looked once more at Rhonda's broken body. She was wearing a high-collared blue blouse, bloody and ripped, exposing an arm with black-red streaks. The arm was limp. So was her neck. Rigor mortis had come and gone. Helen remembered the last time she'd seen Rhonda alive. She'd watched her disappear into the night shadows, an arresting figure in her old-fashioned blouse.

"Rhonda died the night she left work," Helen said. "She wore this blouse. Her mother was right. Rhonda never abandoned her cat. She didn't make it home. She was here in this Dumpster all the time."

"God forgive me for my hard words," Denise said. The big woman seemed to collapse under the weight of her guilt. Even her tight white hair looked pressed down. Cheryl's soft tears continued, an endless reproach.

The back door banged open and Sondra rushed out, a cell phone in her hand. "What's wrong?" she said. "Who's screaming? Is someone hurt?"

"Call 911," Denise said, taking charge once more. "We've found Rhonda. She's dead."

"Dear Lord." Sondra punched in the number while Denise helped Helen out of the Dumpster. Helen's legs were wobbly. She would have fallen off the recycling bin, but Denise caught her. Her jeans were covered with odd stains, and her T-shirt was wet with sweat.

"The police are on their way," Sondra reported. "Nobody can leave the hotel. We can't check in any more guests or let anyone leave until the police question everyone. We all have to stay here. Where's the new guy, Craig?"

"I guess he's getting dressed," Helen said. "I'll go find him before he goes home."

She was glad to get away from Rhonda's battered body, the reeking Dumpster and the weeping Cheryl. The festering stink of death nearly smothered her. Flies hummed a frantic requiem.

Helen checked the laundry room on the first floor. Craig's smock was in the dirty laundry, but there was no sign of him. Did he leave already? She checked the second floor, praying her ex hadn't sneaked back into the hotel during the commotion. No Craig. No Rob, either.

Helen finally found Craig in the third-floor housekeeping room. He was on his knees, his bright yellow head wedged under a storage shelf.

"Craig?" she said.

Startled, he jerked his head up and hit it on the gray metal shelf.

"Ouch," he said. Craig backed out slowly, giving Helen a heavenly view of his hindquarters. What's the matter with me? she wondered, angry at herself. Rhonda's lying dead outside and I'm staring at some guy's buns.

"I'm sorry," Helen said. "I didn't mean to surprise you."

"You can surprise me anytime," Craig said. "But there are more interesting ways. I dropped the cap to the spray polish. It rolled under the shelf." He stood up, dusted off his knees, and held up the yellow plastic cap, treating her to his bad-boy grin.

Helen was in no mood to flirt. "Listen, there's a problem," she said. "There's been an accident. We found a dead woman in the Dumpster."

"You're kidding," he said.

"I'm not. It's the maid you replaced, Rhonda. The police don't want us to leave the hotel. You can wait with us downstairs."

"Why do I have to stay?" he said. "I didn't know her."

"It's what the cops want," she said. "Denise sent me to get you."

"OK," he said, and shrugged. He trotted alongside her like a puppy. But now Helen had no thoughts for her cute companion. Rhonda's death—no, murder—had finally sunk in. The police were on their way to the Full Moon. They'd be Seafield Village cops. Would they know the Lauderdale police? She'd had bad luck finding bodies. She didn't want the homicide detectives getting too interested in her.

In the sun-flooded lobby, a gaunt older man was violently shaking the hotel's front door.

"Why is this door locked?" he demanded. He had bird legs, Bermuda shorts and an angry red complexion. "I demand an explanation."

Denise came hurrying in, making soothing sounds. "I'm sorry, sir, but there's been a problem. The police have requested that all staff and guests remain in the hotel for a short time."

"What? I'm a prisoner? What kind of problem? I'm not here for problems. I'm on vacation."

"One of our maids was found dead, sir," Denise said. "The police are on their way."

"What does that have to do with me?" he said.

"I'm sorry for the inconvenience," Denise began.

"Inconvenience! I have dinner plans at the country club. This isn't my problem. I don't talk to the help."

You're talking to the help right now, you old creep, Helen thought.

"I'm sorry, sir, but our instructions are—"

"I'll make sure this hotel loses its stars and AAA rating, young lady," he said. "This is an outrage. I can't believe I'm delayed for a maid." He spit out the last word, then stalked over to the elevators, leaving behind an ugly silence.

"I'd better stay at the front desk in case more guests show up," Denise said. "Sondra's guarding the Dumpster and talking to the 911 operator on her cell phone. She has to stay on the line until the police arrive. Helen, will you and Craig go into the laundry room and fix Cheryl a cup of tea?"

Tea. Denise's remedy for everything from man trouble to murder. Rhonda had been the last person dosed with hot tea, after she found the body in room 323. Now we've found her body. It was a sickening thought.

Cheryl was sitting on a pile of unfolded sheets, still sniffling. Craig threw himself down on a wide laundry table.

"Don't get too comfortable." Helen filled a cup with tap water and handed it to him. "Go find a tea bag in the breakfast room and nuke this."

Craig did not look pleased to be an errand boy, but Helen was not going out in the hall. She couldn't risk running into Rob.

Cheryl's eyelids were swollen and puffy, and her cheeks were wet with tears. Helen patted her back, like a mother soothing a sick baby. Cheryl is a kind person, she thought. She must feel really guilty about the mean things she said about Rhonda. But we all said them. I blurted something far worse in the Dumpster.

Craig returned with the tea, then went back to sprawling on the laundry table. Helen added three packs of sugar to the cup and took it to Cheryl.

"Here," she said. "Drink this. You'll feel better. Cheryl, don't blame yourself. We all said things we wish we hadn't about Rhonda. We didn't know she was dead."

Cheryl took a sip of tea, wiped her eyes, and said, "I feel bad about Rhonda, but that's not why I'm crying. When the police get here, they're going to find out about my record."

"What record?" Helen said. She looked at Cheryl's curly brown head and innocent eyes and wondered what kind of trouble the little maid could get into.

"I got busted for shoplifting right after Angel was born," Cheryl said.

"What did you take?" Helen asked.

"Disposable diapers."

Craig burst out laughing. It was a hard, cruel sound. Suddenly Helen didn't think he was quite so cute.

"It's not funny," Cheryl said. "Diapers are expensive. Angel's daddy wouldn't give me any money and I didn't know what to do. The store prosecuted me and I got probation."

"We're not laughing at you," Helen said. "But you aren't exactly Ted Bundy. You were just a mom with money worries. This is murder. The police are going to be looking for someone who did more than boost diapers."

Someone like me, she thought, who keeps finding dead people.

Cheryl took a gulp of tea this time. "You're right. I feel guilty saying nasty things about Rhonda. Three days ago she offered me a hundred dollars to buy presents for my little girl. I turned her down because I didn't want to be beholden to anyone. How could I be so mean? She was just trying to be nice." Her voice wobbled, but this time she didn't cry.

Helen wondered where Rhonda got a hundred bucks—and the fifty she flashed with her dinner invitation. Who was paying her, and why? Was it the mysterious boyfriend?

Or did she find the bank robbery stash? The Full Moon was one giant treasure hunt. Illegal, illicit, ill-gotten money trailed through the hotel, making people crazier than crack. It had sensible Denise looking in the potted-palm pot and Sondra taking apart the air vent. Cheryl admitted she'd searched every room in the hotel. They were all obsessed with finding that money.

Suppose Rhonda had found it and refused to share the wealth? Would a coworker murder her in a burst of rage?

Helen thought of plump, solid Denise. Could she kill for cash? She was strong enough to beat Rhonda to death. What about Cheryl, hoping for a better life for her child? Would mother love drive her to murder? Did clever Sondra, working long hours to make it through school, finally snap? A cold cash compress could cure their ills.

Suddenly Cheryl was crying again. Her loud wails were joined by the sirens. The police had arrived.

CHAPTER 11

To meet the homicide detective, Helen donned her cloak of invisibility. The hotel cleaning smock had amazing powers—it could transform a hot babe into a hag. When Helen put it on, she felt like she'd been cursed by an evil witch. Her shoulders slumped, her waist thickened, and her hips widened. Its mustard color turned her skin the tone of old curry.

Helen had winced the first time she'd seen herself in a hotel mirror wearing the ugly yellow smock. Rhonda had stood behind her, pouring vitriol in her ear. "You look like hell in that," Rhonda'd said. "We all do. It's designed that way, to keep us in our place. Men will still hit on you, but it's no compliment. They grabbed poor Naomi's ass, and she looked like your granny. They think we're one of the hotel freebies. Wash your hair with the free shampoo, plug your computer in the free port and stick your dick in the maid."

Helen had laughed then. Now she heard the bitterness in those words.

Oh, Rhonda, she wondered. What did you do to escape the life you hated? Did it kill you?

Helen couldn't ask the homicide detective those questions. He'd interviewed the weeping Cheryl and the cell phone–wielding Sondra first. Denise stayed out by the front desk to handle surly guests, with a police officer standing nearby. Helen and Craig were sent to separate rooms, and Sybil sat in her smoky office. Helen thought the Full Moon's owner must be cured like a ham, she spent so much time sitting in smoke.

Helen was glad she had to wait for her interview in the laundry room. She washed her face and hands and cleaned the Dumpster stink off her shoes with a powerful disinfectant. She couldn't do anything about her stained jeans, but she changed her dirty smock for a fresh one.

Then she paced for nearly forty-five minutes, thinking about battered Rhonda, the bastard Rob and about herself. Her ex-husband was closing in, and Rhonda's death made it easier for him to find her. She had to stay away from the reporters. She couldn't risk having her face in a TV shot or a newspaper photo. She couldn't attract the attention of the police, either. She had to make herself so bland and uninteresting the police would be convinced she didn't know anything about Rhonda's murder.

I don't know anything, she told herself. I have no idea how she died.

But you have your suspicions, a voice whispered inside her head. It was almost as if Rhonda were standing behind her again, pouring out her poison.

"Detective Mulruney will see you now."

Helen jumped when she heard the stern woman police officer. She felt like she was being called into the principal's office. As she followed the officer, Helen told herself, I'm not guilty, but I am timid and self-effacing. I am a humble maid.

The police officer marched her to the breakfast room. The homicide detective sat at a square table by the bulk bins of raisin bran, oatmeal and cornflakes. Helen looked longingly at the coffee machine, but the pots had been washed and put away.

"Sit down," he said. "I'm Detective Bill Mulruney, Seafield Village homicide."

Helen took a chair and folded her hands in her lap. She kept her eyes lowered, but she sneaked some peeks at Mulruney. The homicide detective had a face like an old leather pouch. The sun had burned his skin reddish brown. The color and texture would horrify a dermatologist, but Helen thought weather-beaten skin was attractive. He had bags under his eyes, sags in his cheeks and crevices from his nose to his mouth. Deep lines were hacked across his forehead and cut around his eyes. He didn't look old so much as well used.

The brown eyes that shone out of his sagging face were frighteningly alert. They also seemed bored. Mulruney asked Helen her name, date of birth and address, like a clerk at an insurance office.

She gave the name she used now, shaved two years off her age and said her right address.

She watched his eyes for the predator's flicker of interest that meant she'd set off the cop radar. There was nothing.

Helen was a good liar. She knew exactly how much to say to sound innocent. The hardest part was trying not to fidget or look around for her ex-husband. She was terrified Rob would blunder in on them. She knew two uniformed police officers guarded the hotel's front door, and others were stationed at the side entrance. The Dumpster area was swarming with police and evidence technicians. Right now no one was coming into the Full Moon. She tried to relax.

"When did you last see Rhonda Dournell?" Detective Mulruney asked. He seemed barely awake.

"I waved good-bye when she left work three nights ago," Helen said. "She went toward Federal Highway. I went home in the other direction."

"What time was this?" Mulruney asked.

"About six o'clock," she said. "We had to clean a flooded room and it took longer than usual."

"Was she acting suspicious in any way?"

"No," Helen said.

"Did you see anyone hanging around the parking lot?"

Do they suspect Rhonda was raped? Helen wondered, and suppressed a shiver. Was that how she died, fighting off her attacker? She flashed again on Rhonda's blood-streaked body.

"Any unusual cars or activity? Could she have surprised someone breaking into a vehicle?"

Helen pictured the parking lot that night. She saw a cluster of cars near the lobby entrance, but the rest of the lot was a blacktop wasteland.

"No," Helen said.

"Did she have a boyfriend?"

"Not that I know of." The detective didn't seem to notice her weasel words. Helen hadn't actually seen the rich boyfriend or the fat biker Sam.

Mulruney needed a shave, unless he was cultivating a *Miami Vice* stubble. Judging by his beige polyester jacket with the pills on the lapels, he thought Armani was a town in Italy.

"Did the victim ever mention any family trouble, money problems, gambling issues or drugs?" The detective sounded like he was reading from a checklist. Helen sneaked a peek at his notes. They were unreadable scribbles.

"No," she said. Having a fifty-dollar bill wasn't a money problem.

"Any idea why anyone would want her dead?" Detective Mulruney said.

"No," Helen said.

"Any trouble here at work?"

"No." Helen didn't mention that Rhonda's coworkers had called her a whiner and a slacker. She didn't say they were glad when she didn't show up. Helen was sure the guilt-ridden staff would paint Rhonda as Mother Teresa with a mop.

Helen didn't tell him about the hotel's permanent

floating treasure hunt, either. Maybe Denise really was checking that palm tree for root rot and the elegant Sondra enjoyed rummaging in dirty air-conditioning vents. Helen couldn't prove otherwise. Besides, if she had the police looking too hard at her coworkers, they might mention Rob.

"What about the hotel deliverypeople? Did she fight with any of the suppliers? Did any of them seem interested in her?"

"No," Helen said. "I never saw her talking to any deliveryperson."

"Any reason why a hotel guest would want to cause her harm?" Detective Mulruney asked.

"No."

"Did you ever have any problems with the victim?"

"No."

"Ever hear her talking on the phone and maybe she sounded concerned or worried or like she was having an argument with someone?" Mulruney asked.

"No. She never used the phone around me," Helen said.

The detective seemed to lose interest in Helen completely. "That will be all, Miss"—he looked down at his notes, and various pouches and bags wobbled—"Hawthorne. You're free to go."

Helen had to use all her strength to keep from running out of the room. She'd lost her craving for coffee. Now she wanted a stiff drink. Once out of Mulruney's sight she sprinted down the hall to the laundry room, on the lookout for Rob. Sybil was still in her office, cigarette smoke seeping out from under the door.

Helen wondered how this murder would affect the hotel's business. Would it bring in the morbid types or make the guests start packing? Would it send Rob running back to St. Louis? Helen hoped so. She couldn't afford an encounter with her ex in a hotel crawling with cops.

Back in the laundry room she dialed Rob's room, then let the phone ring until the hotel voice mail picked it up. He wasn't in his room. She hoped that meant he wasn't in the hotel.

Helen threw off her smock, grabbed her purse and headed for the front desk. Sondra was back on duty. For once her impeccable clothes were wrinkled and her hair stuck out in odd clumps.

"Any reporters hanging around outside?" Helen asked.

Sondra checked the hotel's security cameras. "No reporters. No ex-husbands, either. You're safe."

"How is everyone?"

"Denise is being interviewed now," Sondra said. "Craig is still waiting, pacing like a caged panther. The police finished with Cheryl and she hurried home, worried sick about Angel. She had to get her mean old mother to watch her child, and that witch will take it out on Cheryl."

There are people with worse problems than me, Helen thought. But her stomach still felt like it was being squeezed by icy fingers.

Helen thanked Sondra and left by the same side door that Rhonda had slipped out of three days ago, when she'd disappeared into the shadows.

The dead hotel maid didn't rate a single TV truck. Even the homicide detective had seemed bored with her murder. That maid's smock made Rhonda invisible in life and death.

The hotel parking lot did have a zillion police vehicles, all parked at crazy angles. Most of the hotel lot and lawn were roped off with crime-scene tape, and the Dumpsters were screened by the stockade fence. That didn't stop a crowd from gathering, strange misshapen people with wild hair, watching with avid, feral eyes. They looked like they'd been breeding in the mangrove swamps.

They didn't care about Rhonda, either. They were

there to feed on her death. Helen slipped past them, unable to suppress a shudder. She hoped none of the swamp creatures noticed her. A block later she looked over her shoulder, but no one was following her. It was nearly seven o'clock by the time a dazed Helen found a pay phone. She called Margery and told her about Rhonda's death.

"This complicates things," Margery said. "At least there's no sign of your ex here at the Coronado. Come home and keep your mouth shut. I'll be out by the pool with Arlene. As soon as she goes in for the night, we'll talk."

Rob hadn't found her home. Helen leaned against the pay phone, weak with relief. It was too late to call Millicent at the bridal salon, but at least she was safe tonight.

At the Coronado, Margery was waiting by the pool with a stiff glass of white wine and a ham sandwich. "You need to eat," she said.

"Nobody ever tells me that," Arlene said, and gave a braying laugh. Margery stretched her lips into a smile. Anyone who didn't know Margery would think she was relaxed in her chaise longue, but Helen saw her rigid back and neck. Instead of savoring her cigarettes, Margery chain-smoked Marlboros, lighting one from the end of the other. Helen could almost hear her landlady mentally wishing Arlene to go inside 2C.

Arlene had brought chips and a jar of Paul Newman salsa. She wore a muumuu the size of a pup tent printed with giant red poppies. Matching poppy earrings bled from her ears. She made Roseanne Barr look like a preppie princess.

Arlene was knitting a fluffy yellow sweater "for my niece's new baby." Helen watched, half-hypnotized, as the red earrings swayed with Arlene's every move.

"Ladies my age are invisible, no matter how loud we dress," Arlene said. "That means I can have more fun than the young ones. I went to the Montero Dunes

Hotel in Lauderdale. I've always wanted to stay at that exclusive beach hotel, but I'm no millionaire. I sat in the lobby for a while. Security chased off the young folks, but they didn't notice me. After they got used to seeing—or not seeing—me I went out and sat on their private beach in a big teak chaise. The cutest pool boy brought me a mai-tai. I spent the afternoon lounging like a rich lady. I had all the advantages of a guest and none of the bills."

I'm hidden by a menial job, Helen thought. Age is Arlene's cloak of invisibility.

There was nothing invisible about Peggy. She fluttered out of her apartment in a brilliant emerald dress and glided across the green grass like a runway model. Her shoulder looked oddly bare, and Helen realized she was without the faithful Pete.

"Don't you look dramatic," Margery said. "I gather the coffee date worked out."

"Glenn's taking me to Mark's." Peggy did a graceful little twirl, an achievement in her skyscraper ankle-strap spikes.

Margery and Helen whistled. Arlene looked puzzled.

"Mark's is one of the most expensive restaurants in Lauderdale," Margery said. "The chef is Mark Militello. The *New York Times* says he's a hot new chef."

"What kind of food does he serve?" Arlene said.

"American cuisine with local ingredients," Margery said. "The menu changes all the time. If you get a chance, try the cracked conch with black-bean-mango salsa and vanilla-rum butter. For a main dish, the prosciutto-wrapped veal with wild mushroom polenta and porcini mushrooms is spectacular."

"I don't eat veal," Arlene said, her voice heavy with disapproval.

"He does wonderful things with yellowtail snapper," Margery said. "I've had it with black-bean-and-ginger sauce, and also with clams, fennel and chorizo."

Helen looked at her limp ham slapped on dry white

bread. She would have sworn Margery knew more about yellow mustard than yellowtail snapper.

"When did you dine there?" she asked.

"I get around," Margery said.

Helen never doubted that.

"There's Glenn's limo now," Peggy said, and her runway model walk turned into an excited little skip.

"Only way to go to Mark's," Helen said.

The black limo glided into the Coronado parking lot. A uniformed chauffeur opened the door. Helen couldn't see the man in the backseat, just his cigarette glowing in the dark interior.

"Wow," Helen said. "A limo. I'm impressed. This one is rich."

Margery gave a sinus-busting snort. "He spends money," she said. "That's not the same thing. If I were Peggy, I'd stick to lottery tickets."

Arlene folded her knitting into a straw bag. "Well, you ladies always keep me entertained. But I think I'll go watch my television." She gathered up her salsa jar and chip basket, her earrings seesawing wildly. Helen admired the woman's astonishing grace. She couldn't have stood with such ease.

After Arlene closed her door, Margery said, "Okay, tell me what happened. The whole story."

Helen did. Margery listened and smoked thoughtfully, blowing nicotine clouds toward the palms. "Whoever killed her had a real mean streak," she said. "He beat that poor woman to death. You stay out of this, Helen. This person likes to kill. Have you told Phil what happened?"

"His light isn't on," Helen said. "He must be out walking. Either that or he's asleep. I don't want to bother him."

"Hah. You don't want to tell him. You're in the soup. You need all the help you can get. The cops are going to be on your tail. Soon that jerk you married will be the least of your worries."

"I didn't have anything to do with Rhonda's death," Helen said.

"No, but you didn't tell that detective everything, and that will piss him off."

"I couldn't," Helen said.

"Maybe not. But he's going to be running off in six different directions, when you could have sent him the right way the first time."

Helen handed Margery the plate with the half-eaten sandwich. "It's been an awful day. I'm tired," she said. "I appreciate your help, but I think I'll turn in now."

"You can shut your door on me, but you can't make this go away," Margery said. "It's going to be there in the morning."

Helen knew Margery was right, but she still wanted to barricade herself in her apartment. She opened the door, and Thumbs demanded a scratch and dinner. The cat distracted her for a whole ten minutes.

The rest of the night she kept thinking of Rhonda. The red-haired maid was now a hundred pounds of spoiled meat. Who killed her and why? Rhonda wasn't pretty. She wasn't exciting. She was just one of the workaday people who kept the world running, at least until the last day of her life. Then Rhonda had been suddenly generous, bragging about a rich boyfriend, though she didn't seem the kind of woman who attracted rich men.

Now she was dead.

Where did Rhonda get the money—and the man? When she disappeared for three days, why didn't her lover look for her? He should have called her mother or the hotel. Where did Rhonda meet him? Did Sam the biker see her with another man and beat her up? Or did her dream lover turn into a nightmare man?

I should have said something to the police, Helen thought, as she twisted the sheets into guilty knots. How could the cops catch Rhonda's killer if they didn't have the right information? Her pillow felt like a stone. Her covers slid off the bed, but she fell into a restless sleep before she could retrieve them.

In her dreams she was trapped in the stinking Dumpster, running from the dead Rhonda. Helen slapped at the flies and slipped in the slimy trash.

She woke up alone and shivering, drowning in guilt and tormented by stinging questions.

CHAPTER 12

....

*P*ound. *Pound. Thud.*

"Helen, wake up! It's seven thirty."

Who was hammering on her door at this hour of the morning? It had to be bad news. Helen shrugged into her skimpy robe and staggered to the door, groggy with sleep. She flung it open, then realized she should have checked the peephole.

"Good morning, sunshine," Phil said.

Any other woman would have been delighted to find Phil on her doorstep. He was freshly showered and shaved. The sleeves of his blue shirt were rolled precisely two inches below his elbows. How did he do that at seven thirty? Helen always had one sleeve longer than the other.

She blinked at the bright sunlight and made a noise somewhere between a grunt and a whimper. Phil was relentlessly cheerful in the morning. He hummed, he sang, he threw open the windows and greeted the morning. Worst of all, he had a big, sweet smile.

"Don't you have to be at work at eight thirty?" Phil asked. He kissed her and she caught the luscious scent of freshly ironed clothes and hot coffee. He had a paper bag in one hand. Her traitorous cat, Thumbs, curled around Phil's legs and begged for scratches.

"That's right," Helen said. "Which means I sleep until seven thirty-eight."

Phil ignored her snippy tone. "Today you're going to spend eight minutes having breakfast with me. Call it quality time."

He barged into her tiny kitchen in two strides, reached into the bag, and put two hot cups of coffee and a warm apple strudel on the table. Now her kitchen was fragrant with cinnamon. He helped himself to a pile of paper napkins and pulled up a chair. Helen plopped down. Thumbs jumped into Phil's lap.

"The strudel is from the Edelweiss German bakery on East Commercial," Phil said as he stroked the cat. "That's to remind you of your St. Louis roots. But you don't need any reminders, do you, Helen? Rob's in Lauderdale, looking for you."

Suddenly Phil's smile wasn't so sweet. There was a hardness under it. Thumbs jumped off Phil's lap and ran for the bedroom. Helen wished she could run, too. She was trapped in her own kitchen. Margery must have ratted her out.

"It's too early to talk about Rob," Helen said. She burned her tongue on the too-hot coffee.

"And tonight it will be too late," Phil said. "Then it really will be too late, because that bastard will be here and I won't be able to protect you."

"I don't need your protection," Helen said.

"Right. You've done a terrific job of taking care of yourself. That's why he's hunting you down like a dog. Don't let him do this, Helen. Face him in court. You can win. I can help, if you'll let me. You can't keep living like this."

"I owe him thousands in alimony!" Helen burst out. "He's entitled to half my earnings and he doesn't have to lift a finger. Is that your idea of justice?"

"No," Phil said. "No reasonable judge would think that."

"There's no such thing as a reasonable judge in a divorce court," Helen said.

"You're wrong," Phil said. "There are good judges—and good lawyers, too. I can find you one. I'll prove Rob lived off you. I'll—"

Helen looked at him, so earnest in the new morning. His eyes were a sincere blue. His white hair was a shocking contrast with his young face. She traced a finger along the bridge of his slightly crooked nose. "You really believe in the system, don't you?" she said.

"Yes. The law makes mistakes, but it works if you give it a chance."

"I gave it a chance, Phil. It took my money. Next time it can take my freedom. That's too big a risk."

"You won't try?" He was angry now.

"No," Helen said.

"Then Rob's won," Phil said.

"Technically," Helen said. "But what did he get? My empty bank account. He spent more money on detectives than he ever got from me."

"But you had to run," Phil said. "Are you going to skip again?"

"If I have to," Helen said.

"What about us?" Phil said.

A long silence stretched between them, the kind of silence that said too much.

"I hope you'll come with me." Helen could feel her heart tearing inside. She'd lost so much. Now she would lose Phil, too.

"I love you," he said. "I'll help you face him. But I won't run."

He stood up and walked out of her home.

"You just ran now!" Helen screamed at the closed door.

She gulped down her coffee. She thought of tossing the strudel, but decided not to take out her anger on an innocent pastry. She ate the whole thing. Then she threw on some clothes, fed the cat, and slammed her door.

The walk to work was quicker than usual. Helen was

on fire with anger. How dare that man try to run her life. She'd traded one controlling male for another. She'd—

Helen stopped abruptly at the hotel parking lot. The building looked like it was under siege, surrounded by enemy TV trucks and reporters.

Helen panicked. She couldn't be seen on television. She ran to the pay phone down the block and tried to call the hotel. The line was busy. It took half an hour of dialing and pacing before she could get through.

A frazzled Sondra answered the phone. "Where are you? We need you. It's crazy here. We've got radio, TV and newspaper reporters. Two shock jocks did a routine about how you could check out but you could never leave the Full Moon and played 'Hotel California.' Now all the nice quiet guests want to leave this very moment and a bunch of raggedy-asses want to stay at the murder hotel."

Sondra never talked like that. Her nerves were seriously frayed.

"They're acting like we're some sort of theme park," Sondra said. "None of the rooms are cleaned, and we're shorthanded. Craig called in sick, so we're down to Denise and Cheryl."

"I'm at the pay phone by the Shell station," Helen said. "I can't get any closer or the reporters will see me. If I'm on TV, Rob will find me for sure."

"We'll sneak you in," Sondra said. "I'll send Denise. Watch for her blue Toyota."

While she waited, Helen called Millicent's bridal salon.

"Helen!" Millicent said, and suddenly Helen saw her former boss, with her bloodred nails and cantilevered breasts. "I've missed you, dear. How have you been? Is your life calmer since you left the bridal craziness behind?"

"Actually, I'm dealing with some personal wedding fallout," Helen said. "My ex-husband is after me. He wants to know where I live or work."

"He won't get it from me," Millicent said.

"Rob is tricky," Helen said. "He tells people he's a lawyer with an inheritance for me."

"If Ed McMahon walked in with a million dollars for you, the answer is still no," Millicent said. "Don't you worry. I'm used to handling difficult men. Oops. Here comes the bride. Gotta go."

Helen laughed. Millicent thrived on the wedding whirlwind. She'd dealt with too many delicate bridal situations to be flummoxed by a lightweight like Rob.

Helen hung up the phone, bought a soda at the gas station, and paced in the hot sun, wondering if she'd been abandoned. Finally, a battered Toyota rattled onto the lot. Helen thought the paint between the rust spots was blue. She spotted Denise's white hair and large, calm form. Help had arrived.

Denise rolled down the window and handed Helen something that looked like a skinned poodle. "Here, put this on," she said.

"What is this thing?" Helen said.

"It's an Eva Gabor wig," Denise said.

"Where did you get a wig so fast?" Helen asked.

"From the hotel's lost and found."

"Eeuw," Helen said.

"Are you worried about cooties or your ex-husband?" Denise said.

Helen put on the curly white wig, tucking her own hair underneath. The wig's curls wobbled like Slinky toys. "I look like Medusa with a home permanent," she said.

"You don't look like Helen Hawthorne. That's the point." Denise handed her black cat's-eye sunglasses sparkling with rhinestones, and the hotel's mustard yellow smock. "That should do it. You're disguised."

"I'm disgusting," Helen said.

"Vanity is a sin," Denise said, and for a moment Sister Mary Justine was with them. Except Sister J. never had that impish gleam in her eye.

"We're locked on the target," Denise said, barreling across the Full Moon parking lot. "Prepare to exit." She kept the bucking, wheezing car on course, heading straight for the side entrance. Denise was aiming for the TV reporters who blocked the door. A startled cameraman leaped sideways, yelling, "Hey, watch it!"

"Hah! Missed. Too bad. I'd like to run them all down." Denise stopped, and Helen ran for the door, head down. Reporters hurled questions at her. She flung herself at the door. It was locked. Helen banged on it, and Cheryl threw it open. She said, "I'm sorry, ma'am, but you—"

"It's me," Helen said, pushing her way inside. She pulled off the wig and sunglasses. Her hair was flat and sweaty, but she was in.

"Thank goodness," Cheryl said. "The hotel is a mess. You'll have to clean the third floor by yourself. I'm alone on two, and Denise is tackling one. Your ex is still in his room, so scoot upstairs before he comes out."

The third floor was hot, dirty and smoky as a sports bar. Some guests had checked out in an obvious hurry and left things behind, especially in the refrigerators. Helen found three cans of Coors, a peach nectar, and two frozen chicken pot pies. They would go into the maids' community stash. Whoever wanted the left-behind loot would take it home.

Cleaning the whole floor by herself was exhausting, but Helen was glad. She had no time to think about Rob or Phil. Just reciting their names sent her into a heated frenzy of scrubbing.

At eleven thirty Helen's walkie-talkie squawked. "All clear. Your ex has left the hotel," Denise said. "But I don't have time to check his room today."

"That's fine," Helen said. She'd already blocked his search.

The next thing she knew, it was three thirty. Only the honeymoon suite was left. Helen wearily trundled her cart to the door. She found Cheryl and Denise already at work in the huge suite.

"We finished our floors and came up to help," Cheryl said, pulling the sheets off the king bed.

"Thanks," Helen said.

"Don't thank us too much," Denise said, wiping a mirror with broad, practiced strokes. "We saved the Jacuzzi for you."

Judging by the housekeeper's knowing grin, it had to be a doozy. Helen stepped past mounds of wet towels and groaned. The Jacuzzi looked like a giant empty ice-cream-sundae dish. Globs of whipped cream, streaks of chocolate sauce, and squashed maraschino cherries were smeared on the white surface.

"Ohmigod," Helen said.

"That cherry juice is stickier than honey," Denise said.

"Maybe we should make a list of the six stickiest things you can clean in a hotel room," Cheryl said.

Helen's stomach gave a lurch. "Let's not go there," she said. She crawled into the awful empty sundae bowl and started scrubbing. It took an hour and two broken fingernails to get it white and sparkling again.

"Tell me the happy couple left a tip," Helen said.

"I found a penny on the dresser," Cheryl said.

"I hope their mother-in-law moves in with them," Helen said.

Denise came in, a dust rag slung over her shoulder. "Helen, we're going to Rhonda's mother's house after work to pay our respects. I bought a sandwich tray at the supermarket. We took up a collection. You can chip in if you'd like. There's no funeral time yet because of the autopsy, but we thought we should make a condolence call."

"I'd like to go," Helen said, "but my T-shirt's a sweaty mess."

"There are some decent blouses in the lost and found," Denise said. "Your jeans look OK. They'll dry out by the time we get there. Rhonda's mom will understand you're coming from work. But she won't understand if you don't show up."

Helen found a plain white blouse that was fairly clean. It was a little tight at the neck, but she opened the two top buttons and rolled up the sleeves (crookedly). She rode in Denise's creaky car with the sandwich tray on her knees. Cheryl followed in an old red minivan.

Rhonda's mother lived in a cinder-block house that looked like a bigger cinder block painted a peeling pink. It had a flat stretch of dusty yard and a discouraged palm tree. A metal hurricane awning hung halfway off the picture window.

Rhonda's mother looked like her daughter, except she seemed made out of leather. Her skin was tanned dark brown and creased with wrinkles. Her red hair had faded to a rusty gray, and she'd pulled it off her face with a rubber band. Helen couldn't bear to look at the woman's eyes. She was afraid she might drown in so much sorrow.

"I'm Shirley." She held out a strong, calloused hand for Helen to shake. "Thank you for coming."

"I didn't know your daughter nearly long enough," Helen said.

"None of us did," Shirley said.

Helen stepped into a living room fat with furniture. A huge plaid couch, two plump chairs, and a burly oak coffee table hogged the room. Cheryl, Denise and Helen sidled over to the couch and made awkward small talk.

"Did the police talk to you all?" Shirley said. "Do you think they're taking her murder seriously?"

"They asked me if Rhonda had changed in the last week or two," Helen said. "I didn't know her well enough to answer. Did your daughter seem suddenly worried or happier? Did she come into some money?"

You really are low, Helen told herself. Now you're pumping a grieving mother.

"She was no more worried than usual," Shirley said.

"Happiness didn't follow Rhonda around. As for sudden money, my daughter never had two nickels to rub together."

Shirley didn't seem to know about Rhonda's cash windfall. Her daughter never gave her the plane ticket to Mexico. Poor Shirley. That dream was dead, too. Helen felt another stab of sadness. She didn't have the nerve to mention the handsome boyfriend.

A white cat came out of the kitchen and sat down in front of the three women, meowing piteously. "That's Snowball," Shirley said. "She's been like that since I found her. She's looking for Rhonda."

Cheryl started crying.

Helen heard a thud of boots and a jangle of chains, and a fat biker came out of the kitchen with a beer in one hairy hand. "Looking for food is more like it," he said. "That cat doesn't care about anything but dinner."

"That's not true," Shirley said. "Snowball loves Rhonda. She's hardly touched her food since—" Shirley stopped, unable to go on.

"Who's that creep?" Helen whispered.

"Sam, the biker boyfriend," Denise said. She spoke so low her lips barely moved.

Cheryl stopped crying abruptly and stared at the man. Helen thought he looked familiar, or maybe he looked like every mother's nightmare. His gut flopped over his belt. His dirty hair was braided. A full beard nearly hid the stains on his Sturgis T-shirt.

Then Sam took a gulp of beer and Helen saw the tattoo on his wrist—Seminole Sam. The recognition was like a gut punch. This was the scuzzy guy from room 323 with the two women and the strap-on dildo. Helen wondered who'd used it.

Denise stood up. "We have a little something for you from everyone at the hotel." She put the envelope in Shirley's worn hand and patted it.

"Rhonda always spoke so highly of you all," her mother said.

Helen didn't dare look at Denise and Cheryl. She wanted to crawl away.

As Shirley shut the front door in a flurry of blessings and thanks, Helen heard Sam say, "Shirl, could you loan me twenty?"

Back in the car, Denise said, "I feel like slime. I want to eat every ugly word I ever said about Rhonda."

"I'd get a fork and help," Helen said. She used Denise's cell phone to call Margery. "There's no sign of Rob," Margery said. "Come on home."

Denise dropped her off at the Coronado with barely a good-bye. They felt too low and ashamed to say more.

Out by the pool, Helen drank more wine than usual. She tried to follow Arlene's chatter, but she kept seeing poor, battered Rhonda. When Arlene finally went inside, Margery smoked in silence and Helen stared at the black night sky.

Peggy came dancing back to the Coronado about ten o'clock. "We made it an early night because Glenn has an appointment at six in the morning." Her voice was soft with suppressed happiness. "We had dinner at a little French bistro, then walked along the water."

"Sounds romantic," Helen said.

Margery said nothing.

"Except Glenn kept taking calls from Japan," Peggy said. "Some deal he's doing there." She seemed secretly proud that her man had business half a world away.

"Sounds like a real wheeler-dealer," Margery said.

Was that sarcasm? If so, Peggy missed it. "Oh, yes," she said. "He's involved in a big deal. He's talking about millions." She chatted for a few more minutes, then was gone in a rustle of silk.

Helen heard a car door slam and sat straight up. "Is that Rob?"

"Let me look," Margery said. "You stay behind this bougainvillea."

Margery came back a few moments later. "Arlene

was getting out of Glenn's limo. What was she doing with him?"

Helen didn't have to speculate. Arlene was running toward them, almost as excited as Peggy. Her outrageous striped dress looked like a circus tent in a windstorm.

"I've always wanted to ride in a limo," Arlene said, "so I went out and introduced myself to Peggy's boyfriend as he was leaving. He gave me a ride down Las Olas. The limo has fabulous upholstery and a built-in bar with Waterford crystal. I felt like a queen. Glenn was so nice to me. That's what I like about being old. Nobody takes you seriously."

Margery said, "It beats the alternative." Then she blew a great cloud of smoke.

CHAPTER 13

··

The army of reporters had deserted the Full Moon the next morning. Helen wondered what had lured them from the murder hotel. She slipped in the side entrance and found Craig and Cheryl in the laundry room, listening to a radio turned low.

"What's happening?" Helen asked.

"Shh!" Craig said. "It's Bad Barry and Big Andy."

"The nasty shock jocks who did the 'Hotel California' routine yesterday," Cheryl added, as if Helen could forget.

"We're waiting to see if they do their routine again."

Craig flashed his boy-star smile and turned up the radio a notch. Helen and Cheryl leaned in toward the speaker. She heard maniacal laughter, followed by jackass brays.

"You're shitting me," Barry said. "Sweet Cindy, the Channel 19 anchor, was really decapitated?"

"Just confirmed," Andy said. "Happened on I-95 this morning. A beer truck rolled over her convertible. Way to go, Cindy!" Andy could hardly get the words out. He was snorting like a mad bull. Helen wondered if he pawed the studio floor.

"Gives new meaning to 'talking head,' Andy," Barry said. The pair laughed like demons.

Cheryl looked stunned. "I can't believe they'd joke about that," she said.

"I can," Craig said. He had an odd little grin.

Denise walked in and switched off the radio. "I'm sorry that poor young woman died. But at least we won't have to spend another day with all those reporters. They're on to the next tragedy. Now, everyone go to work. Cheryl, you and Helen start on three. Craig and I will clean on two."

Craig followed Denise quietly, like a puppy off his feed. Maybe he really had been sick yesterday.

Up on three, Helen and Cheryl went about their work swiftly. Soon they were in the zone, dusting, sweeping and scrubbing with hardly a word between them. The thrill seekers had checked out, leaving behind mounds of beer cans and pizza boxes.

"The beer cans are all empty," Cheryl said. "You'd think they could have left us a couple of full ones if they weren't going to tip."

Helen kept sticking her head out the room door, looking for Denise. The head housekeeper had promised to search Rob's room. It was nearly noon when Helen saw her in the doorway of 312, hands on her hips. Apparently Denise had struck pay dirt, with the accent on *dirt*.

"I waited until Craig was on break," Denise said. "It wouldn't do to have a trainee see me violate the rules. Your ex-husband left about ten this morning. I just now had the chance to go through his room. Does Rob swing both ways?"

"No," Helen said. "He only inflicts himself on the female sex."

Cheryl turned off the water in the bathroom and leaned against the doorjamb to listen.

"Well, he's got a guy's name and phone number on his dresser today—a Jeffrey Tennyson Barker," Denise said. "There's also a newspaper story about this Jeffrey. I don't want to sound prejudiced, but Jeff looks a little light in the loafers."

Helen sat down hard on the queen bed she'd been making. "Ohmigod. Jeff. Yes, he's gay. He was also my boss at my last job, the Barker Brothers Pampered Pet Boutique. I've got to get to him before Rob does."

What was I thinking? Helen asked herself. Why didn't I call Jeff yesterday, after I talked with Millicent at the bridal shop? Phil wasn't the one who underestimated my ex.

Denise handed Helen her cell phone. "Here," she said. "Make the call now."

She stood so close, Helen could smell her old-fashioned soap. Camay? Denise acts like I'm going to bolt out the door, Helen thought. She wished she could. Suddenly Helen wanted to be far away from this hotel. She felt a brief stab of nostalgia for Jeff's dog boutique, with Lulu the well-dressed beagle-dachshund.

"Hello," Helen said into the cell phone.

Jeff recognized her voice even before she identified herself. "Sweetie, how are you?" She could hear frantic barking. "Lulu, quiet! I'll give you a treat, but only if you're a good girl." The barks turned into hopeful whines.

"You must have been a very good girl, Helen, for someone to leave you nearly a million dollars," Jeff said.

"Rob was at your store." Helen gripped the phone as if it would leap out of her hand. She tried to make her voice sound normal, but it skidded up and down like a teenage boy's.

"Yes, he was. Such a cutie," Jeff said. "Nice buns on that boy, and bearing gifts, besides. Aren't you the lucky one? We're so sorry we couldn't remember the hotel where you're working now."

Helen let out the breath she didn't know she was holding.

"But we remembered the name of the divine little Art Deco apartment building where you live," Jeff said.

"Irk," Helen said.

"Don't thank us," Jeff said. "Although any part of that

million you want to give us as a token of your regard will be just fine. Lulu, don't nip the nice customer. Helen, I have to go."

The line went dead. Helen felt like her brain had been disconnected at the same time.

"Rob found you," Denise said.

"He found my home," Helen said. "I need to call my landlady."

Helen's fingers fumbled so badly with the phone buttons she couldn't make the call. After the third try Denise took the phone from her hands. "What's the number?" she asked.

Denise punched in Margery's number and hit send, then handed Helen the phone.

Margery answered on the first ring. "He's here," she said, her words flat and clipped. "Outside by the pool. I'm making him a drink. Call me in an hour." She hung up before Helen could ask anything. If Margery made him a drink, Rob wouldn't be able to cause trouble this afternoon. Her screwdrivers could anesthetize a rhino.

Helen spent a miserable hour trying to clean the rooms. She knew she was doing a terrible job. The beds were lumpy. The freshly polished furniture looked like it was smeared with grease. Cheryl kept straightening the bedspreads and wiping down the dresser tops after her.

At one o'clock Helen called Margery. "All clear," her landlady said. "Rob's gone, but I don't think he's going back to the hotel right away. I'll give you the details when you come home. Don't worry. You're safe."

Helen didn't feel safe. She stumbled through two more rooms, tripping, dropping things, and putting the sheets on sideways. When Helen sprayed a mirror with furniture polish, Cheryl said, "You need to go home."

"I don't want to leave you alone with all this work."

Cheryl looked at the oily film on the dresser mirror. "No offense, Helen, but I'll finish faster working alone.

Room 323 has the *Do Not Disturb* sign up, so I won't have to clean it."

Helen started to go, but hesitated. Cheryl had too much to do on her own.

"Don't feel guilty," Cheryl said. "When Angel gets a tummy ache at school, I'll have to leave you in the lurch. You've had a bad fright. Go on, get out before your ex comes back. I'll clear it with Denise."

Helen felt more relieved than guilty. She left her stained smock in the laundry room and slunk home like a felon, watching for Rob as she rounded every corner and passed every clump of trees. She kept away from Las Olas, in case he was lunching at a sidewalk café.

She saw no sign of her ex, but she did see a pale, skinny figure with long orange-red hair strolling along the sidewalk.

"Rhonda!" Helen said, surprised but happy.

The woman turned around. She looked nothing like the murdered maid.

"Sorry," Helen mumbled.

When someone died suddenly, you saw them everywhere for a while, Helen thought. That's natural. Then why did it feel so unnatural?

Margery met her with a screwdriver in an iced tea glass. Helen figured it held nearly a pint of vodka and orange juice.

"Drink," her landlady said. "You're a wreck."

Helen took a stiff swig. Margery handed Helen a ham sandwich and a bag of chips.

"Where's the black-bean-mango salsa and vanilla-rum butter?" Helen said.

"I can slap on some French's mustard," Margery said.

"I prefer the indigenous local products," Helen said.

"Good. You've got your sense of humor back. Come on out by the pool, where we can talk. Arlene and Peggy are both gone."

Her landlady clip-clopped back to the pool in purple-heeled sandals. There weren't many seventy-six-year-olds who could wear a lavender halter top, but Margery had smooth, tanned shoulders. She artfully lit a cigarette and took a deep draw that would have left Helen choking on the smoke. Margery looked sophisticated.

It was one of those perfect afternoons that made Floridians realize why they endured the roasting summers. The fine weather was wasted on Helen. She'd turned cold at the thought of Rob. He'd been here at her home. He'd probably sat on this very chaise.

"He really thinks he's slick," Margery said. "He thought he was conning me the whole time, pouring on the charm for an old lady who'd be grateful for a man's attention, no matter how phony.

"I batted my eyelashes and told him you'd moved out. I said you went to Sarasota, on the other side of the state. Two can play the lying game. Well, I did tell the truth, sort of. I said you were short of money, and couldn't even afford a car. I made it clear he wasn't going to get much out of you, even if he did find you."

"Didn't Rob say he could solve all my problems with that million-dollar inheritance?" Helen said.

"He's smart enough to know that wouldn't work on me," Margery said. "He looks about as much like a lawyer as I do. Rob claimed that he was dating someone else and only wanted to reassure you there were no hard feelings. He wanted to make amends."

"He's a lying scumbag," Helen said.

"I know that. I could see it in his eyes. He's eaten up with greed and anger. It's ruining his looks. I said I'd try to get a message to you, but I couldn't promise anything. It would take time."

"Do you think he believes you?"

"I don't know," Margery said. "Waiting will cost him money, and I don't know how much he has. I'll keep an eye out for him. If I find him hanging around here, I'll call the police and report him as suspicious. That should take care of him."

"Do you really think he'll go away?" Helen said, unable to hide her hope.

Margery stared into the turquoise pool, then said, "No. The man is obsessed with you. He was used to cheating on you, and then you fooled him. The biter got bit. He can't stand it. You need to get rid of him. I may have a solution."

"What?" Helen said. "I wish he was dead, but I can't kill him."

"Don't be such a drama queen," Margery said. "Your ex thinks he's quite the ladies' man, doesn't he?"

"Yes," Helen said. "He's made a career of living off women. I mean, besides me."

"Then we may be able to get rid of him easier than you think."

"How?" Helen asked.

"I'll let you know." Margery blew out another stream of smoke. "How are you and Phil getting along?"

"Not so good," Helen said. "We quarreled this morning."

"Was it serious?"

"He wants me to go to St. Louis and clear my name."

"He's right."

"You're taking his side?" Helen said.

"I'm taking your side. I can think of better things to do with that man than fight." Margery held up a liver-spotted hand. "Look at me. You'll be as old and dried up as I am before you know it. You won't remember the stupid fights, but you will remember the good times. You'll need them to get you through a cold old age."

Margery stubbed out her cigarette.

They heard the slam of a car door. Both women jumped up. Margery ran to check out the parking lot. "It's that limo. Peggy is out with that damned four-flusher again," she said.

"You don't think he's really rich, do you?" Helen said.

"He's another user. I can smell them a mile away."

"Why is Peggy being so stupid about this man?" Helen said.

Margery raised her eyebrows.

Why was I so stupid about Rob? Helen thought. Why is any woman dumb about a man? It's always easy to see through someone else's lover.

"She's young, she's lonely, and she wants to believe what he's telling her," Margery said. "How long can she hang out with a parrot?"

"Pete's better than that guy any day," Helen said.

"Not in bed," Margery said. "Quiet. Here she comes."

Peggy floated across the lawn and settled on the chaise, light as a leaf. "Another wonderful night," she said, and sighed. "Glenn took me to dinner again at Mark's. I felt guilty about him picking up the dinner tab, so I bought him a silver cigarette lighter."

"Was this your idea or his?" Margery said.

Helen had the same thought.

"Mine," Peggy said. There was a touch of defiance in her voice.

"How did you know whether to get him silver or gold?" Margery said.

"I saw him admiring a man's lighter in the cigar bar the other night. It was a silver Cartier."

My ex-husband used to do that, Helen thought. He admired a Cartier tank watch, a Rolex, a four-hundred-dollar Egyptian cotton shirt, a Tiffany lighter and an SUV, among other things. I bought them all, like a fool.

"Of course it was your idea," Margery said. This time Peggy couldn't miss the acid in her landlady's voice.

"Don't be that way," Peggy said.

"What way?" Margery tried to look innocent and failed.

"So suspicious," Peggy said. "Glenn is wonderful. He's dynamic and smart. He's putting together a big international deal. He talked to a London banker this evening."

"How do you know?" Margery said. "He could have called Time and Temperature."

"I saw the country code on his cell phone."

"He could have called London Time and Temperature," Margery said.

"Glenn is a successful financier. He knows money. Why do you think he has a limo?"

"Any high school kid can ride in a limo," Margery said. "It proves nothing."

"It tells me he has money and style," Peggy said. "He says if I give him twenty thousand dollars, he can make me rich."

"The only one he'll make rich is himself—by exactly twenty thousand dollars," Margery said.

"I can't talk to you. You're so cynical. You've forgotten how to love," Peggy said. Her anger was fierce and heartbreaking. Peggy stood up, stumbled slightly in her sky-high heels, then ran to her apartment. She shut the door quickly, as if Margery's doubt might creep in.

"No fool like an old fool," Margery said. "Except a young one."

CHAPTER 14

．．．．．．．．．．．．．．．．．．．．．．．．．．．．．．．．．．．．．．．

"Finally," Cheryl said. "The *Do Not Disturb* sign is off the door to room 323. It's been hanging there for two days. I dread going in there."

The brown wood door looked like all the others, but it seemed to pulse as they stared at it. Helen had seen too many horrors in that room. But this morning would be different. She knew they would not have to deal with the curse of 323.

"Don't worry." Helen's voice was rich with smug certainty. "There's nothing bad waiting inside today. That room was rented by a nice suburban mom. Sondra told me. She decided we needed a break, so she put the woman in 323. She was wearing a Ralph Lauren blazer."

"The problem isn't what she had on," Cheryl said. "It's what happened when she took it off."

"No one complained about any noise," Helen said.

"Those are the worst," Cheryl said, as she unlocked the door.

The room was black as a coal mine, but a poisonous cloud of spilled booze, vomit and cigarette smoke boiled out. Helen's heart sank. The blazer was no protection. Mrs. Lauren must have gone on a tear.

"Brace yourself," Cheryl said. "I'm flipping on the light."

The room was wrecked. A broken-backed chair leaned against a crippled dresser. The mirrors were smashed. Lamp shades were torn. The headboard was split in two. The king mattress had unspeakable stains, and the sheets were dragged across the floor. All the pillows were slashed.

"Ohmigod," Helen said. "Call the police. The woman was attacked."

"Here's what was attacked," Cheryl said, throwing open the bathroom door. "Watch your shoes. Someone barfed on the floor."

The room was crammed waist-high with cases of Pabst Blue Ribbon and boxes of booze: Smirnoff Twisted Green Apple, Twisted Mandarin Orange, Twisted Cranberry.

Helen's stomach twisted at the thought. "She drank all that?"

"No, those are kid drinks. She rented this as a party room for her high school kids," Cheryl said.

"You're joking," Helen said.

"I'm dead serious. You'd be surprised how many dimwit parents want to be pals to their teens. Our hotel won't rent a room to underage kids, so Mom or Dad gets it for them. The parents don't want the little darlings wrecking their place. Instead they ruin ours."

"The parents were here for this party?" Helen said.

"No, they dropped the kids off and made them promise not to drive. Usually the parents pick up the kids, too. They sneak in the partyers while the hotel is busy. As long as the kids keep the noise down, we don't know until the damage is done and they're gone. You could have had an army carousing in 323 and nobody would hear. It's off by itself in the back of the hotel."

"What happens now?" Helen said.

"I go downstairs and break the news to Sybil. If this mom is like the others, she'll deny all knowledge of the damage. She'll say someone else must have used the room after she checked out. We'll have to sort through the wreckage and find proof."

Helen looked at the shattered furniture and cigarette-burned carpet. "It's hopeless," she said.

"Nope, we'll get her." Cheryl's brown curls bobbed confidently. "I'll send Craig up, and he can start hauling out the booze boxes and empties. You clean up the broken glass before someone gets cut. If you find any papers or receipts, save them for me."

Craig looked refreshingly clean-cut this morning, a poster boy for young-adult virtue. His blond hair had a golden glow. He whistled when he saw the room. "These dudes partied hearty."

"I'll give them references as wrecking balls," Helen said.

"I'm supposed to carry out all the dead soldiers."

"Take the beer and liquor bottles straight to the Dumpsters," Helen said. "The crime-scene tape should be off them."

Helen could hear the clank and rattle as Craig went to work. He soon left on the first of many trips with two huge bags.

Cheryl was back before Craig. "Sybil was fit to be tied," she said. "She checked the security tapes. A blue minivan pulled up at the back entrance and let out six strapping young men, who hauled the booze up the back stairs. They arrived about the same time as that bus tour from Wisconsin."

"Seventy oldsters sharing rooms on their AARP discounts," Helen said. "No wonder we didn't see the party arrive. Well, you've got the woman."

"Not quite," Cheryl said. "She gave us a fake license tag number when she registered, and we can't see the driver of the minivan on the tape. We'll track her down, but we need more proof. Let's see what we can find. Be careful where you step."

The room was booby-trapped with dozens of red plastic cups, most half-filled with booze and floating cigarettes. "I can't believe this," Helen said. "They used the headboard to open the beer bottles."

Craig popped in the doorway, back from his beer-hauling expedition. "You won't believe what I found out by the death Dumpster," he said.

Cheryl winced. Rhonda's murder wasn't a joke. Craig's eyes glittered with something. Malice? Excitement?

"Two used condoms," he said. "Some sickos screwed by the Dumpster where they found the dead woman. Is that disgusting or what?"

"I don't want to talk about it, Craig," Cheryl said. "It's too horrible."

A subdued Craig went back to filling trash bags with bottles. Helen and Cheryl sifted through the room rubble.

"Aha!" Helen said, as she lifted an abandoned twelve-pack. "A credit-card slip is stuck to the bottom." It was from a liquor store.

"Jeez," Helen said. "It's for three hundred dollars."

The slip was damp with beer and some print was smudged, but Cheryl looked at the signature. "That's her—the idiot who rented this room. I'll run this down to Sybil. Thank goodness for slobs," Cheryl said. "That woman will pay for this damage. If she refuses, I'll report her to the police for serving liquor to minors. She's lucky one of those kids didn't OD. Then she'd have that on her conscience."

"Why would a grown woman buy liquor for young boys?" Helen said.

Cheryl shrugged and her pretty brown curls bobbed. "She's forty going on twenty, an older woman trying to prove she can make the young guys twitch."

"It's enough to drive you to drink," Helen said.

But Helen was grateful to Mrs. Lauren. The room was such a wreck, she spent the whole morning without worrying about Rob. Now the words were back in her mind like a drumbeat: He found me. He found me.

The only thing standing between Rob and ruin was Margery's skill at lying. Her landlady was a good liar, but so was Rob. This was a grudge match between titans, with her life as the prize.

Helen was almost sad when Cheryl closed the door on room 323. She felt her last bit of peace was shut out.

"We've done all we can," Cheryl said. "This room will be out of service for a day or two, while Sybil brings in new furniture and puts down new carpet."

"Maybe it will break the curse of 323," Helen said.

"That room feeds on disaster," Cheryl said, rolling their cart to 322. "It will be worse than ever after this."

Helen saw a pale figure at the end of the hall with long limbs and red hair. It was Rhonda, the old-fashioned girl with the crisp new fifties. Helen stopped dead for minute, then realized it was only a trick of the light. No one was down there.

"Are the construction workers still staying here?" Helen asked, to cover her odd hesitation.

"They checked out yesterday. We have a bunch of businessmen now."

"Right. I saw them down in the lobby this morning," Helen said. "Looks like they took over most of the hotel for a meeting. I hope the businessmen are an improvement. The construction workers drank loads of beer and were pretty messy."

"Hah," Cheryl said, unlocking the door to 322. "The construction workers will seem like a ladies' sewing circle. Individual businessmen are all right. In a group they are demanding, difficult and dirty. Look at this room."

The guest's suitcase must have exploded. Dirty socks and soiled shirts were tossed everywhere. Papers, folders and brochures were dumped on chairs. A pair of muddy running shoes were flung on the dresser. Ashtrays were heaped with butts.

"At least the furniture is still intact," Helen said. "But this guy is a slob. He's got cigarette ash all over everything."

"Have you seen the conference rooms where they're holding their meetings?" Cheryl said, hauling in her bucket of cleaning supplies. "It looks like a pack of wolves is having a seminar. At least the construction workers left us the beer they didn't drink. All we'll get from these guys are their dirty butts."

"Uh, you mean cigarette butts, right?" Helen said. She wasn't sure anymore.

Cheryl giggled. "Mostly."

Helen picked up a liquor bottle about one-fourth empty from the nightstand. "This guy treats himself well," she said. "Johnnie Walker Black. Looks like he had a couple of ounces last night. Maybe he's lonely. He keeps a family photo on the desk."

Cheryl examined the photo. "How do fat guys get such pretty wives?" she said. "She's blond and skinny and he's forty pounds overweight."

"He has the money," Helen said. "Does this company stay here often?"

"We get lots of businessmen. Sybil offers a special seminar deal in some business magazine. But I think it's the first time for this particular corporation," Cheryl said. "Although some of the guys look familiar."

"You mean they all look alike," Helen said. "I never saw so many bald heads, white faces and power ties."

She picked up a blue bathrobe on the unmade bed. "Hey, this guy puts his Phi Beta Kappa key on his robe. Can you believe that? What an ego."

There was a crash and a soft curse.

"What's wrong?" Helen said.

"I've got the dropsy. Knocked over the spray cleaner bottle and the lid wasn't on tight," Cheryl said. "It's going to ruin this desktop."

Helen rushed over. The two maids patted, sprayed and rubbed the desk. "No damage," Cheryl finally declared. "I'm tightening every bottle top. I can't believe—"

Her walkie-talkie went off with a squawk, and she answered it.

"What's up, Sondra?" Cheryl said.

Helen could hear the front desk clerk's voice through the static. "It's the police," Sondra said. "They want to see Helen downstairs. Now."

CHAPTER 15

· ·

Helen felt herself split into three pieces. The small, feral part wanted to scurry for the nearest hole. Another was sick and shriveled with fear. It wanted to whine and beg and slink like a whipped dog.

But one small piece of her still had courage. Helen held on to that, and tried to banish the slinking, scurrying parts. I will get through this, she told herself. I've done nothing wrong.

Except lie, the whipped dog said.

"Helen," Cheryl said. "Do you want me to go with you?"

"No, no," Helen said. "I'm fine."

Double-dog liar, the whipped cur said.

"Then you'd better go. You don't want the police to get mad." Cheryl gave her a slight push toward the door.

Helen looked carefully up and down the hall, like a preschooler crossing the street alone for the first time. Even her hotel smock, the cloak of invisibility, wouldn't protect her if she ran into Rob head-on.

The small, feral part urged her to scuttle down the back stairs and out of the hotel for good. Helen stepped on it, squared her shoulders, and headed for the elevator.

Don't look nervous, she told herself. The police will see you as guilty.

Detective Bill Mulruney was leaning against the front desk, flirting with Sondra. Another old white guy plaguing pretty Sondra, Helen thought. But it was a good sign. At least the man was human.

Then Mulruney turned that baggy face toward hers and Helen changed her mind. She might as well be looking at a tree trunk for all the feeling he showed. His face was hard as oak.

"Let's go into the breakfast room, where we can talk, Miss Hayworth."

Hawthorne, Helen nearly corrected him, and then stopped herself. If he wanted to make life tough for Helen Hayworth, that was fine with Helen Hawthorne.

He took the same seat as before, and Helen found herself staring once again at the bin of breakfast cereal. She wondered how many Cheerios were in there.

Detective Mulruney said nothing, just turned that solid oak stare on her. Helen started counting Cheerios. One, two, three . . . There were twenty-seven in the first row, though it slid down a little on one side. Did those go into row two? She gave up guessing how many Cheerios were in the bin. Maybe she should try counting the fissures and wrinkles in Mulruney's face. The man looked like a topographical map of New Mexico.

Mulruney pulled out a plastic evidence bag with a crisp fifty-dollar bill inside. Now he didn't look bored. He was way too interested in Helen.

"We found this in the victim's purse," the detective said.

"Yes?" Helen said. She wondered if it was the same fifty Rhonda had flashed.

"Did you ever see Miss Dournell with a fifty-dollar bill?"

Tell the truth, Helen decided. There's less to remember. "Rhonda offered to take me out to dinner. I said I was broke and she said she had money. She showed me a fifty."

"When?" Mulruney said.

"The night she—the last time I saw her."

"Why didn't you tell me this before?" the detective said.

"I didn't think it was important," Helen said.

Mulruney slammed his hand down on the table so hard the sugar container jumped. So did Helen. "I told you everything was important," he said. "Everything. Especially if it happened the night she died. Do you know where she got this money?"

"No." Helen looked him in the eye, or rather the eye pouch. It was sort of the truth. She hadn't seen Rhonda's dream lover, much less watched him hand her money. Helen had encountered Sam the biker only once, and he had been more interested in borrowing money than giving it away.

If Helen mentioned Rhonda's new lover, the police would be all over her like ants on a chocolate bar. She had to stay dull. She was just a poor, dumb hotel maid who didn't know nothing about nothing.

"What's wrong with having a fifty-dollar bill?" Helen said. "I'd like a few myself."

Good move, smart mouth, the whipped dog whined. Helen kicked it away.

"It's counterfeit," the detective said.

Helen felt like she'd been punched. This was trouble. She wouldn't have to worry about one small-time police detective. If Rhonda had stacks of counterfeit cash, she'd bring the feds down on the Full Moon.

Suddenly Helen saw a lot more reasons why someone would want Rhonda dead. Was she passing bad money, or did she find out someone else was? Did Rhonda think that fake fifty was the key to easy money? Was that how her man was going to get rich quick?

Or did Rhonda find out her precious fifty was funny when she went to dinner that night? Many Florida shops and restaurants routinely tested fifties before they accepted them. Did she confront the man who gave her the bad money? That would be a good reason to kill her. Helen could see Rhonda doing it, too. She was a seething volcano of rage, and this would send it pouring out.

"Anything you want to add?" the detective said.

He noticed my reaction, Helen thought. Did I fidget, turn red, look away? For all I know, my eyes popped out like a cartoon character's. I don't have a poker face.

Don't sit there squirming like a schoolgirl who has to use the restroom. Answer him.

"Counterfeit fifties are a problem in South Florida," Helen said. "We've had so many bad fifties at this hotel our front desk won't take one without testing it first. Have you seen how many Florida businesses have signs saying they won't change fifties?"

The hotel was the perfect place to pass fake fifties, Helen thought. You couldn't put the funny money in the till. Sybil made the desk clerks use a counterfeit pen. Mark a suspect bill with the pen, and if the mark turned dark brown or black, the bill was a fraud. But the pen didn't always work. The banks used more sophisticated methods and confiscated any bogus bills. The Full Moon's chain-smoking owner would give off real fire if she lost a fifty because it was bad. Sybil had drummed it into poor Sondra's head to test every fifty-dollar bill.

But there was a way around Sybil's precautions. Sondra could give the bogus bills as change. People who paid for their rooms in cash were often at the hotel for a fling. They wouldn't complain if they got bad money. They couldn't. They'd been sleeping in the wrong bed.

Passing fake fifties would be the perfect setup for Sondra, providing quick cash for college. It would save her years of labor behind the front desk, placating old white guys. What if Rhonda had figured out the scam and said something?

"You know, we're aware there's a counterfeit problem in this area," the detective said. "But we're interested in this particular bill belonging to this particular victim."

"Do you think Rhonda was passing bad money?" Helen said. "Is there just the one?"

"We thought you could tell us," the detective said.

That probably meant the police had found only one counterfeit bill. "Rhonda wouldn't be involved in anything illegal," Helen said.

As soon as she said it, she wondered if that were true. Rhonda was sick of cleaning muck out of the honeymoon Jacuzzi. When a young woman made minimum wage, free fifties looked tempting. Especially when the handsome tempter promised love and riches.

Helen waited for Mulruney to mention the plane ticket to Mexico, but he didn't. The cops never found it, she decided. Otherwise Mulruney would have asked if Rhonda planned to leave the country.

"How did Rhonda die?" Helen said.

"She was beaten. Someone beat that poor woman to death."

Helen gasped. She couldn't help it. She'd seen the body. She wasn't surprised by the news. But it seemed worse now that she heard it. It was Rhonda's death sentence.

"We'd like you to sign a statement for us," the detective said.

"Uh, I'll be happy to," Helen said. "Anything to help Rhonda." She sounded sappy and insincere. "May I ask why?"

"You found the body," Detective Mulruney said. "We need to make sure of the facts. So why don't you write them down for us?"

He thinks I'm lying, Helen thought. Her heart was thudding. Her mind was racing. Run, screamed the feral creature. Whine and beg, the whipped dog said.

"Sure," Helen said, but she felt her courage seeping away.

"If you're not telling the truth, we'll have you on perjury." Detective Mulruney smiled like a hungry predator, and his pouches and wrinkles underwent a seismic shift. He looked genuinely scary now. He handed her a yellow legal pad and a hotel pen. Helen's hands shook when she took them.

Mulruney left her alone while she wrote, but he didn't go away. She could see him out of the corner of her eye, laughing with Sondra. Helen labored over her statement as if it could save her life. She wrote, rewrote, crossed out and added words, then tore up the whole statement and started from scratch. She tried to say only the truth, and she did. But not the whole truth.

Helen signed and dated her statement and wished she had a lawyer. She'd betrayed poor Rhonda. She didn't say anything about the plane ticket. She didn't mention the man who gave Rhonda that fifty.

Except no one had seen the dream lover. He didn't exist. He couldn't exist. Rhonda never said his name. All Helen had was a vague schoolgirl description: He was handsome and he listened to Rhonda.

Maybe if I'd listened harder, I'd know something useful, she thought.

But there was nothing to know. Sam the biker was the only man in Rhonda's life, and he was a taker, not a giver.

Poor Rhonda had cracked under the strain of her dreary life. She'd cleaned one too many honeymoon suites and created her own personal romance novel, starring a handsome hunk who wanted to carry her away to a castle by the sea. He was a fantasy man for a fantasy life. He existed only in Rhonda's lonely mind.

But telling herself that didn't make Helen feel better. Her pulse pounded out another message: He's real. He's a real killer.

She saw Rhonda's body in the trash, a pathetic tangle of lank hair and stick limbs. Rhonda didn't deserve that death. She was a good woman. Or was she? What did Helen really know?

Only this: If she was going to live with herself, Helen would have to prove Rhonda's dream lover didn't exist.

CHAPTER 16

....

"What about those two?" Phil said.

Helen and Phil were playing their favorite game: Who Are You?

To play, they picked out people and tried to make deductions about them. It was Phil's turn this afternoon. He pointed to a couple in the restaurant, the Blue Moon Fish Co. There were half a dozen like them at nearby tables. The Blue Moon was a romantic spot on the Intracoastal Waterway near a drawbridge. The bridge was an improbable face-powder pink, the water was Crayola blue, and the yachts were white. Phil was another picture—tan and lean, with his dazzling white hair pulled back in a swashbuckling ponytail. He got admiring looks from the women and a few from the men, including their waiter.

"Two for one?" Helen said.

"It's only fair, considering where we're lunching," Phil said. The Blue Moon was famous for its two-for-one lunches.

Helen studied the pair at the next table. The woman was blond, about thirty-five and exquisitely turned out. The man was a vigorous fifty-something with silver hair that looked sculpted. They held hands and gazed into each other's eyes, then laughed and talked in hectic spurts.

"What do you think of her?" Helen said. She was picking through a huge crock of mussels in white wine. Phil had the salmon gravlax.

"Basic blond Barbie, getting a little long in the tooth," he said, neatly forking a piece of salmon on his bread, then packing it with onions and capers. The tomato sat untouched. "Not much else I can say."

A horn blared, the call for the drawbridge to go up. Tall yachts and sailboats bobbed and circled while they waited for the bridge. Helen was fascinated; a whole street was moving out of the way for the whims of the rich.

She tore off a chunk of focaccia, smeared it with roasted garlic and dipped it in olive oil. She noticed the blonde left the luscious bread untouched. The woman had superhuman powers. Helen watched her remove a morsel of yellowtail snapper with surgical precision and slowly chew it.

"There's plenty that I can say," Helen said. "They're dating. That's a no-brainer. She's hoping for another marriage."

"How do you know about the first?" Phil said.

"She's taken off a ring on her left hand recently. She still has a tan line," Helen said.

"Good," Phil said, packing more salmon with capers and onions.

"She's not a gold digger," Helen said. "But she wouldn't mind a man with money."

"Where do you get that idea, Sherlock?"

"She's high maintenance," Helen said. "That's a salon pedicure and wax job on her legs."

"Nice legs," Phil said, staring at them a little too long.

"Ah-hem," Helen said. "If I can continue. Those sandals are this season's and cost at least two hundred bucks. The clothes are expensive and up-to-the-minute. But her face doesn't have quite the hardness of a real gold digger's. My guess is she's trying to make a quick strike before her money runs out, but she's a tad desperate."

"Why is that?" Phil folded a slightly too large slice of pink gravlax and somehow got it in his mouth.

"She's laughing a little too hard at his jokes," she said.

"He's laughing at hers," Phil said.

"Not so loudly. She's a little shrill and her laughter's forced."

"Very nice," Phil said. "What about him?"

Helen pried the meat out of a mussel while she studied the man with the sculpted hair. "Typical middle-aged guy dating a woman twenty years younger." She dismissed him with a shrug. "South Florida is crawling with men like him."

"You see, Watson, but you do not observe," Phil said. "I would say he's also divorced and on the prowl. Look at his belt. See where those two notches are worn and he's set it back on a new notch? That means he's lost weight—twenty to thirty pounds. When a man his age has a sudden weight loss, he's usually newly divorced or having an affair. This guy's not wearing a ring and there's no tan line on his ring finger."

"Lots of married men don't wear rings," Helen said.

"Yeah, but he wouldn't be flirting with a woman so openly at the Blue Moon, even on an out-of-town trip. The place is too popular. It's easy to run into someone from back home who would tell his wife."

"Good deduction," Helen said. "What else?"

"He looks firm and toned despite the weight loss, so I'm guessing he works out at a gym or possibly has a personal trainer. Judging from his tan and his nails, I'd say he's connected with some type of construction."

"Where did you get that?" Helen said. "What's unusual about his nails?"

"That's a manicure," Phil said. "Most guys his age get clear polish when they have a manicure. He didn't. I'm guessing he doesn't want the construction crew to see him wearing nail polish. He'd lose their respect. But he's a boss or meets with big-money types, and they'll look at his nails. So he gets a manicure, but that's his compromise—no polish. Also, his tan is not from a salon. The back of his neck is too red. He's outdoors a lot."

"Good theories," Helen said. "Too bad you can't prove them."

"Watch this," Phil said.

He stood up and went to the tan man. "Excuse me, but didn't I meet you at the American Home Builders Convention in Chicago? You're Bill Donnelly."

"You got the wrong guy, buddy, but the right industry," the tan man said in a booming voice. His blond companion smiled adorably. "I build homes up the road in Boca." He took out his card. "Here. If you and your lady friend are in the market for a good deal on a custom-built luxury home, you come see me."

"Thanks," Phil said.

"You win," Helen said when he got back to the table. "I'll buy the next round of drinks. Any more deductions?"

The lunches were two for the price of one. The wine was not. Helen was about to drink half a day's pay. It should have bothered her, but it didn't. It was odd, but the less money she had, the more she didn't care about it.

Phil waited until the waiter brought their wine. "I've made one more deduction," he said. "I know something is wrong, Helen. Don't lie to me. You're nearly frantic trying to hide it from me. I love you. Please tell me what it is. Is it your ex-husband? The murder at the hotel?"

Helen didn't know how to say it was both. She didn't want another "I can fix it" lecture about Rob. Phil didn't know Rob was at her hotel and she couldn't tell him. She was afraid Phil would go straight there and make a guy scene.

Helen looked up and saw the waiter. She'd never been so happy to see a man with a dessert menu. "Did we save room for dessert?" he said. "We have our icky, sticky caramel tart with Chunky Monkey ice cream, or crunchy-top crème brûlée, or some very evil chocolate."

Helen wanted to discuss the delicious desserts in intimate detail—anything to avoid the unappetizing can of worms Phil had just opened. But he was too quick. Before Helen could answer, Phil said, "Could you give us a minute, please?"

Could you give us a month? Or a year? She watched the waiter's back disappear in the crowd, with the longing of a castaway watching a rescue ship sail by. Helen was all alone. She had to give Phil something. She settled for a small slice of the truth. "It's Rhonda. That detective came back to talk to me again about her murder."

"What kind of questions did he ask?" Phil said.

"Pretty standard ones, mostly: When did I last see her? How long did I know her?"

"What wasn't standard?" Phil's voice was sharp.

"The detective also wanted to know about a counterfeit fifty he found in her wallet."

"Just one bill, or was there a stack of bad money in her effects?"

"One bill," Helen said. "At least, from what I can tell."

"You've got a good detective," Phil said.

"What do you mean by that?"

"I thought you had another retired cop from up north who took a cushy job with a small force," Phil said. "But this one actually found a funny fifty. I don't mean to put the police down, but most wouldn't notice that fifty when they did a property inventory unless it was fairly low quality. Bad money usually goes right by your average copper."

"I saw the bill," Helen said. "Looked normal to me. I'm no expert, but at least it had President Grant on it."

"Then the detective probably spotted some flaw he noticed in a flyer from the Secret Service. He's sharp," Phil said.

Helen's heart sank. This was not what she wanted

to hear. She'd thought Detective Mulruney was bored the first time she met him. Did she read him wrong? It wouldn't be the first time. Her track record with the male species was not good.

"What else did he ask about the money?" Phil said.

Distract him, she reminded herself. "Why would the Secret Service care about a bad fifty? Aren't they the president's men?"

"They're also charged with investigating funny money," Phil said. "Maybe your detective got stuck with a bad bill himself. If there's counterfeit money involved, someone definitely had a motive to kill that woman, especially if she paid for something with bad money."

Phil was way too interested. Helen didn't want him poking around the hotel, where he might run into Rob. That sharp detective would certainly notice Phil.

Think, she told herself. She had to ask Phil for some help, but keep him far away from Rob. Then she had an idea. "I need your help, Phil." Helen's voice shimmered with sincerity. "I lied to the police and now I feel guilty. Well, it wasn't a lie, really. More like an omission."

Like what I'm doing now, she thought.

"I didn't tell the detective about Rhonda's rich, handsome lover. I didn't believe he was real. I still don't. But I need to know for sure. Did Rhonda really have another lover? I've closed off that part of the police investigation by not saying anything, and I don't feel right about it. Rhonda's killer has to be found. He treated her with such contempt. I saw her body. He beat up that poor woman and then threw her away."

Helen's eyes filled with tears, but she didn't know who she was crying for. "You could put my mind at ease if you'd tell me there is no dream lover."

"And if there is?" Phil asked.

The waiter was at their table again. "Have you decided?" he said.

"Yes," Helen said. The waiter stood there, pen poised. "I'll go to the police and let the chips fall."

CHAPTER 17

Helen woke up in Phil's arms. The sun was shining low through her bedroom window. She checked the bedside clock. Five in the afternoon. Now that was how to spend a day—a long, wet lunch followed by a lazy session of love.

Phil was still asleep. She studied his eyelashes. Not too long and girlie, but not short and bristly like a doormat. He had strong eyelashes, if that was the right word.

She liked the arms that held her and the chest she leaned against. Well tanned, well muscled and not too much hair, just enough to know he was a man. Oh, yes. Phil was definitely a man. He never wore jewelry, and that was good, too. Helen didn't like pinkie rings, bracelets, or gold chains. They made men look like mobsters.

One foot stuck out of the sheets. Phil had nice feet, slender and neat. Rob's feet were hairy, with gnarly yellow toenails. Her ex looked like a bear coming out of hibernation. She'd bought Rob an expensive pedicure set as a hint, but he'd laughed at her. "I don't need to fix my feet," he'd said. "Women find me attractive right down to my toes."

It didn't occur to Helen till later that Rob never wore sandals or hung around the pool. So how did these women see his naked feet?

Why am I tormenting myself with memories of Rob when I'm in bed with another man? Helen wondered.

Because Rob can take me away from all this: The afternoons with Phil. The poolside wine sessions with Margery. My new life could be destroyed tomorrow.

"What's wrong?" Phil said, sitting up suddenly. "You were twitching, like you were angry at something."

"Why do you say that?" Helen said.

"First, because you woke me up," Phil said. "Second, because whenever you want to avoid a question, you answer it with another question. You were thinking about Rob, weren't you? He's the only person who can upset you like that. But you won't talk about him with me."

"One man at a time is enough," Helen said.

"You also use jokes to avoid the subject," Phil said.

Helen rolled on top of him and licked his ear with light little flicks. "I'm not wasting another moment of my life on that man," she said. "Not when I have someone as tasty as you." Her tongue worked its way down his neck.

"Sex," Phil gasped, "is another avoidance technique."

Helen was down past his waist. "Does it work?" she asked.

"Oh, yes," he said. "Yes, yes, yes."

It was six o'clock when Helen woke again to the sound of gentle snoring. She was still in Phil's arms, but her lover and her cat were snoring a duet. Both had the same whistling after-wheeze. Helen giggled, and Phil and Thumbs both woke up, blinking in the waning light and looking slightly offended.

"What's so funny?" Phil said.

"You and Thumbs were snoring together."

Thumbs sat up and butted her hand, then meowed loudly.

"I don't speak cat. What's he want?" Phil said.

"Dinner," Helen said. "He's hungry."

"Me, too. How about if I get us carryout from the Lotus Chinese Kitchen?"

"Shrimp with snow peas?" Helen said.

"Kung pao chicken with lots of red peppers for me," Phil said.

"You like it hot," Helen said.

"Tell me about it." Phil slapped her rump as he started to dress. He was out the door a few minutes later. Helen slipped on a silk robe and went about the house in a dreamy glow, picking up the clothes she'd left scattered on the floor. She was stripping her bra off a lamp shade when she heard a knock on her door.

This time she was alert enough to check the peephole. It was Margery, in a purple off-the-shoulder top and eggplant short shorts. Helen couldn't see her landlady's shoes, but she did see a big plate of strawberries dipped in chocolate.

"You can bring those anytime," Helen said when she opened the door.

"Figured you'd worked up quite an appetite, judging from the moans coming out of this apartment. Nice bra."

Helen looked at the flimsy black lace and blushed. The residents of the Coronado lived like boaters in a marina, pretending not to see or hear their neighbors.

"Hey, I'm glad you took my advice about Phil," Margery said. "Where is he?"

"Phil went to get dinner," Helen said.

"I told you that man was a find," Margery said. "Do you know how many men would expect you to cook for them afterward? Now that lover boy is gone, I wanted to tell you my plan to get rid of your ex."

"You have a plan?"

"All nice and legal," Margery said. "And almost guaranteed. I'm going to introduce him to a rich widow friend. Marcella—I'm not sure which last name she's using now—is in town this week. I've arranged to have her meet Rob for drinks by my pool tonight."

"Is Marcella staying with you?" Helen asked.

Margery laughed. "With me? Helen, she has a yacht in Port Everglades with a helicopter, a pool and a cook."

"Ohmigod," Helen said. "Maybe I should meet her."

Margery gave one of her sinus-busting snorts. "Stay inside between nine and midnight. I want this meeting to take place by moonlight. Marcella will look her best then. I'm sure you can find some way to keep yourself occupied."

"Margery, I'm speechless with gratitude," Helen said. "But why would you sic Rob on your friend?"

"Marcella can take care of herself. She's about sixty, but looks forty. She likes men his age, and she throws around money. Rob will love her."

"Rob will live off her."

"Exactly," Margery said. "She's an old-fashioned girl. Like Liz Taylor, Marcella has to marry the men she sleeps with. Once Rob is married to a moneybags like her, he'll forget all about poor you. He won't even be in Lauderdale. Marcella sails the Caribbean in that yacht. She'll take him away from here. They'll stay at the finest island resorts. You won't have to worry about him ever again."

Margery stood there, smiling. With a lit cigarette for a magic wand, she made an unlikely fairy godmother. But Helen knew her landlady could perform magic. "I hardly know what to say, except Rob doesn't deserve this. But I'll repeat it: Do you want to do this to your friend?"

"Marcella knows how to handle spongers," Margery said. "She's used to them in her world. She's a big girl. I think he's just her type."

"Well, she's your friend," Helen said.

"And you're my friend," Margery said. "You've lived in fear of this rat for too long. It's time you got a little help. I'll knock on your door and give you the all-clear when they're both gone."

She stopped suddenly. "I hear someone clomping down the sidewalk. I hope that's Phil. I'd better put more citronella candles out by the pool. I don't want this romance nipped in the bud by hungry mosquitoes."

Helen laughed. She never expected a happy ending to her Rob problem. She wouldn't mind her ex flitting from one island to another if she never saw him again. She peeked out the blinds to make sure it was her man, then ran to open the front door. Phil was carrying two steaming take-out bags.

"Hello, handsome," Margery said.

Phil gave his landlady a kiss on the cheek. "What have you got for me?" he said.

"Dessert," she said, holding out the plate of strawberries.

Phil popped one in his mouth. "Want to join us for dinner?" he said. "We have plenty of food."

"You don't want an old lady like me hanging around," Margery said, batting her eyelashes outrageously. "Have fun."

She was out the door. Helen was relieved. Even with gray hair and wrinkles, Margery could cast a spell over men.

Helen brought out plates and silverware, and Phil opened the take-out cartons. They ate huge mounds of Chinese food and fed the leftovers to the cat. Then they fed the strawberries to each other.

"Oops," Phil said. "You dropped some chocolate on your chest. Let me help clean it up."

That led to another long, slow session in the bedroom. It was nearly nine o'clock when Phil said, "What did Margery really want?"

Helen was in a love stupor, too languid and lazy to consider her words. "She's fixing my ex up with a rich older woman." Helen pulled Phil closer to her.

Suddenly Phil was in no mood for love. He sat straight up in bed. "What? You know where Rob is staying in Lauderdale? Why didn't you tell me? I'll go over there and beat that creep to a pulp."

"You will not," Helen said. "There's no need to act like a caveman. Margery has a foolproof plan."

"With that fool, Rob?"

"Calm down," Helen said. "Margery is a first-rate matchmaker. If this works out, Rob will be out of my hair forever."

"And if it doesn't?" Phil said.

"We'll worry about that later," Helen said.

"Can I at least see this guy?" Phil asked.

"Sure. He should be passing by this window any minute. He's meeting his date by the pool."

Helen turned off the lights and cracked the miniblinds. They waited in the dark. Phil tickled her neck and held her close. "Helen, I love you," he whispered in her ear. "I don't want you to live on the run anymore. Let me help you. This is what I do for a living."

Helen heard footsteps on the concrete walkway. "Shush," she said. "It's him."

Phil peeked out the window. Helen did, too. The man who'd ruined her old life was strolling down the sidewalk, whistling out of tune.

"That's Rob?"

Helen nodded.

Phil gave a harsh laugh. "You married that dork?"

CHAPTER 18

"**H**e's bald," Phil said.
    "He is not," Helen said. "His hair's just a little thin on top."
    "A little thin?" Phil said. "His hair's a little thin the way Mr. Clean is a little bald."
    If Rob reached through that window, he could touch me, Helen thought. It was creepy that her ex was so close. He'd give anything to lay hands on me, and I'm within his reach. Rob ambled by her apartment unaware.
    Phil and Helen crouched below the windowsill, arguing in whispers.
    "He looks like an elf," Phil said. "His ears are pointed."
    "They are not," Helen said. "Rob is no movie star, but that's the secret of his success. Men like him because they think he isn't a threat. They let him hang around with their wives because they see him as safe. Women think he's cute. He makes them laugh. You'd be surprised how many women would rather have a good laugh than a good body."
    "In my case, they get both," Phil said.
    Helen was in no mood for jokes. "Everyone underestimates Rob. A woman starts out treating him like a brother, and the next thing she knows she's committing incest."

"Oh, come on," Phil said. "You make him sound like a chick magnet. He has a potbelly."

"Only a little one," Helen said.

"Why are you defending him?" Phil said.

Why am I? Helen wondered. She didn't care about Rob. But she couldn't stand that Phil thought she was a fool for loving Rob. She wanted him to see Rob's attraction.

"Look at that loser," Phil said. "This is the man you've been running from? He couldn't find the beer at a Super Bowl party."

"Shut up, Rob," Helen said.

"Rob?" Phil said.

"I mean Phil," Helen said.

Helen peeked out the window again. She could see her ex-husband sitting by the pool, charming Margery, while she and Phil hissed at each other like caged snakes. Rob always left unhappy couples in his wake.

"I admit I'm upset at seeing him," Helen said. "But there's no need for us to argue. I thought we'd settled this. Rob is meeting Margery's rich friend tonight. Hopefully they'll like each other and get married."

"Helen, that's a ridiculous plan. What intelligent woman would marry that feeb?"

"I did," Helen said.

"You were young," he said. "It wasn't your fault."

"I'm so glad you forgive me," Helen said. "But I was forty years old when I walked out on Rob."

"I didn't mean it that way," Phil said.

"Which way did you mean it?" Helen said.

Phil finally seemed to realize he'd been tactless. "Helen, I will do anything to help you. Anything. Let me take care of this guy for you."

If Phil had taken Helen in his arms then, she might have said yes. Instead he gave her an annoying smirk and said, "Besides, how hard can it be? He looks clueless."

"I warned you, don't underestimate him," Helen said. "Rob tracked me to the Coronado. He won't go away. He needs money in the worst way. He's bankrupt if he can't work out some sort of settlement with me. That's why Margery is trying to fix him up with Marcella. If he's busy chasing her money, he won't try to get the little bit I earn."

"Why would Margery do that?" Phil asked.

"Because she cares about me."

"I know that," Phil said. "Why would she do that to Marcella?"

"She says Marcella is older and can take care of herself."

"She's probably smarter about men."

He did it again. He treated her like a moron. Hot anger flared up in Helen. "What did you say?"

"I'm sorry, Helen," Phil said, but he didn't sound sorry. "I can't believe you let this twerp ruin your life. How could you give him so much power?"

"I didn't give him any power. The court did," Helen said.

"You should have stayed and fought. Thanks to Rob, you're working way below your capacity."

"He did me a favor," Helen said. "If Rob disappeared tomorrow, I still wouldn't go back to a corporation."

"I didn't say you had to work for IBM," Phil said. "But you don't have to be a hotel maid, either."

"What's wrong with making an honest living?" Helen asked.

"Nothing. But ask yourself: Do your coworkers have your education? People don't do hard labor unless they can't get easier jobs. Do you think the maids work those jobs so their children can clean hotels? They don't want their kids to have their life. You have a college degree, Helen. You can use your mind. You don't have to break your back."

"I like the exercise," Helen said. "I hate panty hose, memos and meetings. I'd rather break my back making beds than sit through one more brainstorming session. I'm free of the corporate rat race. I like my new life. I love you. I wish you would try to understand me."

"I wish I could understand you," Phil said. "But I'm not sure that's possible. I think I'd better leave before I say something worse."

He kissed her on the forehead, as if she were an old woman, and slipped out the door. Phil left with hardly a sound. Helen sat alone in her living room in her sexy silk robe, feeling foolish and angry. She threw the sofa pillows at the door, followed by the newspapers and magazines on the coffee table. She thought of throwing something breakable, but she didn't want to lose her security deposit. Besides, she loved the fifties furniture—the turquoise Barcalounger, the lamps shaped like nuclear reactors, the boomerang coffee table.

In her old life she would have sneered at it as tacky. Now she thought it belonged in this apartment with the speckled terrazzo floors. So did she. If Margery's plan worked, she'd be able to stay here forever.

It wasn't a crazy plan. OK, it was crazy. But Margery had pulled off more improbable schemes. Helen shouldn't have mentioned it at this early stage. Rob and Marcella hadn't even met yet. But Helen could hope. She wanted Marcella to sail off into the sunset with her ex-husband. She didn't envy Rob his supposed rich life. People who married for money worked for it.

But Rob would finally find work that suited his talents.

Helen brooded alone in her living room, morosely scratching her cat's ears. She wanted to open the box of cold wine in her fridge, but drinking wasn't a good idea in her current mood. Instead she picked up the tossed pillows and papers. It was good for her waistline. Physical labor gave her muscles, but not sculpted gym muscles. Helen had strong arms and hands, but her waist and thighs needed work. She brooded on that, too.

At eleven o'clock that night, Helen heard a knock on her door. The all-clear signal from Margery was an hour earlier than expected. Helen sighed. The matchmaking hadn't worked. She'd invite Margery in for a postmortem.

She checked the peephole, but instead of her land-lady she saw Peggy, gorgeous in a pale green dress. She looked like a luna moth Helen had seen in a book—beautiful and fragile, with huge graceful wings the color of a new leaf. Something so lovely could be easily hurt. Helen was afraid for her friend.

"I know it's late—" Peggy began.

"Quick, come in," Helen interrupted, and dragged Peggy in the door. "I don't want Rob to see you. Margery's introducing him to her rich friend, Marcella. They're out talking by the pool."

"Can I see him?" Peggy said, in the way you'd ask to look at a new kitten.

Helen turned off the living room light and gently lifted the blinds for Peggy.

"Marcella has her back to me, but I can just make him out by candlelight," Peggy said. "He's cute in a teddy bear kind of way."

Helen was pleased that Peggy saw Rob's attraction. Then she realized Peggy's choices in men were even worse than hers.

"Think your ex will go for her?" Peggy said.

"I hope so," Helen said, putting the blinds back down and turning on the light again. The late-night light made Peggy's red hair flame. "Normally I'd feel guilty about unloading him on another woman. But Marcella can afford the lawyers to keep Rob in line. Have a seat. Can I get you some wine?"

"No, I've been drinking pisco sours with Glenn. I'm a little giddy already. I'd better not mix drinks. I wanted to give you my news. Please don't be mad at me. I know how you feel about Glenn." Peggy was glowing with happiness.

This is going to be bad, Helen thought. Peggy has done something she's going to regret.

"I'm not mad," Helen said. "Margery and I are worried about you, that's all."

Peggy plopped down a little heavily on the couch, the only sign that she might be tipsy, and stroked Thumbs. She looked oddly incomplete without her parrot, Pete, on her shoulder. "Why?" she said. "Glenn is a great guy."

"He seems to make you happy," Helen said, choosing her words carefully.

"Why wouldn't I be happy, dating a rich, charming and successful man?" Peggy suddenly stopped petting the cat. "You don't think Glenn is a success. You think he's a hustler, riding around in a big limo, everything for show. Margery doesn't think he makes international deals. She said he could fake those calls to London by dialing Time and Temperature. But he didn't. He made them on a Vertu Signature phone."

"What's that?" Helen said.

"It's the Rolex of the cell phone world. It costs almost twelve thousand dollars. It has gold keys with ruby bearings and a sapphire-crystal face."

"Sounds like a real gem," Helen said.

"A fake can't afford a phone like that," Peggy said.

Helen wasn't convinced. Glenn could have rented, borrowed—or stolen—the phone. Like the limousine, it was overpriced and overdone.

"Have you seen his office in Lauderdale?" Helen said.

"He pointed out the building to me. It's in a big, expensive tower off Las Olas, where all the major corporations are."

"Did you go into his office? See his name on the door?"

"Why would we go to his office on a date?" Peggy said.

Anyone can point to a skyscraper and say they have an office inside, Helen thought.

"He gave me his card and the company brochure," Peggy said. "They both have his office address."

You can get those printed up for a hundred bucks, Helen thought.

"I know what you're thinking, but you're wrong," Peggy said. "Glenn is a great guy and a smart business-man."

Helen's stomach dropped about ten stories. "You gave him your twenty thousand dollars," she said.

"He's going to make me rich and happy," Peggy said. "He promised. He'll take me away from this and we'll have a boat and a big house on the water."

Helen had heard those words once before—from a dead woman.

CHAPTER 19

. . . .

Helen heard flirty laughter and sexy giggles out by the pool, then a man's deeper chuckle, like some answering mating call.

Rob and Marcella. Margery's matchmaking was working. In the candlelit garden, by the waterfalls of bougainvillea, the courtship dance had begun.

Helen lifted the blinds, feeling like a nosy old woman. By the primitive light, Helen could see Rob and the woman lying on chaise longues. Their bodies were relaxed. No, not relaxed—abandoned, yielding. Though they were both fully dressed, they seemed naked. The woman's back was to Helen, but her hair was too dark to be Margery's. The landlady had disappeared.

Would Peggy interrupt them? Helen hoped not. Peggy was so exotic, the sight of her would wilt this tender young romance. Peggy would remind the couple of what they should be and what they used to be. The soft night air would suddenly grow heavy with regret.

Helen saw a movement over on the edge of the property. Peggy was flitting across the Coronado lawn to her apartment, carefully skirting the pool. She was too much of a friend to ruin Margery's plan.

Helen watched, fascinated. Marcella lay back in her chaise, waxed legs glowing in the flickering light. Rob leaned slightly forward, as if she were drawing him toward her. She had the power and he acknowledged it. Rob listened with his whole body. Helen expected a pang of jealousy, but she felt nothing. She only prayed this romance would work.

How sad is that? she thought. I want my former husband to run off with another woman.

Marcella's voice was too low to carry, but she moved her hands as she talked, as if conducting their conversation. Rob held a wineglass. He seemed bewitched.

In our end is our beginning, Helen thought. The first time she saw Rob was at a party. He was holding a wineglass and charming another woman. She was a model-thin blonde with cornsilk hair and bored glamour. When Rob saw Helen, he left the blonde in midsentence and introduced himself. "As soon as I saw you, I had to know you," Rob had said.

Helen was dazzled. No man had ever treated her that way. She felt powerful, sexy and meanly triumphant when she saw the blonde alone in the corner.

Rob had had more hair and less gut then, but he hadn't changed much in nearly twenty years. She was the one who'd changed. Helen was wiser in ways she never wanted to be.

Rob had been the blonde's lover the night they'd met, but he'd abandoned her for Helen. "Once I saw you, there was no one else in the room," he told Helen.

At twenty-two, she thought that was exciting. Now Helen knew better: The way a man treated his old love was the way he'd treat his new one. Rob cast aside his old lover without a second thought, but he never let go of his wine.

Rob had wanted to go home with Helen that night, and she'd wanted him in her bed. Her desire was a compulsion, a love sickness. She thought she'd die when she told him no. But on some primal level, she knew Rob only wanted what he couldn't have.

So she won this empty prize. At twenty-two she'd felt superior to all the other women he'd slept with. Now she was smart enough to know she'd lost that night. Wiser women realized Rob wasn't husband material. They had him for a romp in the sheets, then left. Helen mistook her naïveté for moral superiority.

Three months later Helen had an engagement ring and a deposit on the church. Rob committed his first infidelity before the wedding, though she wouldn't find out until years later. He had an affair with her maid of honor, a curvy, freckled brunette named Kate.

When they were planning the wedding, Helen had asked Rob if he found Kate attractive. "If you like cheerleaders," he'd said. "She doesn't have your legs."

Whatever Kate had, Rob wanted it. He got it, too. But Helen's love was blind. She saw Rob admiring other women. She believed him when he said, "Baby, I'm just looking, like any red-blooded man. It's you I married. Don't you trust me?"

She should have said no. But Rob was so passionate, Helen thought he couldn't have any energy left for another woman. It took her a long time to understand the real thrill for Rob was cheating on her.

Marriage made his bed hopping so convenient. Rob set the rules, telling his women right up front, "I won't leave my wife. We have an understanding."

My wife understands she's the faithful one. You understand we'll have a little recreational sex, but don't come running to me, honey, if you're sick, lonely or need me. I'm married.

After her marriage unraveled, Helen spent the long nights trying to count all the women Rob had betrayed her with. She stopped at sixteen. She was overwhelmed by memories of sly smiles from strange women. She recalled Rob's explanation for the motel matchbook in his pocket: "John gave me that when I asked him for a light." The lipstick on his collar was waved away with: "I got that on my shirt at a good-bye party for Sonya. You remember sweet little Sonya. She's getting married and moving to San Diego."

Helen remembered the women who called their home. "Just a telemarketer," Rob assured her. "I said I didn't want any."

Helen couldn't look in his eyes. She was afraid of what she'd see.

Then one afternoon Helen came home from work early and walked in on Rob with their neighbor Sandy. No, he wasn't with Sandy. He was deep inside her, groaning and pumping. There was no way Helen could close her eyes to that. Something hot and red exploded inside her, and she was permanently cured of her blindness. Helen picked up a crowbar and started swinging, while Rob scurried for the protection of his Toyota Land Cruiser like a cornered rat.

She'd killed Rob's SUV. She'd pounded it into scrap, while a naked Rob cowered inside, begging her to stop. She did stop, after the cops arrived and the car was destroyed.

But Helen never stopped beating up on herself for being so blind, so stupid, so in love with a man who didn't love her. When she ran from St. Louis, she didn't just leave Rob behind. She tried to shed her old, gullible self.

Now she was in Fort Lauderdale, watching the man she'd slept with for seventeen years try to bed another woman—and hoping he'd succeed. Five years ago she would have been shocked speechless. But she was a different woman then, a good little corporate creature who saw only what she was supposed to.

I have to quit staring out this window, she thought. I'm going to burn a hole in Rob's shirt. Helen shut the blinds and settled in with a book. She read the same paragraph over and over, although she had no idea what it said. Only Thumbs sitting on her legs kept her from pacing restlessly. She ran her fingers through his fur until he nipped her.

At midnight she heard a knock on the door. She expected Margery, but when she looked out the peephole, there was Phil with a rose and a bottle of champagne. "Let me in," he whispered. "If you don't, I'll make an awful scene."

She did, but not because she was afraid he'd betray her. A man who knew how to apologize was irresistible, especially when he wore her favorite blue shirt.

Apologies did not come easy to Phil. He squared his shoulders and took a deep breath, as if he were about to give a speech. "I'm sorry," he said. "After what I married, I have no business criticizing anyone's choice of a mate."

Kendra. How could Helen have forgotten about Phil's ex-wife, that stiletto-heeled vixen? If she'd remembered Kendra, Helen would have thrown his trashy ex in Phil's face.

"The fact that you didn't mention Kendra makes you a saint," Phil said.

Helen wasn't too good to take credit for her accidental virtue. "I hope you're not planning to limit your apology to saintly activities."

"Well," he said with a sly smile, "I thought I'd start by getting down on my knees."

He slowly unzipped her jeans. Helen moaned. "You need to apologize more often."

It was nearly three in the morning when they were awakened by a man and a woman laughing and talking outside Helen's apartment. Phil sat up in bed, startling Thumbs. The big-pawed cat jumped off the bed with a graceless thud and sent the empty champagne bottle rolling across the floor. At least the rose in the wineglass was safe.

"Who's that?" Phil said.

"Shssh," Helen said. "I bet it's Rob and his new honey. Let's get a look at her."

They tiptoed to the window. The lights were off. Helen carefully lifted the miniblinds from the bottom and peeked outside. She nearly dropped the blinds. Rob was less than a foot away, leaning against her wall and kissing a brunette. Her ex had quite a lip grip.

Helen thought the woman was about forty, but when her face came under the hard yellow porch light, Helen saw she was actually a well-preserved sixty. She was handsome, but she looked a little harsh in that light. Her hair was a shade too dark, her eye makeup a little too black and her lipstick a fraction too red. Her clothes cost more than Helen made in six months. Their exaggerated cut could only be couture. Rob was pulling down the gold zipper on her blouse with one hand. The woman didn't remove it.

Margery, you old cupid, Helen thought.

Your turn, she mouthed to Phil. He grinned at her, then looked out the window. The grin disappeared. Phil stared for a second, then dropped the blinds with a crash. The couple leaped like startled deer and ran laughing toward the parking lot.

"Holy shit," Phil said. "That's Marcella, the Black Widow."

"Who?"

"The most notorious female serial killer in South Florida."

"Who did she kill?" Helen said.

"Her husbands," Phil said.

CHAPTER 20

"**R**ob is kissing a serial killer," Helen said. "We have to warn him."

She was relieved she'd said that. Inside her, the divorced devil-wife was screaming, Good! I hope he dies slowly and painfully. I hope Marcella removes his manhood with a rusty knife and fries it with fava beans.

Helen was thankful her good side won out this time. She was sure the divorced devil-wife would scare the pants back on Phil. He was deliciously naked, but she was too upset to enjoy the view.

"We can't warn him," Phil said. "We can't say a word against the woman. Marcella would slap us with a slander suit. She can afford to hire every lawyer in Lauderdale. We wouldn't have a leg to stand on."

Helen had a sudden vision of pin-striped lawyers presenting Phil's legs to Marcella, like Salome receiving the head of John the Baptist.

"Besides, would Rob believe you if you did warn him?" Phil said. "And how are you going to warn him?"

Oh. That. Helen could see herself knocking on her ex's hotel door and saying, "Hi, Rob. It's me. I know I've avoided you for a couple of years, but now I'm worried about you. Remember the woman you were smooching last night? The rich one with the yacht and more houses than a Monopoly game? She has this unusual hobby. She likes to collect husbands and kill them."

Her speech would drive Rob into Marcella's arms. "You're right, Phil," Helen said. "It was a stupid idea."

"I like it when you say I'm right." He smiled and his eyes crinkled. Helen loved when Phil's eyes did that. She had a naked man with eye crinkles in her living room, and all she could think about was her worthless ex. Rob was a better chaperone than a convent full of nuns.

"Maybe we could tip off the police," Helen said. "I could make an anonymous call from a pay phone and let them know Marcella is in town. They could watch her."

"Why?" Phil said. "There are no outstanding warrants against her. She's never been charged with a crime. She's a fine upstanding multimillionaire—and a multiwidow."

"How does she get away with it?" Helen said. "I couldn't even kill one husband."

"Her story takes some explaining," Phil said. "Throw on some clothes and let's go for a drive."

Helen's front door opened onto a silent world. The Coronado looked as if it were under a spell. The late-night moon turned the old building's dazzling white walls a frozen blue. Mist swirled across the grass. Even the midnight cats were no longer on the prowl. At this hour, Helen could believe any story, no matter how fantastic.

They tiptoed down the sidewalk to Phil's dusty black Jeep. He started the engine, but didn't turn on the head-lights until they were on the deserted street.

"How did you know about Marcella?" Helen said.

"Everyone in South Florida law enforcement knows about her," Phil said. "She's a legend. The police believe she's killed at least four men, maybe five.

"Marcella was twenty when she married her first hus-band. She looks expensively lacquered now, but forty years ago her beauty was natural. I saw her wedding pictures. She had long wavy hair and a lush body. In her wedding photos you can see the men staring at her with undisguised hunger. They looked at her new husband with envy. You can almost read their minds: 'How did a geezer with liver spots like raisins get a looker like her?' "

Helen shuddered. "How did he?"

"Her new husband owned a shipping company. Oil tankers, I think. Marcella was a clerk-typist in the office. His wife of forty years had died recently. He was lonely, fabulously wealthy, and fifty years older than Marcella.

"The marriage seemed a success. He enjoyed playing Pygmalion, teaching her how to walk, talk and dress. She liked being an old man's darling. He died of a heart attack ten years later. His death may have been natural, or maybe she got tired of waiting for his money. We'll never know. There was no autopsy. The man was eighty and he had no children to stir up trouble.

"When he died, Marcella inherited half a billion dollars, four houses, a yacht and a teak sailboat. She was thirty. She buried her elderly husband, wore black for six months, then married a twenty-three-year-old Chippendale.

"Her second husband had a great body and all the right moves except one: Chip swung both ways. He had a boyfriend. One of the yacht crew talked too much in an island bar. He said Marcella caught Chip with his boyfriend and made a terrible scene.

"Shortly after that, Marcella and Chip went on a sailboat trip to the islands of Exuma in the Bahamas. She told the police that Husband Number Two had a lot of wine that evening and must have fallen off the boat during the night. When she awoke the next morning, he was gone. She'd searched frantically for hours, but there was no trace of Chip.

"A fisherman found the body two days later. Chip's zipper was open. That detail seemed to confirm her story. A lot of drowned men get pulled out of the water in that condition. Late at night, a drunk takes a whiz off the side of the boat, loses his balance in the shifting sea and falls overboard. He can't catch up with the boat. The guy drowns, cursing his own stupidity.

"The police had heard the rumors and questioned the crew member who'd supposedly witnessed the fight, but he denied it ever happened. The coroner ruled the death accidental. The suddenly tight-lipped crew member started his own charter boat company after the inquest."

"What happened to Chip's boyfriend?" Helen said.

"He disappeared," Phil said.

"Did he die, too?" Helen said.

"Don't know," Phil said. "He was a drifter. If he was smart, he took off."

The Jeep's lights cut through the swirling night mist. Helen noticed the streets were narrower and lined with candy-colored cottages. Tipsy couples strolled down the sidewalk, clutching beer bottles and each other.

"It's a nice night for a walk on the beach," Phil said.

The ocean had always been a place of infinite possibility for them. Helen had first kissed Phil on the water after a wild boat chase. She'd rescued him from drowning, and he'd saved her from the police with a kiss. They had sealed their love on the beach.

Phil parked the Jeep at a shuttered T-shirt shop. Helen slipped off her shoes and rolled up her jeans for a walk on the sand. The beach felt cold and wet under her bare feet. The sand was sprinkled with sharp broken shells. The waves rushing over her feet chilled her. So did their endless shushing sound. Usually Helen found the water soothing. Tonight it unsettled her. What was it like to be lost in that limitless blackness, to feel your body grow colder and heavier as you choked on the water that would soon kill you? Helen shivered.

Phil put his arm around her. "Do you really want to hear the rest of this?" he said.

She nodded.

"Husband Number Three was a member of the yacht

crew. He was another empty-headed stud fifteen years younger than Marcella."

"She was making up for her time with the liver-spotted old man," Helen said.

"She was nearly forty now," Phil said. "You'd think this husband would have learned. But men always thought they were smarter than Marcella until it was too late. Gossip says she caught this one with an island cutie, but nobody would say anything on the record."

"Any new charter businesses start up suddenly?" Helen said. She stepped over an eyeless fish rotting on the cold sand.

"Not that I know of," Phil said. "Two days after Marcella supposedly caught her third husband in bed with another woman, he ate some bad seafood and died in agony. The island police didn't investigate his death too carefully. He was seen eating three lobsters that night in a restaurant in the capital of Georgetown. Two other lobster lovers at the restaurant were also sick, but they survived."

"Did Marcella have lobster?"

"No, she ate steak, the most expensive thing on any island menu. Marcella was once more a widow. After the inquest, she buried her handsome young husband at sea."

What if I'd had the chance to kill Rob two days after I caught him with Sandy? Helen wondered.

The man would be dead meat, the divorced devil-wife said.

You had a chance to kill him when you found him, her good angel said. All you did was murder his SUV.

Helen kept those thoughts to herself. She stepped carefully around the beach trash. Seaweed decorated with busted balloons and lemon halves wrapped in yellow net were strung along the sand. Cruise ship debris, jettisoned illegally.

"Marcella was fifty-two when she met her fourth husband at a bar in the Caymans," Phil said. "That wedding nearly equaled Madonna's extravaganza with Sean Penn. The ceremony was in a pavilion by the sea decorated with ten thousand pink roses. Her off-white gown had a fifteen-foot train embroidered with seed pearls."

"Where did you get that information?" Helen said.

"*People* magazine," Phil said. "The wedding cost nearly a million dollars. Two years later, the groom drowned in a diving accident off the island of St. Christopher. Defective air tank. Some island dive operations aren't the safest. Her fourth husband was only thirty. The investigation found nothing unusual, and Marcella seemed to have no known reason to kill him. But the police think she did, just the same."

"And the fifth husband?" Helen said.

"He died in the Bahamas on that fatal sailboat," Phil said.

"She repeated herself," Helen said. "That's hardly original."

"Husband Number Five didn't come up with an original sin. He was a bodybuilding champ who cheated on Marcella with a sixteen-year-old Nassau girl. He told the girl the rich old bag he married was so grateful, he could do anything."

"Ouch," Helen said. "How did Marcella find that out?"

"The young woman got pregnant and her mother told Marcella."

"Let me guess," Helen said. "The child is now going to Harvard."

"The boy was well provided for," Phil said. "Marcella was generous—and forgiving. She had a very public reconciliation with her fifth husband on Bay Street. It was so touching, tourists and locals alike applauded them. The couple sailed for a second honeymoon on that teak boat. Marcella wanted to picnic on a remote island, just the two of them. The cook packed a basket with caviar, lobster and champagne."

"You'd think her husbands would watch out for that lobster," Helen said.

"Lobster didn't kill this one," Phil said. "Her fifth husband was an inexperienced sailor. The sailboat hit a sudden squall, the boom swung wildly in the wind, and he was cracked on the head. He died before Marcella could get him to a hospital.

"The Nassau police were suspicious. But other boaters reported there had been a squall in the area. The police found blood on the boom. The only odd thing was, the champagne bottle wasn't anywhere on board. Marcella said it must have been lost during the confusion. The coroner ruled that the head wound was consistent with injuries sustained by a blow from the boom. Marcella had the bodybuilder cremated. That was four months ago."

"And now she is looking for Husband Number Six," Helen said.

"Maybe not. She's getting older. Maybe she's tired of men," Phil said.

"She seemed pretty interested tonight," Helen said. "Do you think Margery knows Marcella is the Black Widow?"

"Of course," Phil said.

Helen stared at the dark ocean. "Then she's deliberately sending Rob to his death."

"Margery wouldn't do that," Phil said. "Never."

Helen felt relieved until he added, "But she might set things in motion to see what would happen."

Helen had spent so many nights boiling with hate, thinking of ways to kill Rob, but even she couldn't dream up the Black Widow. She was the perfect trap for Rob. He'd be ensnared by her luxury and his own ego. Like all Marcella's husbands, he'd imagine he could play around on his aging wife and still enjoy her money.

"Helen, relax." Phil kissed her neck. "I don't think that romance will go anywhere. The guy has no technique. He pawed Marcella like a horny teenager."

"Maybe she wants to feel like a horny teen," Helen said.

The sky was lightening in the east. A thin line of silver appeared in the black night.

"Forget him. Watch the sunrise with me," Phil said. "It's the greatest show on earth."

Soon the sky filled with towering pink and gray clouds. The molten morning sun burst above the horizon, gilding the pink with liquid gold. Helen never saw the sun come up in St. Louis, when she was a corporate slave. It was a glorious sight.

"It's a new day," Phil said, and kissed her until he was the only man on her mind.

The sand was warm and the air felt soft when they left to eat breakfast at an old chrome diner. After blueberry pancakes and hot coffee, Helen checked the time. Seven thirty. She hadn't stayed up all night since college. She felt raffish and a little light-headed.

"I have to go, Phil," she said. "I barely have time to shower and change for work. It's been a strange and wonderful night. Thank you."

"Don't worry about Rob," he said, as he kissed her good-bye.

"I won't," she said. In the new morning her fears seemed foolish. They were night fevers. Marcella was no murdering monster. She'd had bad luck with men, that was all.

At eight twenty-five Helen slipped through the side door of the Full Moon Hotel. She was met by a jubilant Sondra.

"You don't have to sneak around anymore," the desk clerk said. "Your ex checked out half an hour ago. He must have used that dating service after all. This woman in a silver Bentley pulled into the hotel parking lot. A Bentley at this place. Can you believe it?" Sondra's brown eyes were wide.

"Her chauffeur paid Rob's bill and put his suitcase in the trunk. Then he opened the door and your ex climbed inside the Bentley. That's when I saw her. She looked like an old-time movie star, that older woman in *Sunset Boulevard*. Remember her?"

"Gloria Swanson," Helen said. "She killed her younger lover."

"Whatever," Sondra said. "You're free. Your ex is another woman's problem."

"Did this woman have dark hair and red lipstick?" Helen asked.

"That's her," Sondra said. "Do you know her?"

"She's a rich widow," Helen said.

And Rob's a dead man, she thought.

CHAPTER 21

. . . .

"Helen, what's the rule for moving a guest's property?" Craig said. The blond boy-band leader was stripping the bed in room 323.

Helen came out of the bathroom, her toilet brush held like a scepter. "We can't touch it," she said. "This room is the guest's home. We must respect his things. If someone piles clothes and junk on a dresser, we can't dust it. We can't even throw away a cup of warm soda. But we can move a newspaper to make a bed."

"What about a handgun?" Craig said.

"Gun?" Helen said. The toilet brush clattered to the floor. "You found a gun?"

Craig picked up the crumpled pillow. On the mattress was the biggest, longest handgun Helen had ever seen, with a barrel like a steel casket and a grip like a black mood.

"That's not a handgun," Helen said, her voice quavering. "That's a cannon. Why would you carry that? In case you ran into an elephant in a dark alley?"

"It's a Smith & Wesson Model 629 Classic .44 Magnum," Craig said, his voice reverent. The boy-band leader had morphed into a weapons expert. "Look at that baby. It's a foot long. A Magnum can do a lot of damage."

He stared at the huge handgun like a man in a dream, then shook himself awake. "So do we move it or not?"

"Did the guest put the sign on the bed that asks us not to change the sheets?" Helen asked.

"No," Craig said. "He tore it into little pieces."

"Hostile," Helen said.

"Very," Craig said.

The gun pulsed, black and evil, the source of dark crimes.

"We're not supposed to touch that gun," Helen said. "A weapon is a little different from a *USA Today*."

"Tell me about it. I'd survive a hit in the chest with a newspaper. Have you seen the guy staying in this room?"

"Yesterday he demanded extra towels," Helen said. "When I brought them, he grabbed them and didn't tip. He's short and muscle-bound, with a thick neck and big red pimples."

"Steroids make you short-tempered," Craig said.

'Roid rage was loose in this room, along with a gun. The Magnum seemed to grow larger. It was at least two feet long now.

"How mad do guests get if we don't make their beds?" Craig asked.

"Extremely," Helen said. "They pound on the front desk, screaming for clean sheets. Sondra tries to explain why beds piled with belongings can't be touched, but the guests see a freshly made bed as their natural right. They pay good money for their room and they want service. At home it takes two minutes to make the bed. They don't even think about it. But on vacation they'll wait all day for us to do it. Even when we offer to make the bed if they'll move their junk, they're still furious."

"Do you want to tell a man with a .44 Magnum why we didn't make his bed?" Craig said.

Helen stared at the gun. Were those notches on the grip, or scratches?

"I think we can make an exception to the no-touch rule," Helen said.

"Right." Craig started to pick up the gun.

"Wait!" Helen said. "What if it was used in a crime? Here, pick it up with this." She threw him a towel.

Craig laughed. "Aw, come on. This belongs to some harmless nut who'd rather fondle a gun than a girl. I can't see a criminal hiding out at the Full Moon with the AARP tours."

"You'd be surprised," Helen said. "We had a bank robber in this room."

"Here?" Craig's eyes widened.

Damn, he was cute. Helen liked watching him pull the heavy spread off the bed. A man doing domestic chores seemed extra attractive.

"It happened before I worked here," Helen said. "The robber holed up in this room and the cops shot him. He tried to escape out that window." She pointed dramatically at the bland glass rectangle.

"What happened to the money?" Craig said.

"It was never found. The cops think he was meeting someone for a drug deal. The other maids say the FBI searched the hotel and tore this room apart, but they never found anything."

"Where do you think the money is?" Craig said.

"I have no idea," Helen said. "There's nowhere to hide it in the room. The pictures and headboard are bolted to the wall. You can't stick it under the bed. All the beds have wooden barriers to keep items from rolling under the mattresses. The robber could stash the money in an air-conditioner duct or hide it in a housekeeping room. The only other hiding place would be in the laundry room."

And those have been searched by the staff, she thought.

"Huh," Craig said. "So you don't think it's still in the hotel?"

"No," Helen said. "My guess is his accomplice got away with the money. The robber was killed before he could run."

"Makes sense," Craig said. "Especially since no one's

found it." He leaned over and kissed Helen lightly. She was suddenly aware that she was alone in a hotel room with a young hunk and a big bed. Now the king-size bed was pulsing. It seemed to spread across the room, an acre of white sheets.

"Have a drink with me after work." Craig's voice was husky.

"I'm seeing someone," Helen said.

"No strings," Craig said. "Just for fun."

"Sorry," she said.

Helen was sorry, and wished she wasn't. An uncomplicated fling had a sudden strong allure. How can I even think that, after last night with Phil? she scolded herself. I must be overtired. Maybe I'm running from commitment. No, I sound like a talk-show expert. Maybe I'm just a talk-show guest—on *Jerry Springer*.

"We'd better get going." Helen loaded her spray bottle and cleaning rags on the cart. "We have to leave for Rhonda's funeral at two."

There. A little death should take care of any lingering lust.

"Uh, count me out," Craig said.

"You're not going?" Helen said.

"Funerals aren't my thing," he said.

"Are they anyone's?" Helen said.

"Look, I didn't know the woman," Craig said. "Who cares anyway? She was just a maid. She didn't own the hotel. She cleaned it. It's no biggie. No one will miss me."

"I sure won't," Helen said. She didn't care if he heard her. No wonder she thought Craig was in a boy band. That's what he was—a boy, not a man. Someone with no sense of responsibility. She wouldn't get that little frisson if he kissed her again. Now he left her cold. She didn't even think he was cute. His eyes were small and shifty and his teeth looked feral and pointed.

"Suit yourself." Helen pushed the cart down the hall to the next room. She and Craig cleaned three rooms in an awkward silence. *She was just a maid,* he'd said. How could he be so callous? Craig got his job because Rhonda died. The least he could do was show up at the church, the selfish jerk. He was getting the afternoon off with pay. Sybil had hired temps so all the staff could go to the funeral. Sybil liked making a buck, but she still did unexpected kindnesses. Maybe that was why the staff put up with the owner's penny-pinching.

Finally Helen couldn't stand her own seething silence. "I need to ask Cheryl a question," she said. "I'll be back."

Craig shrugged, but kept quiet.

Helen didn't care if he had to clean her share of the room. She saw Cheryl's cart parked in front of room 214, but the curly-haired maid wasn't there. In fact, she wasn't anywhere on the second floor.

Helen ran back upstairs and saw the door to 323 propped open. She and Craig had just cleaned it. Did something else go wrong with the trouble room?

Helen tiptoed in and found Cheryl on her hands and knees in the closet. The only piece of carpet to survive the attack of the party animals was in there. Cheryl had ripped it up.

"What are you doing?" Helen pasted on a smile to hide the sharpness in her question.

"Nothing." Cheryl quickly dropped the carpet. "The rug didn't feel right when I vacuumed it the other day and I wanted to check it."

"What was wrong?" Helen said.

"It was lumpy," Cheryl said. "I mean, it was loose. See?" She picked up a corner with one hand.

But Helen saw Cheryl's other hand sliding over to cover something. Helen couldn't tell if it was one dollar or a fifty, but she'd recognize that shade of green anywhere.

"Find some money on the floor?" Helen said. She tried to keep her voice light.

"Why, yes," Cheryl said. "No. It wasn't on the floor."

Her pretty pink complexion flushed an ugly red. "It's twenty dollars. It was in your ex-husband Rob's room. Either he left it or the rich lady's chauffeur put it on the dresser. I never got a tip that big, not ever. I'm afraid to let go of it, in case it disappears. But I feel guilty. I should split it with you, since he's your husband."

"Ex-husband," Helen said. "You can have it—and him."

Rob had never left a twenty-dollar tip in his life. What was Cheryl doing in room 323? Was she on another Full Moon treasure hunt? Didn't the FBI look under the carpet in the closet? Rhonda's funeral must be making the hotel staff crazier than usual.

Helen couldn't face Craig on an empty stomach. She was ashamed of her hot flare of lust. She went downstairs to the lobby vending machines and bought a bag of pretzels.

The sight in the lobby stopped her short.

Arlene was sitting on a pink couch with her knitting and her video camera. The Coronado resident had dyed her hair egg-yolk yellow. She wore an eye-burning fuchsia pantsuit. Helen thought she looked like an angry zit.

"Helen, I didn't know you worked here!" Arlene said. Her penciled-in eyebrows bounced up and down on her forehead and she started talking faster. "I told you about my hotel lobby hobby. You know I love to hang out in the lobbies and people-watch. I bet you see some sights here."

"Not really," Helen said. "This hotel is kind of quiet." Except for the murder.

"The quiet ones are the best," Arlene said.

"I'm not sure there's much to watch," Helen said. Unless you count my ex-husband, who made quite a spectacle crawling into a Bentley with Marcella.

Arlene was shoving her yarn and needles into a giant straw tote.

"You don't have to leave," Helen said.

"Oh yes I do." Arlene gave Helen a big lipsticked

smile. "It's nearly two o'clock. I need to go home and take my afternoon nap. We old gals have to keep to our schedules. See you out by the Coronado pool tonight."

She was gone, just like that. Helen envied the big woman's grace as she rose and ran lightly to her car. She waited until Arlene pulled out of the parking lot before she went over to the front desk. Sondra wore somber gray today. Helen appreciated this mark of respect for Rhonda.

"What was that woman doing in the lobby?" Helen asked.

"Nothing much," Sondra said. "Typical tourist. She watched people for a while, but she never talked to anyone. She knitted something pink and fluffy. Then she got out her video camera and took pictures of everything, the way tourists do. Shot the palm trees and the flowers, the lobby and the pool, the pay phones and the vending machines. You think they don't have vending machines back home?"

"Who knows?" Helen said.

But she knew this: Arlene lived in 2C at the Coronado, and that set Helen's alarm bells ringing. Too many crooks had stayed in that apartment. She also knew Arlene was in a hurry to leave once when she saw Helen. Did she really rush home for a nap? And was she really surprised to see Helen? She couldn't remember if she'd told Arlene the name of this hotel.

There was one more question Helen couldn't answer: Why was Arlene at the Full Moon hotel the day of Rhonda's funeral?

CHAPTER 22

J ESUS SAVES was painted on the cracked plate-glass window of the derelict drugstore.

"Does he have any bargains on Maalox?" Helen whispered to Denise.

The head housekeeper glared at her.

Helen opened the door to the storefront church and was hit by a refrigerated blast of rubbing alcohol, adhesive tape and mint.

"A church in a drugstore is taking the opium of the people too far," Helen said.

"You're going to hell," Denise said, sounding like Sister Mary Justine. "Now shut up or I'll make you walk home." She settled her ample body on a dented folding chair. Helen prayed it wouldn't collapse.

Helen knew why she was cracking bad jokes. She hated this grim church. She stared at the broken tile floor, gray with dust and blotched with old gum, and remembered her grandmother saying, "We were never so poor we couldn't afford soap." Someone could have mopped the floor, considering what Rhonda did for a living. No cleaning woman should have a funeral in a dirty church.

The altar was a barren table with a Bible and a black cross. Rhonda's cheap gray casket seemed to suck the light from the room. The wilted gladioli looked like they'd been pulled out of a Dumpster. Like Rhonda.

Helen desperately wanted to believe that Rhonda's funeral had simple dignity, but it was stark and sad. There were thirty people in the church, including the hotel staff. The black-clad mourners huddled together like crows in a rainstorm.

Rhonda's mother, Shirley, was yellow and dry as an old bone. Her battered black hat looked stepped on. Next to her sat a plump woman who patted Shirley's sticklike arms. Rhonda's mother leaned against the woman as if she might collapse. Was she a sister, an aunt or a friend? Helen was glad Shirley had someone to comfort her.

Helen also saw who wasn't there. There was no dream lover. The only men were two skinny retirees and fat Sam the biker. No, make that four. Leaning against the back wall was Detective Mulruney, his suit as wrinkled as his face.

The bony preacher with his frock coat could have stepped from a nineteenth-century daguerreotype. He offered cold comfort, reading from Job in a dead monotone: " 'Man is born unto trouble, as the sparks fly upward.' "

Helen wanted to shout, "This is not a man's funeral. Rhonda is a woman. Can't you say something about her?"

But the preacher never did. He read his hopeless texts until Helen wept in frustration. No one had noticed Rhonda when she was alive. She was thrown away in death. Now she was ignored at her own funeral.

I will find who killed her, Helen vowed. She knew it sounded childish, but at least her tears stopped.

The funeral party followed a dusty hearse to the cemetery, squeezed between two truck terminals in Lauderdale. The graveyard was flat and treeless. Helen stared into the hole prepared for Rhonda. The thin, lifeless dirt was dotted with rocks, evoking sermons on seeds and stony soil.

Helen looked at the desolate grave and wanted to ask, "Is that all there is?" She knew the answer.

After the burial, Helen, Denise, Cheryl and Sondra rode back to the Jesus Saves church in stunned silence. They still had to endure what Rhonda's mother called a "cold collation"—stale sandwiches and soggy cookies. A coffeepot was set up on the former pharmacy counter. Helen poured herself a cup to warm her hands. She felt chilled inside and out.

The Full Moon staff formed a miserable quartet. They scattered when Sam approached, his plate piled high with gray turkey sandwiches. Helen was left alone with Rhonda's biker boyfriend. He wore an awkward suit. The sleeves were too short to cover the Seminole Sam tattoo on his wrist. His dark hair was salted with dandruff.

"Guess you never expected to see me like this," Sam said.

Helen flashed on the vision of Sam and his two skanky girlfriends leaving the Full Moon. How could he take those trashy women to the hotel where Rhonda worked? Was he trying to humiliate her? Then Helen had a sudden horrible thought and slopped her coffee on the floor. What if Sam knew it didn't matter because Rhonda was dead in the Dumpster?

Sam didn't notice Helen's trembling hands or the coffee puddle at her feet. He was still munching the pile of aging turkey. "I mean, you must be surprised to see me in a suit," he said through a mouthful of masticated turkey.

"Yes," Helen said. One word was all she could manage.

"Got it for my court appearance," Sam said. "Figured it would come in handy again, so I kept it. It's the least I could do for Rhonda."

"And I'm sure that's what you did for her," Helen said.

Sam hesitated, as if he wasn't sure he'd been insulted.

Then he backed away, protecting his piled plate from her venom. Helen heard a soft snicker behind her.

"He deserved that."

Helen turned to see a woman who could have been Rhonda's blond sister. She was tall and scrawny, with a long face and big teeth. Her brassy hair hung in banana curls, a style some twenty years too young for her. Then she smiled, and was transformed. Energy and charm overcame bad hair any day.

"I'm Amber." She stuck out a long, thin hand. "I'm just about Rhonda's best friend. I mean, I was. Well, I still am but she's—" Amber abandoned the hopeless tangle of syntax.

"I worked with Rhonda at the Full Moon," Helen said.

"I liked the way you gave Sam hell, even if he was too dumb to know it," Amber said. "He's a prick. And wasn't that a sorry excuse for a funeral?"

"Amen," Helen said. "Let's get out of here."

"Rhonda used to drink at Biddle's Corner Bar up the road," Amber said. "I could use a beer. Let's give her a proper send-off."

Helen rarely drank beer, but in the dusty little church a cold brew was tempting. She said her good-byes to Shirley and told Denise she'd find her own way home. The head housekeeper seemed relieved.

Biddle's Corner Bar turned out to be a dingy cinder-block building halfway up the street. At three thirty in the afternoon, it was deserted except for a bartender polishing glasses. Amber went up to the bar for two draft beers and a pack of Planters peanuts.

Back at the table, Amber held up her frosted glass. "To Rhonda," she said. "She deserved better in this world. If there is a God, she'll get it in the next."

Helen clinked glasses with her, then took a bitter sip of beer. It settled the dust and soothed her soul. A handful of peanuts helped, too. "You said it better than the preacher."

"Damn preacher," Amber said. "He was as cold as his church. Maybe if he'd cut back on the air-conditioning he'd have money to clean the place up." She took a long drink. "Rhonda would have been better off without any religion. Never did anything but make her feel guilty."

A skinny guy with homemade prison tattoos banged through the door and sat down at the bar. Rhonda could really pick places to meet men, Helen thought.

"I'm trying to understand Rhonda," Helen said. "But I can't get a handle on her."

"Nobody could," Amber said. "She spent every Friday and Saturday night in this bar and all Sunday in church. She dressed like a nun, but she liked men and they liked her. I should talk, but she was built like a broomstick. It didn't matter to the guys. There was something about Rhonda that men noticed and women couldn't see."

The way men can't see Rob's appeal, Helen thought.

"Why did she date Sam?" Helen said.

Amber drew thoughtful water circles on her beer glass. "She didn't think she deserved any better. Isn't that what they say on *Oprah*? She'd go out with a nice man, but it never lasted. She thought nice guys were wimps. If they had a mean streak like Sam, she figured they were real men."

"She didn't have a high opinion of men, did she?" Helen said.

"Most women don't." Amber swallowed a third of her beer.

Helen took a longer sip and crunched another peanut. "The day she died, Rhonda talked about a handsome boyfriend. Was he real or did she make him up?"

"I never knew Rhonda to lie about men," Amber said.

Helen felt her heart shrivel. She was wrong. She'd ruined the murder investigation and sent the police in the wrong direction.

"Who was he?" Helen said.

"I never saw him. But she talked about him constantly in her last weeks."

"Did you know this mystery man gave her money?" Helen said. "At least fifty dollars."

"Men were always giving her little presents: flowers, perfume, a cultured pearl necklace. Even her cat Snowball was a gift. Sam gave her that. He found the kitten on the road. Trust him to give her something she'd have to support. Rhonda thought it was wrong to accept gifts from men, but she took them all the same, then flogged herself on Sunday. She never told her mama. I used to say she needed a man who'd give her diamonds and condos, but she just laughed at me."

"Did you know that the fifty was counterfeit?"

"Doesn't surprise me," Amber said. "I'm a waitress. Do you know how many bad fifties are floating around South Florida?" She took another gulp of beer, then burped delicately.

"Do you think she was passing bad money?" Helen asked.

"No, she wasn't that kind of girl. She wouldn't get involved in a counterfeit ring. She liked sex, but she wasn't greedy for money. Otherwise she would have sold it instead of giving it away, you know what I mean?"

"Can you tell me anything about her new boyfriend?" Helen was practically begging.

"I wish I could," Amber said. "But she wouldn't even tell me his name, and usually she told me more than I wanted to know about her men friends. She said he was really special, but she had to keep him a secret for a little while. Rhonda seemed happier and more confident in her final weeks. She didn't spend Friday and Saturday nights in this dive. She kicked Sam out when he asked for another loan till payday. Since Sam didn't have a job, she knew payday was a long time away."

"Did she describe the man at all?" Helen said.

"All I know is he had dark hair and a tattoo on his wrist."

"Like Sam," Helen said. "Maybe there wasn't any new boyfriend. Maybe he was just a cleaned-up version of Sam. An imaginary lover who was kinder, handsomer, and gave her money instead of sponging off her. If he was real, he never bothered coming to her funeral. He never even called her mother and said he was sorry."

"Maybe he was a butthole, but he's as real as this beer," Amber said.

Helen looked at the chilled glass. It was empty.

It was still daylight when Helen lurched out of the tavern, blinking in the brilliant sun. She took the bus home. It chugged along the traffic-clogged streets until she wanted to barf. Helen arrived at the Coronado, sick with remorse and too much beer.

She felt sicker when she saw the two people she least wanted to talk to sitting out by the pool. Margery and Arlene were stretched out on chaise longues, with wineglasses in their hands. Helen tried to slip around the side of the building, but Arlene called out, "Yoo-hoo! Come try my shrimp dip."

There was no escape. Arlene was still wearing the same hot-pink eyesore she'd had on at the hotel, but she'd abandoned her knitting bag. "It was such a surprise to see you today," she said. "But you work at a nice, clean hotel."

"We try," Helen said, taking a seat.

"Wine?" her landlady said.

"Not thirsty," Helen said. Wine on top of the beer would give her a raging headache.

"Shrimp dip?" Arlene said.

Helen's beer-soaked stomach did a barrel roll. "Not hungry, thanks."

"You young things are always on a diet," Arlene said. "I have to ask you, since you're in the business, how clean is the average hotel room?"

"In some ways, it's cleaner than your own home," Helen said. "Most people don't dust, vacuum or scrub the bathroom every day. They also don't change their sheets and towels daily."

"I sure don't," Arlene said.

"The bedspreads are the weak link. Even most well-run hotels only change them every two weeks. Some wait longer."

"And people have s-e-x on them," Arlene said.

Helen wondered why she spelled out the word. "They're also diaper-changing stations."

Arlene wrinkled her face. Margery sat behind a screen of smoke, grinning at Helen.

"I wouldn't sleep on a hotel bedspread if you paid me," Helen said. "I'd avoid the in-room coffeepot, too. We had this absentminded maid who cleaned the coffeepot with the toilet rag."

"Eeuw. I wish you didn't tell me that. I need my coffee in the morning," Arlene said.

"Then order it from room service," Helen said. "Or walk to the nearest coffee shop."

"Uh, thanks," Arlene said. She was a not-so-hot shade of green. It clashed with the hot pink. "I've had a lot of hotel coffee in my lifetime. Now I wonder what I drank."

This time she didn't rise from the chaise with her usual grace. She ran for her apartment with an ungainly lope.

"I finally get a decent tenant in 2C and you have to make her sick," Margery said.

"She's a crook like all the others," Helen said.

"Awwk!" Pete the parrot said. Peggy was drifting toward them like a lost soul, a sulky Pete riding on her shoulder.

"We'll continue this conversation after Peggy leaves," Margery hissed. She looked up at Peggy and said, "You look like forty miles of bad road."

Peggy was on her cell phone again. She shook the phone, then checked the display screen and snapped it shut.

"What's the matter?" Helen said.

"I can't find Glenn," Peggy said. "I haven't been able to reach him all day. I've called and called. He usually talks to me four or five times a day."

"Maybe he had a business trip," Margery said.

"He would have told me," Peggy said. "He could be sick or hurt."

"Do you want to go to his apartment and check on him?" Margery said. "We'll go with you."

"No, I don't want to be too clingy. That scares a man away. He's entitled to a day away from me."

Helen fought to keep from looking at her landlady. She knew Margery's thoughts were the same as her own: I told you so. He took your money and ran.

The silence grew louder, until Helen couldn't stand it anymore. "You won't believe who I saw at work today."

Margery glared at her. She didn't want to hear more bad news about 2C.

Tough, Helen thought. She had other bones to pick with Margery in private. She told them about Arlene's visit to the Full Moon.

"What do you think she's doing in those hotel lobbies?" Helen asked.

"Spying on people?" Peggy said. "Blackmailing someone? Maybe she's a private eye."

"She didn't photograph many people," Helen said. "Sondra at the front desk said Arlene took the typical tourist videos of trees and flowers, then shot the pay phones and the snack area, the pool and the lobby. The Full Moon lobby isn't anything to write home about, much less video."

"Damn. I've been snookered again," Margery said, stubbing out her cigarette. "I wish I knew why she hangs around hotels."

"She's too old to be a hooker," Peggy said. "Maybe she's a pickpocket or a thief. Any reports of theft or break-ins at your hotel?"

"No," Helen said. "She didn't talk to anyone at the

hotel, didn't approach any guests, and didn't go toward the room elevators. She spends time at other hotels, too, remember? She told us about her day at that beach hotel."

"She's up to something," Margery said. "I wish I knew what it was."

"Awwwk," Pete said.

Peggy checked her cell phone for the tenth time in five minutes. "I think I'll go inside," she said. The brilliant butterfly was gone. Peggy's shoulders drooped and her hair needed a wash. Even Pete seemed downhearted.

Once Peggy was inside her apartment, Margery said, "Your ex and my friend Marcella really hit it off. She called me, absolutely ecstatic about her night with Rob. She's letting him move in with her."

"How soon before she kills him?" Helen said.

Margery tried to look innocent. "I'm not sure what you mean," she said.

"Phil says your friend Marcella is the Black Widow," Helen said. "She's killed at least four husbands."

Margery laughed. "Your man has quite an imagination. Marcella is a single woman, just like you."

"Not exactly. My ex is still alive. What happens if Rob dies?"

"You're being ridiculous. But what if he did, just for the sake of argument? The world would be a better place and you could quit slinking around. Why do you care? Right now your ex is living like a pasha and you're cleaning toilets. Rob is like a cat. He'll land on his feet. Aren't you tired of being a martyr?"

"I like my life," Helen said stubbornly.

"Then you should have a talk with Phil. He'd better be careful about spreading vicious gossip. Marcella has never been accused of anything."

"She married a lot of dead men," Helen said.

"She was unlucky," Margery said.

"Not as unlucky as they were," Helen said.

CHAPTER 23

"**H**ey, Dean," the man bellowed outside the hotel room. "Get your ass in gear. We've got a plane to catch."

The man stood in the hall, pounding on the door to room 322. This section was infested by the business conference.

No wonder the maids hated corporate types, Helen thought. Not only were they slobs, they were rude. Look at this one, making a racket in the hall at nine in the morning. Didn't he know this was a tourist hotel? Some people liked to sleep late on vacation.

The man shouted and slammed the door with the flat of his hand. *Boom! Boom!* The wooden door sounded like a kettledrum. He'd wake up the whole hotel.

"Dean, this isn't funny," he screamed. "Get your butt out of bed. We're late, damn it."

Cussing. The AARP tourists would love that. Helen had to stop this tantrum. She abandoned her cleaning cart and ran to 322.

The door pounder wore a gray pin-striped suit, a power tie and an air of impatience. A small bald spot sat on his head like a crown. He was not used to being ignored. A younger man with more hair and a cringing air held the door pounder's topcoat. They must be headed for a colder climate.

The suit was about to batter the door with his fully loaded briefcase when Helen said, "May I help you, sir?"

The door pounder dropped the briefcase. The coat holder picked it up.

"We're trying to wake up Dean," the suit said. "He won't answer his phone and he won't come to the door. My name is Richard. That's Jason."

The boss gave the coat holder a nod, and the young man showed his teeth in an obsequious smile. The attention made Jason bold. "If Dean doesn't move soon, we'll have to call him the late Dean Stamples," he said.

The boss's silence was arctic. Jason gulped.

"Will you open the door for us, miss?" Richard the boss said. It wasn't a question. It was an order. "We have to be at the airport in half an hour. We have a rental car to return."

"I can't open the door, sir, but I can call the manager to help you. I'll be right back."

Helen didn't wait for the elevator. She raced down the stairs to the front desk. Sondra was facing a long, impatient line of businessmen looking at their watches and talking importantly on their cell phones. The bow on Sondra's blouse was slightly crooked, the only sign the impeccable clerk was frazzled.

"I need to see you," Helen said, and dragged Sondra into the back office. "We've got a problem. The guy in room 322 won't pick up his phone or open his door."

Sondra groaned. "The curse of 323 is spreading."

"Hey! Are you girls going to gossip or are you going to wait on me?" The balding pin-striped man at the desk could have been Richard's clone.

Sondra came out to the front desk. "I'll find the hotel owner to personally serve you, sir," she said.

The pin-striped man puffed out his chest.

"Serves him right," Helen said. "Wait till Sybil lands on him."

Helen enjoyed watching the man's face fall as the short, gnarled Sybil creaked out of her lair, trailing ashes and smoke like an escaped demon.

"What's your problem?" Sybil said, in a tone that meant there'd better not be one.

"I'm trying to get my bill," Mr. Pinstripe said.

"Well, things will go a lot faster if you'll quit nagging my staff," Sybil said. "They're moving as fast as they can."

Sondra pulled Helen into the back room again. "We'll call the guest from here," she said. The phone rang six times, but there was no answer from room 322.

Helen didn't expect one. "A phone call isn't going to disturb that guy," she said. "His boss made enough noise to wake the dead."

Sondra stared at Helen. "I hope this isn't what I think it is. We'd better get up there fast." She grabbed her passkey card and rushed past a cluster of tourists with fat flowered suitcases waiting for the elevator. Sondra pounded up the stairs. Helen ran two steps behind her.

"What do you know about the guest in this room?" Sondra asked as they climbed.

By the second floor, Helen was short of breath. Her words came out in quick asthmatic wheezes. "It's a guy. One of the businessmen. Cheryl and I cleaned his room two days ago. He was a slob and a smoker. He had the *Do Not Disturb* sign on the door yesterday, so we didn't have to clean the room. We slipped a card under the door so he could call housekeeping for clean towels, but he never did."

"I don't like this," Sondra said. "I dread opening that door."

"I'll go in with you," Helen said, as she paused to catch her breath.

They tumbled out into the third-floor hall. Richard the boss was pacing outside room 322. Jason circled in his wake, lugging the boss' coat and briefcase. His own were piled on the floor.

Richard looked pointedly at his watch, but he gave Sondra a bright smile. Few men could resist her. "We've got a little problem waking up our friend Dean," he said.

Jason leered at Sondra. "If you go in there, that will really wake him up."

Sondra ignored him and knocked on the door. "Hello? Sir? Anyone in there?" she said.

Silence.

Sondra snicked her card through the slot and the room door swung open. Cold coppery air poured out, with a strong liquor stink underneath. Bourbon? Scotch? Something foul and sour was in that room.

Richard wrinkled his nose in disgust. The boss did not approve of booze. Helen thought she saw a sly smile flicker across Jason's face. She wondered if Dean was an office rival.

Richard tried to bull his way into the room, but Sondra blocked him. "Please stay outside, sir," she said. "I'm not authorized to let other guests inside an occupied room."

The boss paced in the doorway, irritated at being refused.

The room was so dark, Helen expected to find bats on the ceiling. She braced herself for an unpleasant sight as Sondra flipped on the light.

The bed was empty. Helen let out an involuntary sigh of relief. Dean wasn't dead in his bed.

"Maybe he stepped out for coffee," Sondra said.

"We told him we'd pick him up at nine," Richard said from the doorway. His tone said any other alternative was unthinkable.

"Maybe Dean forgot," Jason said. "He skipped part of the conference to score some serious sightseeing. Maybe he's on the beach now."

"I don't think he left the hotel," Helen said. "His wallet is on the dresser and his pants are on the chair. His shoes are by the bed."

"I'd like to see old Dean running around naked," Jason said, and giggled.

I bet you would, you little suck, Helen thought. She'd worked with her share of Jasons during her corporate years.

The bathroom door was closed, but a yellow sliver of light shone under the door. Helen listened for running water, but all was quiet. The carpet was dry, and no puddles seeped under the door. That was a good sign.

Sondra knocked on the bathroom door. "Hello? Hello, sir? Are you OK?"

More silence.

"Hope he didn't do an Elvis," Jason said. "You know, die on the crapper."

"Shut up," Richard said, and Helen silently thanked him for that executive order.

Jason clamped his jaws closed.

"I'd better go in there," Sondra said. She rattled the handle. The door wasn't locked. "Sir, I'm opening this door. I'm coming into the bathroom."

The silence stretched on.

Very slowly, the door opened. Then it hit something with an odd rubbery thud. Helen saw the glitter of broken glass on the floor and dark red-black splashes on the tile. Blood was everywhere.

"Ohmigod," Helen said.

Sondra backed out of the bathroom, stepping on Helen's foot. "You don't want to go in there," she said, her voice shaky. She closed the door behind her. "Call 911. I'll stay here and guard the room."

Richard was on the threshold, ready to invade. "Tell me what's going on," he said. "I have a right to know. Is Dean sick? Does he need an ambulance?"

"I'm sorry, sir," Sondra said. She stopped and tried to phrase her next words carefully. "I'm very sorry. Your friend is beyond that kind of help."

"Shit," Richard said. "What am I going to tell his wife?" He was wringing his soft manicured hands.

Jason turned dead white. He stared at his foot. Maybe he was eager to put it in his mouth again. But he was a well-trained corporate minion. He'd been ordered to say nothing. Jason slumped against the wall and hung onto the boss's coat as if it were a life preserver.

"Helen!" Sondra said. "Don't stand there like a statue. Call the police now."

Helen ran on wobbly legs to the room she'd been cleaning. She felt sick and sad. She'd made the dead man's bed and picked his towels off the floor. She'd dusted his family photo. What was Richard going to tell Dean's pretty wife and two smiling children?

They wouldn't be smiling today.

How did Dean die? Where did the broken glass come from? Blood was spattered all over the walls. Did that mean it was murder or suicide? Maybe it was natural causes. Maybe he broke a glass and bled to death. Helen wished she'd seen the body, but it was too late now. Sondra was guarding the door like a pit bull.

She hoped it wasn't murder. If the hotel had another violent death, the Full Moon would turn into a media madhouse. The press would be permanently camped in the parking lot. The dead man wasn't a minimum-wage maid. He was a businessman and a visitor to South Florida. Murder was bad for the tourist industry, and it got lots of official attention. Helen had helped find the body—again. Her name and picture would be splashed all over. Her ex-husband would see her for sure—unless he was still with Marcella the Black Widow.

Now there was an ethical dilemma the nuns never discussed: To save yourself, could you pray that your ex-husband kept sleeping with a serial killer?

Helen pushed aside the cleaning cart blocking the door and dialed 911 on the room phone.

"Is this a medical, fire or police emergency?" the operator asked.

"Police," Helen said. "I'm at the Full Moon Hotel. There's a man dead in room 322. Blood and glass are all over the bathroom. I don't know how he died, but he has two little kids."

"May I have your name, please?" The operator was unnaturally calm.

"I forgot," Helen said, and slammed down the phone.

CHAPTER 24

. . . .

"So, you found another body," Detective Bill Mulruney said.

This time the homicide detective didn't seem bored when he talked to Helen. He was way too interested in her.

"Not really," Helen said. "The boss couldn't wake the man up. He asked me for help."

Helen and the homicide detective were back in the hotel breakfast room, sitting at the same table with the view of the cereal bin. This morning Mulruney had a face like an unmade bed. Helen itched to put a pillow over it and press down hard. If the detective could read her thoughts, he'd arrest her.

Be calm, she told herself. Be careful. If you leave here doing the perp walk, you'll be smeared all over TV. Rob will find you for sure. If you want your nice life with Phil at the Coronado, then watch what you say. Snappy answers are luxuries poor maids can't afford.

Helen concentrated on the Cheerios in the Plexiglas bin. Staring at the hundreds of holes had a soothing effect. Each one was a crispy little "ohm." The Zen of breakfast cereal.

"Miss Hawthorne," the detective said, "you seem to be helpful when there are dead bodies to be found."

She took a deep breath and said, "Two guests at the hotel were banging on a room door, trying to get their colleague out of bed. I was afraid they'd disturb everyone on the floor. I asked if I could help them. They wanted me to open the door, but I'm not allowed to do that. I ran and got Sondra at the front desk. She found the body."

"But you were there with her in the room," the detective said.

"Yes, but—"

"And you found the other victim, Miss Rhonda Dournell. In fact, you climbed in the Dumpster and went looking for that body."

"Yes, but—"

"We found out that you were present at another murder earlier this year. You discovered the body at that big wedding. Your fingerprints were all over that scene."

"Yes, but—"

Did he know about the other murders? Helen was sweating now. She wondered if the cop could see the drops popping out on her forehead like zits at prom time.

"But what, Miss Hawthorne?" the detective said.

"There was no connection between the wedding murder and the hotel murder," Helen said.

"Except you," he said.

"Me?" Her voice spiked to an un-Zenlike squeak.

"We've found your prints in the victim's room," Detective Mulruney said.

"Of course," Helen said. "I cleaned it. My prints are probably in every room in the hotel."

"When was the last time you saw the victim alive?"

"I'm assuming the dead man is Mr. Dean Stamples."

"That is correct."

"How did he die?" Helen asked.

"Why don't you tell us?" Mulruney said.

"I didn't see the actual body," Helen said. "Just the

blood on the walls and the glass on the floor. Was he murdered?"

"We're treating it as a suspicious death," Mulruney said. "You've avoided my question again. When was the last time you saw Mr. Stamples alive?"

"I never did," Helen said. "I mean, I never saw him alive. Or dead, either. Sondra wouldn't let anyone see the body. She shut the door. I never saw the dead man when he was alive, except for a photograph on his desk. He was in it. In the picture, not the desk."

Helen realized she was twisting her name tag on her smock. She also wasn't making any sense. She took a deep breath and tried to explain. "I may have seen Mr. Stamples in the hall or on the hotel elevator, but I didn't know it was him. He was just one more businessman who threw his towels and socks on the floor and left cigarette ashes all over his room."

"And you resented that," the detective said.

"No!" Helen said. "That's what people do when they stay at hotels. They act like slobs."

"And slobs make you angry," he said.

Helen studied the Cheerios, hoping they would give her the minimum daily requirement of patience. "I get paid to clean up after them. I'm better off than their wives, who have to do it for free."

"When was the last time you were in the victim's room?" Detective Mulruney said.

"A couple of days ago," Helen said. "Cheryl and I cleaned it about eleven o'clock. You can check the exact time. It's in the housekeeper's records in the office. We keep a list of rooms that needed to be cleaned and the times we did them. I didn't see him then. He wasn't in the room."

"What was the condition of the room?" Mulruney said.

"It was a smoker's room, a little messier than most," Helen said. "He slept alone."

"How do you know that?"

Helen blushed at the thought of some of the beds she'd seen. "When you've made as many beds as I have, Detective, you can tell." She could see the heaped ashtrays, the ashes coating the furniture, and the lonely bed.

"So, as an experienced bed detective, what did you see?"

Don't let him get to you, Helen told herself. "The sheets were all twisted and one pillow was tossed on the floor. He drank Scotch. He had a bottle of Johnnie Walker Black. It was three-quarters full. There was melted water in his ice bucket."

"Any glasses?"

"Just the four plastic ones we give guests," Helen said. "Three in the bathroom were still in the wrappers. One by the bed was used."

"No signs that he had a second drinker in the room?"

"Not that I could tell," Helen said.

"And you're an expert at that, too," he said.

Helen didn't answer.

"What about food?" Detective Mulruney said.

"We didn't find any pizza boxes or carryout cartons," Helen said. "He didn't eat dinner in the room. He smoked, though. He had ashes all over his desk, the floor and his computer."

"You remember a lot about this room for a man you claim you never saw," the detective said.

"The guy wore his Phi Beta Kappa key on his bathrobe," Helen said. "That stuck in my mind."

"Why?"

"It was kind of pathetic," Helen said. "It was like he had to prove he was somebody, even when he was alone."

The atmosphere seemed to lighten slightly, as if the interrogation had turned a corner. Maybe he believes me now, Helen thought.

"Anything else you remember about the room?" Detective Mulruney said.

"The man kept a photo of his wife and two kids in a folding leather frame on his desk. Some people who travel a lot pack their family photos. This struck me as a particularly nice family."

"So you looked at it?"

"Of course."

"And you picked it up?" The investigation turned the corner and ran into a brick wall.

"I dusted it," Helen said. She shifted uneasily in her chair, and her hand went to her name tag. She pulled it back down. Mulruney didn't need to know the conversation she'd had with Cheryl about powerful husbands and helpless wives. That would sound resentful.

"What did you do after you cleaned his room?" the detective said.

"Cheryl and I cleaned seventeen rooms that day," Helen said. "We took two ten-minute breaks. We finished about three thirty and then I went home."

"What about lunch?" Detective Mulruney said.

"The maids don't eat lunch," Helen said. "Lunch makes us too sleepy to work. It slows us down. We snack on our breaks. I had popcorn on my first break and pretzels on my second."

"What happened when you went into his room yesterday?"

A trick question. The detective enjoyed setting little traps. "I didn't go into his room yesterday. The *Do Not Disturb* sign was on the door," Helen said. "It's a rule that we can't knock or otherwise disturb the guest when the sign is out. We slipped a card under the door giving him a number to call if he wanted fresh towels. He didn't call."

"Did this man know the maid, Rhonda Dournell?"

"I don't think so," Helen said.

"Has he stayed here before?"

"I don't know," Helen said. "The hotel records would tell you that."

Helen remembered the photo. Surely that bland, balding businessman wasn't Rhonda's dream lover. True, he was handsomer than Sam the biker. Or at least cleaner. Maybe when he gave Rhonda fifty dollars that improved his looks. But a man wouldn't travel with a photo of his wife and children and cheat on them with a hotel maid, would he?

Happens all the time, she thought.

"Could the victim have had an affair with Miss Dournell?"

Helen jumped, as if Detective Mulruney had been poking around in her thoughts. "Rhonda? No! She wasn't like that."

How do I know? she wondered.

"How do you know?" the detective said.

Helen was seriously rattled. She concentrated on the beige breakfast food. "Mr. Stamples didn't check in until after Rhonda was dead."

"And how do you know that?" Mulruney didn't bother to hide his contempt. "Oh, I forgot. You're the bed expert, the rumpled sheets specialist. Then how about this one, Miss Mattress Maven? The victim knew her. He got a little nooky whenever he was in Florida on business. Except this time he was killed by her jealous lover."

But Helen didn't think any man was jealous of Rhonda. She couldn't see the skinny, unhappy maid with anyone but scaly Sam, who used her and took her money. The Rhondas of this world were meant for mistreatment.

Except her friend Amber swore that Rhonda had a handsome lover.

"I don't think so," Helen said. "But I really can't tell you much about Rhonda's personal life. I didn't know her outside of work."

"What about your personal life?" the detective said. "You have a talent for finding dead bodies, Miss Hawthorne. Some people just happen to have lives like that.

Some people make their lives like that. Which one are you?"

"I—"

"Why don't you sign a statement for us? Just for the record. In case you happen to find another body."

Helen twisted her name tag so hard, the pin ripped off the fabric. She'd failed. Detective Mulruney thought she was lying. She couldn't look at the man. She might see what he thought of her.

She stared at the breakfast cereal. The Cheerios stared back at Helen like a heap of eyeless skulls.

CHAPTER 25

. . . .

"Another murder today at the Full Moon Hotel in Seafield Village." The reporter looked earnestly at the TV camera, her face professionally serious.

Helen knew that thirty seconds earlier the same woman had been giggling with the cameraman and checking her tight blouse for wrinkles. Its brilliant blue was a perfect match for her contact lenses.

Helen could watch the TV crews on the parking lot from the hotel manager's office. It was weird to see the hotel on the TV screen, while she hid inside the same building.

Helen did not have a peaceful refuge. Sybil was furious that the reporters were back, ruining her hotel's reputation. Her fluffy white hair looked like a puff of smoke coming out of her head.

"This time," the reporter said, widening her eyes, "the victim is Dean Stamples, a thirty-one-year-old businessman from Cincinnati. He was found dead in his room by a hotel employee after he failed to respond to wake-up calls. A police spokesperson said the victim had been slashed repeatedly."

Helen sighed with relief, which made her choke on Sybil's cigarette smoke. This was good news. No hotel employees were named in the news stories.

Sybil muttered to herself and set fire to one cigarette after another. " 'Another murder,' " she said, grinding out yet another lipsticked butt in the monster ashtray. "That TV tart makes it sound like we have one every week."

The reporter told the TV audience, "Last week a hotel maid was found dead in a Dumpster behind this same hotel in normally quiet Seafield Village. That's two deaths in less than seven days."

Sybil let out a bloodcurdling yowl. "You don't have to rub it in, damn it. The viewers can figure it out for themselves. Next you'll bring up the g-d bank robber."

The reporter said, "Six months ago, police shot and killed a carjacker who made off with one hundred thousand dollars and hid out at the hotel. The money was never found."

"Argggh!" Sybil shrieked.

Helen was glad the office door was bolted or there might have been a fourth killing at the hotel. The Full Moon's irate owner looked ready to march outside and tear the blue-eyed, blue-bloused reporter limb from limb.

"It's just TV," Helen said. "Nobody will remember what the reporter said in a couple of days."

"Hah!" Sybil said. "They're ruining me. I don't trust myself to talk to the lying buggers."

The one smart thing Sybil did was barricade herself in her office when the reporters showed up. She was furious, but she had enough sense to know she'd lose her temper with the press and make the situation worse. That left Sondra besieged by the reporters, with only a terse "no comment" to fend them off.

Helen was hiding out with Sybil. She was sorry to abandon Sondra, but she couldn't go out there and wind up on TV.

"What time is it?" Sybil asked.

"Six twelve," Helen said.

"The vultures will start packing up by the time the

sports reports come on. We'll have to stick it out another ten or fifteen minutes."

It had been a nearly endless day. Most of the guests had tried to check out as soon as they'd heard about Dean Stamples' murder. A dead maid might add a little excitement to an otherwise ordinary hotel, but a murdered guest was too close to home—or rather, too close to their rooms. A crazed killer cut up a guest in the bath. What if that lunatic got loose in their room? They weren't looking to star in their own personal *Psycho* movie.

The police made the guests stay for questioning, keeping the surly crowd in their rooms for most of the afternoon. It had been a waste of time. Nobody had seen anything suspicious. The last guest had finally cleared out about an hour ago. The police were gone, too.

After her rocky interview with Detective Mulruney, Helen had written her statement with a shaky hand. The letters looked like they were running for cover. By the time she finished, the hotel was surrounded by media. She knew the reporters would be doing live remotes from the death hotel parking lot. She was stuck until after the six-o'clock news, when they would chase some other tragedy.

She'd called Margery.

"I swear, Helen, can't you go anywhere without getting involved in another murder?" Helen could hear the irritation in her landlady's voice, and almost see the cigarette smoke curling around her hair. Or maybe that was Sybil's smoke she saw.

"I'm not involved," Helen said. "It's a hotel. People die in hotels all the time."

"Humph," Margery said. "Stay there and stay out of sight. All we can do is pray you get lucky for a change. I talked with Marcella. She's keeping your ex busy in the bedroom."

Helen winced at the pictures that last sentence conjured up.

"Rob could still turn on the TV news instead of Marcella, and spot you," her landlady said. "There's no guarantee that romance will add up to anything long-term."

Helen felt a strange stomach-tightening lurch. Was she supposed to be glad that her ex was dallying with a serial killer? As long as Rob romped in Marcella's bed, he wouldn't be after Helen. Or should she do the decent thing, and hope the romance died? What did Marcella do with her old boyfriends? Shove them out the door— or throw them overboard?

"Helen, are you there?" Margery demanded. "I'll pick you up at the hotel's back door at seven. If any reporters are still hanging around, I'll figure some way to get you out."

Helen stayed in the hotel's office until six fifty, sucking in Sybil's secondhand smoke and listening to her rant. As predicted, the pesky reporters had disappeared.

But it wasn't Margery who pulled up to the hotel door. Phil rumbled up in his battered black Jeep, looking deliciously cool in black jeans and a tight black T-shirt. Helen rushed out and jumped in the Jeep. Phil drew her close and held her.

"You've had a hell of a day. How are you?" he asked, kissing her hair, neck and lips.

"Better now," Helen said between kisses. "A lot better. You're the best thing I've seen all day."

"I do beat a dead man," Phil said.

Helen shivered. "That was so awful. You wouldn't believe the blood. He had two little kids, Phil."

"Any idea who killed him?"

"The police spent a lot of time tormenting me," Helen said. "They think I had something to do with it."

"Believe me, if they thought that, you'd be sitting in a cell," Phil said.

"No, you were right about Detective Mulruney. He's a cagey one. He's too smart to throw me in jail right away. He'll build a case first, slowly and carefully. He kept asking me why I found so many dead people."

"I'd probably wonder the same thing, if I were him. Coppers aren't big believers in coincidence."

"But it was!" Helen said.

"Shhhh," Phil said, smoothing her hair. "Then we'll have to convince him. That's what I'm here for. What else did he ask?"

"If I thought the dead man knew Rhonda or had had an affair with her. It sounded like he thought there might be a connection between the two murders—the hotel maid and hotel guest."

"Interesting," Phil said. "How did the guy die?"

"I didn't see the body, but there was blood and glass all over. A TV reporter said he'd been slashed repeatedly."

"Sounds like the killer was angry," Phil said. "Wonder if the dead man picked up the wrong woman—or man—and took them back to the hotel room?"

Helen had been cleaning hotel rooms long enough to know even the mildest homebody could misbehave on the road.

"That would make sense," she said. "But it would be hard on his wife and kids." She started to unbutton his shirt, and was surprised when Phil stopped her.

"We can't neck on the hotel parking lot, pleasant as it is," he said. "We have an appointment at seven thirty. I got a lead on Rhonda's boyfriend. I thought you'd want to come with me to talk to the person."

"Who is it?" Helen said.

"Waitress at the pancake house down the road. I got Rhonda's picture from the newspaper's Web site and showed it around. This waitress recognized Rhonda. She waited on her and a dark-haired man. The waitress was too busy to say much when I was in there at dinnertime. She said I should come back at seven thirty, when the dinner crowd died down. I'm hoping she remembers something more about the man except 'he was cute.'"

"You need a translator," Helen said. "*Cute* is a very precise term for females. It depends on how it's used."

Phil eased into the wild tourist traffic, dodging the cars that zigzagged from lane to lane. "What does *cute* mean?" he said. "Puppies are cute. Babies are cute. Guys are not cute."

"Fat lot you know," Helen said.

"Am I cute?" he said. An SUV honked rudely and roared around them.

"No, you're hot," Helen said. "But someone who's cute can also be hot."

"But I'm not? Cute, I mean."

"Well, the back of your neck is cute," Helen said. "And the way your hair falls over your forehead is cute. But basically, no. You're not cute."

"I don't get it," he said.

"I'm glad. If you did, you probably wouldn't be interested in women, and that would be a tragedy." She kissed him lightly on the ear. "I think your ears could be cute, too."

Phil made a left turn across the oncoming traffic to a chorus of horns. The diner was one of the new ones designed to look old. At this hour there was only one other occupied table, but the busboy was clearing away piles of dirty plates. The restaurant must have been a madhouse an hour ago.

Phil nodded at a thirtyish waitress in a cheerleader costume. The short pleated skirt made her thighs look thick, but the outfit was oddly sexy. The waitress's name tag said she was Penny.

"Are you hungry?" Phil asked Helen.

"Starved. I've been living off pretzels and Sybil's secondhand smoke."

Helen ordered blueberry pancakes, two eggs over easy and a side of ham. Phil had a western omelet with extra onions.

"I remember you," Penny said. "You were asking about that woman who was in here a couple of weeks ago." The waitress had eyes like brown velvet and long silky lashes, which she batted at Phil.

Phil put a twenty on the table. "Do you have time to talk now?"

"Let me coffee the other booth, and then I can talk until your order is up," Penny said. Her dark curls bounced with enthusiasm as she rushed off to pour for the other table.

Penny sat down at their table, just a little too close to Phil. Helen's hackles went up, but Phil winked at her. This was no time to get territorial, Helen reminded herself. She needed information if she was going to get the police off her back.

"What were Rhonda and her date like?" Phil asked.

"She was kind of a dog." Penny smiled provocatively. "She dressed like she was religious or something in a high-collared blouse and old lady's skirt. He had dark hair, was about twenty-five and cute."

Phil rolled his eyes. "Anything else you can tell us?"

The waitress shrugged. "He was just a cute guy. We see a lot of them here."

"Cute how?" Helen said. "Tom Cruise cute? Surfer cute? Boy-next-door cute?"

"Not like Tom Cruise," the waitress said. "Cruise is not cute. He's boring. He's what Hollywood thinks women think is cute."

"You got that right," Helen said. "Cruise was totally miscast as the vampire Lestat."

She could see Phil shifting impatiently.

"Cruise had no sense of inner evil," the waitress said. "That would have made him really interesting. The guy with Rhonda was more the bad-boy type, you know what I mean?"

"I do," Helen said.

"He was cute like a surfer, except his hair was dark. You usually think of those California types as blond."

"Anything that made him stand out or seem a little different?"

"Nothing really. Once you got past the cute, he was just another guy. Well, there was that tattoo on his wrist."

"What kind of tattoo?" Helen said.

"Something to do with a cow or a cowboy or a ranch. I'm not sure. I just caught a glimpse of it when he looked at his watch. It was mostly hidden by his shirt. That's all I remember."

A bell dinged in the kitchen and a man at the other table called, "Waitress! Check!" He scribbled in the air.

"Gotta go," Penny said, leaping up from the table and pocketing the twenty in one motion. "Your dinner's up."

"You've been a big help," Helen said.

As he poured ketchup on his omelet, Phil said, "Well, I'm glad you settled the Cruise casting problem. Otherwise we've wasted the evening."

"No, we haven't. The waitress really was helpful," Helen said. "I know exactly what kind of guy she's talking about."

"So what's he look like?" Phil asked.

"I'll know him when I see him," Helen said. "I'm looking for a particular kind of cute."

"I just hope you don't run into him in the shower," Phil said.

"Maybe you should come home with me. I may need protection," Helen said, fluttering her own eyelashes.

"Now that's cute," Phil said.

CHAPTER 26

....

"H i, it's Glenn. I'm sorry I'm not here to take your call. You know how much I want to talk to you—"

Peggy's cell phone speaker blasted her lover's voice mail message around the Coronado pool. She quickly snapped the phone shut.

"He doesn't sound sorry," Margery said. She wore shorts the color of twilight and sunset red toenail polish. Helen wondered how her landlady got the knee-high lace-up sandals to stay up. She was sure the straps would slide down her legs.

"This isn't a joke," Peggy said, and burst into tears.

"Awk!" Pete the parrot flapped his wings. He was upset, too.

Helen was stunned. Peggy never cried, not even when the cops had cuffed her and hauled her off to jail.

Margery stubbed out her cigarette and sat up in her chaise longue. "I'm sorry," she said. "I need to quit flapping my lips for the sake of something to do."

"It's not you, it's me. I'm worried." Peggy sniffled into a crumpled Kleenex. "Glenn hasn't returned my calls for two days."

Ever since you gave him your twenty thousand dollars, Helen thought. But she wasn't going to rub salt into her friend's bruised heart. Peggy had dark circles under her eyes, and her fine porcelain skin was a sickly yellow.

"Maybe it's time we check on him," Margery said.

"No!" Peggy said, too quickly. "I mean, I don't want to bother him."

"He's certainly bothered you," Margery said.

"It's not that. He could be sick or injured."

"Exactly why we need to check on him," Margery said. "I'm going with or without you."

Peggy was trapped. Now she would have to confront her worst fear. "Let me take Pete home," she said, bargaining for a little more time.

"I'll get the car going," Margery said. There would be no escape or excuses. "You're coming, too," the landlady said to Helen, as Peggy and Pete disappeared into their apartment.

"I wouldn't leave Peggy alone at a time like this," Helen said.

"For her sake, I hope the SOB is dead," Margery said.

"Then I'd better stay home," Helen said. "I've found enough dead people lately. The cops are starting to think it's my hobby."

"It's perfectly safe for you to come along," Margery said. "You know damn well what we're going to find. So does Peggy."

But Margery wouldn't say it, and neither would Helen.

Peggy climbed into Margery's big white Lincoln Town Car like a felon being delivered to a federal prison. The death sentence had been passed. All hope for her romance was gone. She was going to witness the final execution.

The ride to Glenn's home was mercifully short. He lived in a row of yellow town houses that looked like they'd been put up yesterday. The paint was fresh and the ornamental palms still had the landscaper's tags on them.

"Is his car parked on the street?" Margery said.

"I don't think he has a car," Peggy said. "We always rode in limos."

Rode, Helen noticed. Past tense. There would be no more glamorous nights on Las Olas.

"Humph," Margery snorted.

Peggy knocked politely on the door to number seventeen, a meek little tap-tap.

"You sound like a sick mouse," Margery said. She pushed Peggy aside and hammered on the door until the windows rattled.

A head popped out of the town house next door like a gopher out of a hole. The guy even had ginger hair and buck teeth. "He moved out yesterday," the gopher said. "Or was it today? It was after midnight. I know that much. He woke me up."

Peggy gripped the porch railing, unable to speak. Helen patted her shoulder.

"Do you know where he went?" Margery said.

The gopher shook his head. "Some bill collector dude has been looking for him. Said he ran up a bunch of bills on a fake credit card. A limo company wanted him, too. They sounded really mad. I was surprised. He seemed like such a nice guy."

"Yes, he did," Peggy said. Her voice was shaky, but she squared her shoulders and walked to the car alone.

When she settled into its plush comfort, she said, "You don't have to say I told you so. You were right. I'm a fool. I gave him twenty thousand dollars and he skipped, just like you said he would."

"I'm not exactly infallible," Margery said. "I think I've rented out 2C to another crook. Helen figured it out. I was blind as the old bat I am. She told you about Arlene. That woman is up to something. I just don't know what it is."

"Where is Arlene?" Helen said. "I haven't seen her—"

"Since last night," Peggy said. Then she started to laugh, except it sounded more like crying. "No, she couldn't. She wouldn't. Please tell me she didn't run off with Glenn. It's bad enough that he stole my money. But if a woman thirty years older stole my man—that is too freaking much."

"I don't think man stealing is the crime here," Helen said. "Maybe Arlene isn't doing anything wrong."

"She is and you know it," Margery said. "She's up to no good in those hotel lobbies."

"I don't think Arlene and Glenn were lovers, but did you ever wonder if there might be some connection between them?" Helen said.

"You think every crook in South Florida is connected?" Margery said.

"Remember that night Arlene rode in Glenn's limo?" Helen said. "She came running back all excited, saying how nice Glenn was to let her ride with him. It got me thinking. Arlene's kind of weird-looking, even for Florida. Why would a man like Glenn let a bizarro like Arlene ride with him unless he knew her? You don't invite strangers into your limo. Suppose she jumped in with him so they could have a little talk in private?"

"It's possible," Margery said. "Your brain's working better than mine. Now tell me why she's videotaping those hotel lobbies. I can't see what it is."

"Maybe we need to see what Arlene saw. Anybody got a camcorder?" Helen said.

"I do," Peggy said. "At home."

"It's still light out," Helen said. "Let's go to the Full Moon and shoot what Arlene did."

Margery raced through the back streets to the Coronado like she had lights and sirens. Helen grabbed the seat and hung on while her landlady drove, cigarette clenched in her teeth. The Town Car screeched in front of the Coronado, and Peggy flung open her door, ready to dash inside.

"Be careful you don't run into Arlene," Margery said to Peggy. "One look at your face and she'll know something is wrong."

While Peggy sprinted across the lawn, Helen said, "Do you really think Arlene skipped with Glenn?"

"Glenn's skipped and we haven't seen Arlene lately." Margery said. "That's not quite the same thing. But I'm worried. Arlene's car isn't here."

"Maybe she's trolling another hotel lobby," Helen said.

"Maybe," Margery said.

They watched Peggy unlock her door and heard Pete's welcoming squawk.

"Do you think she'll be OK?" Helen asked.

"She's strong," Margery said. "Besides, Peggy is used to losing. She plays the lottery."

"But this time she lost her money and her man," Helen said.

"Peggy has a good job. She can make more money. That man was no loss. I'm glad she didn't marry him. We'll just have to make sure we have plenty of wine and time for her until she recovers. Quiet. Here she comes."

"Got it," Peggy said, and threw the camera bag on the car seat. Margery pulled out into the street before Peggy shut the door and forced the car through the honking, lurching traffic. The tires squealed when she pulled up at the Full Moon.

"Look at that," Helen said. "The hotel's parking lot is almost deserted. There're only four cars. It should be packed to the curb."

"Dead guests aren't good for business," Margery said.

Inside they found Sondra sitting at the front desk, reading a thick textbook. There was nothing for her to do.

Then Helen heard giggles and the pounding of wet feet. A little blond girl in a tiny, saggy swimsuit was running down the hall. She looked about six, with adorably wispy hair and a missing tooth.

"No running, sweetheart," Sondra said. "Your feet are wet and you'll hurt yourself."

"Yes, ma'am." The child flashed a jack-o'-lantern grin.

"Ma'am?" Helen said. "Does any kid say that anymore? What's a family doing here? I thought everyone had checked out."

"Shh," Sondra said. "They're from the Midwest, where people still have manners, and they obviously haven't turned on the TV news. It's a mom, dad, two little ones, and a sulky teenage boy who spends all day making calls on the lobby phone and listening to his iPod. The parents and little kids hang out by the pool. What are you doing here? You don't have to be at work until tomorrow morning."

"We're trying to figure out why that odd lady Arlene was hanging out in the lobby the other day," Helen said. "Can we video the same stuff she did?"

"Suit yourself," Sondra said, "but it was pretty boring."

A car pulled up and parked in the darkest side of the lot. A man about sixty got out, and pulled a fishing hat down low on his forehead. A woman, her face in shadow, waited in the car.

"Look how she's keeping her head down," Sondra said. "Bet you anything they're sneaking around."

"What are they doing here?" Helen said.

"They think no one else will be at the murder hotel."

"They figured right, except for Mr. and Mrs. Midwest," Helen said.

"And two other cheating couples who ducked in about half an hour ago." Sondra rolled her eyes. "Now, shoo with that camera. These types are skittish enough, and every room rented keeps us in business."

Helen found Margery and Peggy pacing by the fountain. "Could you take any longer?" her landlady grumped. "The light's going to be gone."

Peggy handed Helen the camcorder. "You use it. You know what Arlene shot."

Helen put her eye to the viewfinder and waited a moment for her vision to adjust to the world in miniature. Then she walked the route that Sondra said Arlene had taken.

"Flowers and trees first," Helen said. She looked at them through the viewfinder. Nothing unusual. Just flowers and trees.

"Pool next." Helen saw the kids splashing in the water. The little blond girl ran out of the pool, suit straps slipping off her shoulders, showing little pink breast buds. Her baby brother toddled after her, his diaper drooping to reveal a bare bottom. They were so beautiful—and so innocent. Was Arlene taking shots of naked children? Helen felt the bottom drop out of her stomach. Please, let me be wrong. She swung the camera around.

"Then the lobby," Helen said. There was the man with the fishing hat, haggling over the room rates at the front desk. His hat was pulled down so low, the top half of his head was hidden.

"Seventy dollars is our lowest senior rate," Sondra told him.

Senior rate? Now, that was romantic. How old was Lover Boy?

"Come on, honey, you can give us a better deal than that," he whined. "Who else is going to stay here?"

"Sixty-seven fifty," Sondra said.

"Done," he said, and counted out the cash. Affordable adultery.

Was that someone else's wife waiting in the car? Helen wondered. Sondra thought the man was sneaking around, and she'd seen plenty of guilty couples. Was Arlene indulging in a little garden-variety blackmail?

Helen swung the camera away from the front desk before the sneaky man saw her. "Snack bar now," she said, using the hotel's grand name for the cluster of vending machines. Helen watched a kid wearing baggy shorts and a rumpled T-shirt try to slide a dollar bill into the soda machine. It spit the money back. Was this some sort of vending machine scam? Why video it? The kid turned the bill around, stuck the money in again, and scored a Mountain Dew. Then he slouched over to the pay phones with a calling card.

"Pay phones." Helen swung the camera to the phones on the wall, while the surly kid punched in numbers.

He looked up, saw Helen with the camcorder, and said, "Hey, bitch, do you mind?" The kid's hand was cupped over the calling card.

"Do I mind what?" Helen said, the video camera still trained on his face. It was blotched with anger and zits.

"Do you fucking mind not shoulder surfing?" Manners evaporated after a certain age, even in the Midwest.

"What's shoulder surfing?" Helen asked, lowering the camera.

The kid clenched his long, skinny fingers protectively over the card face. "You know what it is. Put that camcorder down or I'll call the fucking cops. It's bad enough I lost my cell phone when I got grounded and I'm stuck with a fucking calling card. Now every asshole with a camcorder thinks he can steal my card numbers. I already got ripped off at a turnpike rest stop. My dad bitched me out for being careless. Drop the fucking camcorder or I'll call 911."

The kid's words suddenly skidded to a halt, as if he was surprised to be saying so much. Helen suspected he communicated with adults mostly by grunts and single syllables. She turned off her camera. "Thank you," she said. "Thank you very much."

The kid stood there openmouthed, but that may have been his usual expression.

Helen ran back to Margery and Peggy, who were once more pacing the lobby.

"I've got it! I think Arlene was shoulder surfing."

"What?" Peggy and Margery said together.

"She was stealing calling card and credit card numbers with a video camera."

"I'll be damned," Margery said.

"It makes sense," Peggy said. She was starting to show

signs of life again. Maybe Margery's folly made her feel better about her own mistake. "That's why she hung around vacation hotels and cultivated that harmless-tourist act with the knitting and the video cam. She took a bunch of innocent pictures, then swung the camera toward the phone bank."

"Well, well, it's time to have a talk with her," Margery said.

"Unless she's run off with Glenn," Peggy said. She was getting used to the idea of losing her man.

"Maybe she's at home watching TV," Helen said.

Margery fixed her with a glare. "Do you believe that?"

"Uh, no," Helen said.

"Then let's quit wasting time and go home."

Margery drove to the Coronado as if she got a bonus for running yellow lights. She stopped by her apartment just long enough to grab her passkey.

Helen and Peggy followed her up the stairs to 2C, then stood back while Margery pounded on the door. There was no answer.

Helen felt sick, and leaned against the wall.

Margery looked over at her. "What's wrong with you?"

"I'm getting a complex," Helen said. "Every time somebody knocks on a door, the people inside have either skipped or died."

"If that crook Arlene skipped, she's going to wish she was dead," Margery growled. She banged on the door again. "No answer. I'm going in." Margery unlocked the door with her passkey. The sharp, dizzying odor of bleach, ammonia and lemon polish poured out.

"That's one good thing about renting to crooks," Margery said. "They always clean up any fingerprints when they split."

Helen and Peggy followed her inside. The apartment looked ready to show. The tabletops and counters sparkled. The floor was shiny clean.

"She's gone," Margery said.

"She take the towels?" Helen said. The residents of 2C usually departed with souvenirs.

"Nope. She got my whistling teakettle and the sea-shell mirror."

Helen saw the blank spot on the wall by the front door and the empty stove burner.

"But I got first and last month's rent and a cleaning deposit," Margery said. "I won't lose any money. But I liked that mirror."

"Too bad she got away," Helen said.

"She left," Margery said. "That doesn't mean she got away."

CHAPTER 27

∙∙

"They grabbed those children and ran out of this hotel like the devil was chasing them," Sondra said.

"Who?" Helen said. She'd walked in on Sondra and Craig at the front desk.

"That nice family from the Midwest," Sondra said. "I don't know how they found out about the deaths, but they packed up and left at two thirty this morning. Wouldn't even wait until daylight. Sybil was on duty. She said they acted like she was going to murder them in their beds."

The hotel was unnaturally quiet for eight thirty in the morning. There was no line of impatient travelers at the front desk. No guests waited for the elevator. No one poured coffee or nuked a cinnamon roll in the break-fast room. The room's TV was off, too. The employees couldn't bear to watch the morning news.

"Did the other couples check out, too?" Helen said.

"All gone. The hotel is empty," Sondra said. "All our reservations are canceled for the next month. We have fifty-two rooms to clean today, but then there's no work. Sybil says she'll put you both on vacation pay for a week. After that, you may have to look for another job if business doesn't pick up."

"No," Craig said. "I want to work here."

"We all want to work here," Sondra said. "We'll never find another boss as nice as Sybil. She even let me take off time for important tests at school."

Helen looked down and saw that Craig was holding Sondra's slender brown hand. Helen couldn't blame him. The desk clerk was impossibly lovely in a long cream skirt and silk blouse.

Sondra deftly took back her hand. She was used to dealing with smitten men. "Well," she said, "I have work to do. Cheryl's cleaning on two. Denise said to tell you that you're both working together on the third floor. Room 322 still has the police seal on it, so you can skip it, but you've got your work cut out for you. A boys' soccer team stayed in 323, but they checked out the day of the murder. It hasn't been cleaned yet. Denise said it was trashed. The couple who checked into the honeymoon suite last night carried a bag of fresh produce. They didn't look like vegetarians to me."

"Yuck," Helen said.

"That's why I like the front desk," Sondra said. "Nothing but good, clean complaints."

"I don't know where to start," Helen said, as she and Craig rode the elevator upstairs. "They both sound bad."

Craig pulled out a coin. "Heads or tails," he said. "Heads we do the soccer room first. I want to start there."

"Tails we do the honeymoon suite first," Helen said. "Produce puts me off my feed. I want to get it over with. Loser cleans the Jacuzzi."

Craig flipped the coin. "You lose," he said. "We start with the soccer room."

"I'm afraid to see what those kids did to it," Helen said.

She unlocked the door to 323, stopped at the threshold, and stared. "I don't think you won," she said.

"The little bastards," Craig said.

The room was looped with toilet paper. It zigzagged over the bed and around the lamps. It crisscrossed the chair backs, wrapped around the mirror, and clung to the bathroom fixtures. TP trailed down the shower curtains and ran along the rug. The toilet paper was covered with squiggles of red and yellow Silly String.

Scrawled in Silly String on the bedroom walls was: *We're Going All the Way—State Champs!*

"I hope they lose," Craig said.

"I assume red and yellow are the school colors," Helen said. She looked at the toilet paper draping the desk. "It's stuck to the furniture. Oh, no. It's wet."

"With what?" Craig said. "This was a room full of feral boys." He sniffed the paper. "It's water."

"Don't expect me to thank the little slobs," Helen said. "This is going to be a bear to clean."

"Did they leave a tip?" Craig asked.

"A penny on the dresser," Helen said. "Look at this mess. What kind of men are they going to be?"

"The kind who stay in 323," Craig said.

After two hours of scraping, scrubbing and swearing, they'd stripped off the wet toilet paper and Silly String. Helen cleaned the last sludge out of the tub and stood up, dizzy with fatigue. Craig was looking tired, too. As they pushed the heavy housekeeping cart past room 322, Helen could see fingerprint powder on the door. She was glad the room was still sealed.

"How long do you think it will be before we clean that?" Craig said.

"If we're lucky, the hotel will close first," Helen said. "That fingerprint stuff is worse than Silly String."

The morning was long and hot. Most guests had turned off their room air conditioners to be environmentally conscious. They forgot about the hotel maids, who roasted while they cleaned the steamy rooms. Helen turned the air conditioners back on, but the rooms didn't cool down quickly. She and Craig were both sweating by the time they took their eleven-o'clock break.

At eleven fifteen they were ready to tackle the honeymoon suite. Neither had much enthusiasm for the job. The two randy adults had made almost as much mess as a whole teen soccer team. The sheets had been dragged off the bed. Beer cans littered the tabletops, and a bottle of red wine was spilled on the carpet.

"At least they put the cucumbers in the wastebasket," Craig said.

Helen grabbed the alcohol spray off the cart and studied the Jacuzzi. It was streaked and smeared like a first grader's finger painting. "This is disgusting," she said. "I hate fresh fruit in the Jacuzzi. There's squashed peaches, bananas and strawberries, plus whipped cream, dark chocolate—and dark hair."

"You sound just like Rhonda," Craig said absently, as he gathered up the dirty bedsheets.

Helen was too stunned to say anything.

"Rhonda was always bitching about the whipped cream and shit," Craig said. "Every damn time she had to clean that Jacuzzi, she complained about crawling into the tub. She could gripe for hours. I got sick of listening to her."

"How did you know?" Helen's voice was a croak. "You never met Rhonda. You came here after she was killed." She looked at his sweaty hair. It was blond. But he had dark roots.

"What do you mean?" Craig unfurled a clean sheet across the huge mattress, and the damp Band-Aid flapped up on his wrist. There was no wound. It covered a tattoo— Bart Simpson on a surfboard saying, *"Cowabunga, dude."*

Something to do with a cow, Penny the waitress had said, *or a cowboy or a ranch.* Dude ranches. Dude. *Cowabunga, dude.* Bart's words had gotten a little twisted in Penny's mind, but she was right. There was a tattoo on the cute surfer dude. And he had dark hair that he'd dyed blond.

Helen stared at the tattoo, fascinated. She was looking at the hand of a killer.

Craig's voice went shrill, and he started talking faster. "You all said she bitched and whined."

"No," Helen said. "You said she complained to you. For hours. We never said anything to you about her complaints. Denise is too professional to criticize the staff to a new hire. I sure didn't say anything. After Rhonda died we were all too ashamed of ourselves. We made her into a saint. We would never have told you that."

"Cheryl told me," Craig insisted. "That's right. It was Cheryl." He gave Helen that sun-drenched smile.

"No, it wasn't," Helen said. "Cheryl felt guilty because she'd turned down Rhonda's money. She wouldn't have bad-mouthed her."

She looked him right in his lying hazel eyes. "You're Rhonda's mystery boyfriend. She talked about you all the time. You're her handsome dark-haired man with the money."

"You think I dated that skank?" he said. "You're crazy, bitch."

Helen knew she was right. Craig's odd behavior made sense now. She saw him crawling around in the house-keeping room, giving her a lame excuse about dropping a spray can cap. She heard Craig asking her out—and Cheryl, too. He didn't like older women. He wanted to pump the maids about hotel hiding places.

"You're trying to find the money, aren't you?" Helen said. "That's why you asked us where we'd hide it. You're the dead robber's accomplice. He was shot before he could give you the money."

Craig slammed the sheets down on the floor. "Lady, I don't know what I've done to you, but I don't deserve this."

Helen's brain felt supercharged. She saw connections everywhere. "You wanted Rhonda to look for that money. That's why you hooked up with her. It was easy, wasn't it? She hung out at that bar and had a taste for lowlifes. You started taking her out. Don't deny it. You took her to the diner down the road. A waitress saw you together."

"You're freaking stupid," Craig said.

"I was. But I've smartened up," Helen said. "I can see through you like a window. You gave poor Rhonda promises and cash—more cash than she ever saw in her life. You led her on. What happened then, Craig? Why did you kill her? Was she starting to get suspicious? Or were you too impatient? When she didn't find anything, you killed her and took her place so you could search the hotel yourself. She told you nobody ever quit a job at the Full Moon, so you created a vacancy."

"Helen, look at me. Do I look like a killer?" Craig looked like a minor movie star, golden, handsome, magnetic. His voice was soft and reasonable. His gloved hands were swift. They reached for the broom and swung it at Helen's head.

"Crazy bitch," he shrieked.

Helen saw his eyes flicker a fraction before he struck. She turned enough to catch the blow with her shoulder. The force knocked her into the wall. Craig swung viciously at her head with a black desk chair. She slid down the wall, and he barely missed her. The chair broke apart, leaving a dusty hole in the drywall.

My God, Helen thought. He's trying to kill me. She was nearly blinded by the drywall dust. Helen felt along the floor and found a splintered chair leg and the bottle of alcohol.

Craig flung a lamp at her head. Helen ducked. The heavy brass base hit the wall, and the shade cartwheeled across the floor. The bulb shattered.

"Argggh!" Craig charged again, swinging the shattered chair back. The jagged edges made a weird and lethal weapon.

Helen slashed at Craig with the splintered chair leg, knocking the broken furniture out of his hands. She hit him so hard, the shock ran up her hand.

Craig yelped and crashed to the floor. Helen sprayed

his eyes with alcohol, kicked the broken chair back away, and body slammed herself down on his chest.

"Oof!" he said as the air left his lungs. Craig's eyes were squeezed shut and leaking tears. When he could talk again, he wheezed, "Ow, bitch. I can't see. I'm blind."

"Good," Helen said. "You tried to kill me. Why did you kill Rhonda?"

"It was her fault. She made me do it. My eyes hurt." Craig struggled to sit up. Helen clubbed him with the broken chair leg, and pointed the alcohol spray bottle at his red, watery eyes.

"Stay," she said, as if he were an unruly dog. "Lie down and play dead."

Craig stayed still as a corpse.

Her hand found a sharp shard of lightbulb, and she held it over his left eye. "How'd you like to be really blind?" she said.

Craig's voice was a dry whisper. "We had a deal. Rhonda would search the hotel, and we'd split the money when she found it."

"Some deal," Helen said. "What did she get out of it?"

"I had the hotel plans," he said. "I told her about good places to search—vents, ducts and unmarked storage areas. I gave her money for expenses."

"Fake fifties," Helen said.

"Hey, they spent just like real money. I told her to do anything, pay anyone, to find that cash. I'm a dead man if I don't come up with it by next Thursday. I made a deal with some very bad people. The only reason I'm still alive is they knew the situation. Once I had Rhonda working for me at the hotel, they gave me a deadline to find it—or else. They said they'd cut my heart out and show it to me. I couldn't run. They were watching me."

"Did Rhonda know this?" Helen asked.

"She knew I was desperate. All she gave me was a

bunch of excuses. Then I found that plane ticket in her purse. She was going to take my money and run."

"No, that's what you were going to do, Craig. You were going to abandon Rhonda as soon as she gave you the cash. Or did you always plan to kill her?"

Craig said nothing. Helen made a tiny cut in the tender skin under his eye with the broken lightbulb. Helen stared at the thin line of blood welling up in the cut. That scared her so much, the shard slipped from her fingers.

Craig was too terrified to notice. "Yes, no, I don't know," he shrieked.

"Did she know you were a drug dealer?"

"No. I said I was the son of the architect who built this hotel and I needed the money because I ran up some gambling debts, but there would be enough left over for us. I pretended I knew her from school. She was four years older than me. I said I'd always had a thing for older women."

"You little shit," Helen said. "You use that line on all the women."

"Just the old ones," Craig said.

Helen whacked him again with the chair leg.

"Ow! Fuck. What's the matter with you?" he said.

"Shut up and keep talking," she said.

He seemed to understand that command. "Rhonda took so long, I got suspicious. I was gonna die. When I saw that plane ticket, I lost it."

"You killed her for nothing," Helen said. "She loved you. She bought the ticket for her mother."

He managed a shrug, even with Helen sitting on him. "It worked out. It got me at the hotel, in her job, so I could do the search myself."

It worked out. Helen stared that the creature beneath her. She wanted to hit him again for what he'd done to Rhonda, but she was afraid she wouldn't stop beating him. Time to change the subject. "Tell me why you killed Dean Stamples. Did he catch you searching his room?"

"I never killed him!" Craig screamed.

Helen noticed he didn't deny killing Rhonda.

The room door slammed against the wall. "What's going on here?" Denise, the head housekeeper, entered in a majestic rush, wielding a wet mop. "I heard the screaming two floors down. What happened to this room? Helen, what are you doing to Craig?"

"He killed Rhonda," Helen said. "He was her mysterious dark lover—and the robber's accomplice. He dyed his hair and wore gloves to hide his fingerprints. He's here searching for the lost money."

"So that's what you were doing up on the third floor," Denise said. "Helen told me how you fed her that line about dropping a spray can cap. I knew you were lying."

"No!" Craig said. "She's crazy. She attacked me because I wouldn't screw her. She made up this weird shit about me killing Rhonda. She's menopausal."

Denise whacked him smartly with the mop. "I hate guys who say that," she said.

"Me, too." Helen thumped his arm with the chair leg.

"Ow!" Craig cowered like a hunchbacked Quasimodo, rubbing his stinging eyes and warding off their blows.

"How'd you figure out this lying piece of trash killed Rhonda?" Denise said.

"He said Rhonda complained about cleaning the Jacuzzi," Helen said. "He could only know that if he talked with her when she was alive."

Craig bucked like a bronco and threw Helen off his chest, but he couldn't move fast enough. Denise slugged him with the mop, and he dropped to the floor again. She kicked him hard in the ribs. "That's for Rhonda," she said.

This time Craig didn't move.

"He's out cold," Denise said. "Stand guard while I call the police." She charged out of the room.

Craig lay motionless on the carpet. He had to be unconscious, Helen thought. No one who cleaned hotels would stretch out on that carpet. He knew what had been on it.

She leaned closer. She could barely hear him breathing. His eyes were closed. Sirens screamed in the parking lot. The police were at the Full Moon. That should have made Craig react. She poked his chest with the chair leg. Not a twitch.

It was over. All the police had to do was cuff the killer and haul him away.

"Ahgggg!" Craig butted his head against Helen's. She fell back on the floor, stunned. The man had a skull like a sledgehammer. She lashed out at him with her fist, but he clubbed her head with the shattered chair leg. The blackness closed in on her. There was a buzzing like a thousand flies.

When her vision cleared, she heard Craig pounding down the hall.

Get up! she told herself. He's getting away.

Helen struggled to her feet. The cleaning cart was jammed into the door frame with the mop stick. She tried to shove it out of the way, but she was too woozy.

Helen took a whiff from the ammonia bottle to clear her head. She gagged and coughed, but her head was a little clearer. She threw herself against the jammed cart, and the mop handle snapped. The cart rolled aside and she nearly fell into the hall. Her head ached. Each step shot pain up her neck.

She couldn't let Rhonda's killer escape.

The hall was empty, but she heard the fire door slam, and ran to it. The stairs seemed to sway and twist as she started down, clinging to the rail. Craig was getting away. She couldn't run fast enough to catch him.

Police were pouring into the lobby when Helen staggered to the second-floor balcony and yelled, "Help! The killer's running out the fire stairs on the first floor."

Her shout pierced her brain like glass shards. She looked down and saw Craig race around the corner, holding the black chair leg like a handgun.

"There!" Sondra shouted, and pointed toward the door.

"In the hall," Denise screamed. "He killed Rhonda. He's got a—"

"Police! Stop! Police!" a muscular young officer said, his gun drawn. "Drop the weapon! Drop the weapon! Police!"

Craig was five feet from freedom. He stopped, turned toward the officer, and raised the chair leg like a loaded weapon.

The officer fired.

Craig dropped as if the rug were pulled out from under him. A long splash of red darkened the hall floor.

CHAPTER 28

· ·

Rhonda's killer was dead.

His blood made a dark lake, where Helen could drown her anger. She waited for the hot surge of triumph.

Helen had kept her promise to Rhonda. Her colleague's killer had been brought to justice. The man who'd used her, deceived her and beaten her was shot down like a rabid animal.

Instead she saw Craig, with his hunky body and boy-band hair. Heard him laughing while he cleaned the hotel rooms. Felt the electric *zing!* when he kissed her. His flirtation had been lies, but Helen had still enjoyed it. He wasn't the first man who'd lied to her.

Someone was crying softly. Helen wished it were her. But it was Cheryl, weeping in the lobby. Helen felt only numb. Craig was dead—but so was Rhonda. Her revenge felt empty. She'd helped no one and solved nothing.

Helen had so many unanswered questions: Why did Craig kill Dean Stamples? Did he know the guest in 322? Or had Dean surprised the cleaner in his room?

Helen had no doubt Craig had murdered Rhonda. She saw the fear in his eyes when he denied knowing the maid. She heard his desperate lies after his fatal slip of the tongue. Helen had beaten the confession out of him, but she thought he'd been telling the truth, at least about Rhonda: He'd met her, seduced her, used her and killed her in a hot fury when he thought she'd betrayed him. Maybe he'd intended to murder her all along. But why kill Dean?

She thought she'd pieced together most of the story, but she couldn't be sure. Now she would never know. Craig took those answers with him into the lake of blood.

Time froze. Cheryl's weeping was the only sound. The young cop was standing in the lobby, his face blank with shock. Helen leaned over the balcony and said, "Thank you, Officer. That man beat Rhonda to death. He tried to kill me. You saved me."

Craig tried to kill me, she repeated to herself. Why? Why didn't he shove me aside and run? He could have escaped.

Because he could never come back here again and look for the money. He could run away, but he couldn't escape. He owed that money to the wrong people. He'd die horribly if he didn't find it. He died for it, anyway.

I almost died for it. I would have been beaten to death, like Rhonda and Dean. The Full Moon would have died, too. No one would stay at a hotel where a serial killer stalked the halls.

Once again Helen saw Craig turn and point the chair leg like a loaded weapon at the police officer. Was his death suicide by cop? It was certainly a quicker, easier end than the drug dealers promised him.

"Thank you, Officer," Helen said again.

The cop stared straight ahead. He didn't—or couldn't—hear her.

I wanted to ease his guilt, Helen thought. He's going to suffer, too. Craig has left a trail of pain through this hotel.

Her words seemed to bring the lobby back to life. Now people were shouting, screaming, yelling orders and talking into cell phones. Outside, there were more sirens. The lobby pulsed red from the emergency-vehicle lights, like some weird daylight disco.

Blood dripped on the cream-painted balcony rail—Helen's own blood. It was redder and brighter than Craig's, because she was alive and he was dead. She felt the balcony tilt. She sat down fast on the carpet before she tumbled over the rail.

"Are you OK, miss?" A blond paramedic, who looked like she bench-pressed Buicks, was talking from far away. Helen tried to follow her words, but the hall was blurry and dark around the edges.

"Just dizzy." Helen said every word as if she would be billed for it.

"Are you hurt? Where do you hurt?" the blond paramedic prodded her with questions.

"Head. Shoulder. He hit me."

"We're going to take you to the hospital to check you out," the paramedic said.

Helen didn't resist when two more paramedics loaded her onto a gurney. She couldn't have if she'd wanted to. She'd have to fight three incredible hulks. They slid her into the ambulance and it tore off to the emergency room.

"Do I get a siren?" Helen said.

"You only rate flashing lights, I'm afraid." The fit blond paramedic smiled for the first time. Her teeth were very white.

In the chaos of the emergency room, Helen didn't pass out, but she drifted away to someplace safe. She felt wrapped in thick cotton, instead of the thin hospital blanket. She was far away from Craig and that drowning lake of blood.

It was hours before Helen saw anything sane. She heard the moans of two teenagers who'd been riding in the back of a pickup truck when they bounced out on the highway. A homeless man shuffled through the gurneys and wheelchairs, panhandling.

She heard the wails of a woman who'd been beaten

so badly by her lover that her eye was swollen shut. The woman cop who brought her in was not sympathetic. "What did she expect?" the cop said. "She took up with a known felon."

For a moment the dark lake appeared, and Helen stared at some frightening questions. Why was Rhonda fatally attracted to the wrong men? Did she expect every man who walked into that bar would be trouble? Did Rhonda play date roulette—or even suicide by dating?

Then a doctor was in the ER cubicle, bringing her back to the present with his brisk, cheerful talk. Helen would not drown in the blood lake. Not this time.

The doctor shone a light in her eyes and asked what day it was.

"I've been here so long, I'm not sure anymore," she said.

"You sound oriented to this place," the doctor said.

Helen laughed. She felt like she'd awakened from a bad dream.

The doctor had a round, rosy face, a round bald spot, and a clean white coat. He told Helen his name and she instantly forgot it. "You have a nice crop of bruises on your shoulder," he said. "That cut on your scalp will need stitches. What happened?"

"I ran into a chair," Helen said.

"I want to X-ray that shoulder and order a CT scan for your head," the doctor said.

"She should have her head examined," a raucous voice said. The cubicle curtain was shoved aside, and Margery stomped in wearing outrageous purple ruffles and high-heeled suede sandals. Hospital security was no match for Super Landlady.

"You look like a year's worth of bad news," Margery said. "Who's picking up this bill? You don't have any money."

"Sybil at the hotel," Helen said. "I got clobbered in the line of duty."

"I hope he knocked some sense into you."

The dark lake of blood opened up before Helen. "He—he's dead," she said, and burst into tears. Damn, Helen hated when she cried. It was so girlie. Margery stood there as if she were watching some painful but necessary procedure.

"Head injuries make you emotional sometimes," the doctor said.

Helen couldn't stop crying. "He's dead," she wailed. "I don't know who's going to clean up after him."

"You don't always make a lot of sense with a head injury," the doctor said.

"She sounds like that all the time," Margery said.

"Where's Phil?" Helen asked.

"He's on a job in Miami, and I wanted to get a look at you before I called him. You're fine. I'm not telling him until he gets home later tonight. Otherwise he'll come racing up I-95 and get in an accident, and I'll have to deal with two people in the hospital."

It was nearly seven o'clock when Helen gave a statement to the police at the hospital. She had three stitches in her scalp. Her head was pounding, her stomach was queasy, her shoulder ached, and that deadly gunshot still rang in her ears. The lake of blood shimmered in the distance, but at least she didn't feel like she'd drown in it. She dutifully swallowed the pain pills, but they didn't help. This hurt was much deeper.

"No broken bones in your shoulder," the doctor said, "and no sign of stroke, bleeding or skull fracture. There's a tiny bit of brain edema. I think it's a slight concussion. I'd like to keep you overnight for observation."

"I want to go home," Helen said. "I can sign myself out. Margery can drive me."

"No, I can't. I'm not waking you up every two hours and checking on you," Margery said. "You've kept me awake enough already. Let the pros watch you. Stay here and stay out of trouble. I'll see you in the morning."

At eleven thirty the next morning, a hospital aide wheeled Helen out into the too-bright sunlight. Phil helped her into his Jeep, gave her a kiss and a careful hug that hurt her shoulder, and handed her a rose. A thorn stuck her in the thumb.

She sucked the salty blood while Phil negotiated the traffic in the hospital driveway.

"You nearly got that old woman with the cane," Helen said.

"No points for that," Phil said. "You have to aim for the healthy young ones." He steered the Jeep around a wary mother with a stroller and was out on the street. "I got some inside information from my friends on the force."

"The cops actually told you something?" Helen said.

"You forgot, I'm connected," he said. "Also, the guy is dead and they're going to close two murders."

The Jeep hit a pothole, and Helen winced. The jolt went right up into her aching head.

"Turns out the late Craig was a small-time hustler and drug dealer," Phil said. "He had a long sheet, including assault and battery. He beat up a prostitute when she objected to him not paying."

I never guessed boy-band Craig was violent, Helen thought. Not till he tried to attack me. None of us did. I escaped with cuts and bruises for my mistake. Rhonda paid for it with her life.

"The police found a couple of fake fifties in his apartment," Phil said. "They figure he may have gotten stung in a drug deal and tried to hand off some of the bad money to Rhonda."

"He told me straight out he gave the bad money to Rhonda," Helen said. "He didn't care if she got caught passing it."

"He wasn't your caring kind of guy," Phil said. "But he and Rhonda were definitely an item. The police found his fingerprints all over her apartment, along with a few other jailbird prints."

"She had lousy taste in men," Helen said.

"Looks like it. Unless they were on a Wanted poster, she didn't want them," Phil said. "There were bloodstains at Craig's place, too. He tried to clean away the blood, but it showed up loud and clear with Luminol."

"Was it Rhonda's?" Helen said.

"It's definitely her blood type. They won't get the DNA results back right away, but they think he killed her at his apartment and took her in his car to the hotel Dumpster. I don't know why he didn't dump the body somewhere else."

"I do," Helen said. "I bet he thought he knew everything about that hotel, including the Dumpster schedule. Rhonda's body would have been picked up early the next morning, except Sybil got that trash perfume and changed the pickup schedule. That's how Craig got caught. I found the body. If the trash had been picked up by the old schedule, Rhonda's body would have been carted away early that morning. She would have disappeared and no one would have known she was dead."

"The revenge of the Full Moon," Phil said. "Sounds like a movie."

Helen didn't laugh. Nothing seemed funny. She felt like someone had drained the blood out of her.

At the Coronado, Margery treated her like an invalid. She helped Phil settle her into bed and plumped Helen's pillows. Margery gritted her teeth when Thumbs rubbed up against her legs begging for food (the landlady hated cats) but she fed the big-pawed fellow.

She brought Helen soup, scrambled eggs and toast. Thumbs snoozed on the bed most of the day, while Helen stared at the ceiling and thought about how wrong she'd been about Craig. She saw Dean Stamples' photo of his smiling children and pretty blond widow. If she'd figured things out sooner, would his family still have a father?

At sunset, Phil knocked on her door. "Come sit out by the pool with everyone," he said. "Margery, Peggy and Pete are waiting to hear your story."

"I don't feel like it," Helen said, and gave a dramatic sigh. She wanted to brood.

Two minutes later her door was flung open, and Margery flipped on the light in her darkened bedroom. "We've been patient enough while you've moped around," her landlady said. "Get your ass out here. I've heard bits and pieces of this story from Sybil and Sondra and I saw some confused reports on TV. I want to know what happened."

Margery handed Helen her bathrobe. "You don't have to dress for us."

Helen went outside on wobbly legs. She felt better in the fresh air, but she wasn't ready to admit that. Phil grinned at her and held out a chaise longue. Pete sat on Peggy's shoulder and watched her with beady eyes.

Helen sat down gingerly, favoring her bruised shoulder. Phil put a soft pillow at her back. She looked at the expectant faces of the people who'd helped her through so much. Margery was right. She owed them an explanation.

Helen took a deep breath and started to talk. She didn't cry once. Not even when she said, "Craig was shot dead in front of me. His blood was all over the floor. I think he wanted the police to kill him."

"Maybe it was suicide by cop," Phil said. "Maybe it wasn't. Sometimes the suspects are just doing what human nature designed them to do—look at the sound of the commanding voice."

"Is the police officer in trouble for shooting an unarmed man?" Helen asked.

"Word is he'll be OK. Whoever called 911 made it sound like Craig was killing you."

"He was," Helen said.

"Three cops swore they thought the chair leg was a loaded weapon and Craig was going to fire. The officer identified himself and told the suspect to drop the weapon. He was considered armed and dangerous. He'd already killed two people."

"Rhonda and Dean Stamples, the man in room 322," Helen said.

"How did Dean die?" Margery said.

"Scotch bottle," Helen said.

"Someone forced him to drink too much?" Peggy said.

"No, they hit him in the face with it," Phil said. "When the killer hit Dean, he shoved that cartilage in Dean's nose right through—"

"Awwk!" Pete said.

"I think I know enough," Peggy said quickly.

"Dean's death was probably a spur-of-the-moment thing," Helen said. It was her story, and she wanted it back. "The cops think he caught Craig in his room and accused him of stealing. Craig wasn't stealing. He was looking for the robbery stash, but he would have been fired for unauthorized entry into a guest's room. That would have cut off his access to the hotel and his search for the money. Craig had to find that cash. So he killed Dean."

"That's so sad," Peggy said. "Dean died for nothing."

"So did Craig," Helen said. "He never found the money. It's still missing. And poor Rhonda—her dream lover turned into a nightmare. All that pointless death."

The setting sun had turned the Coronado pool into a blood-tinged lake. Helen tried not to look. She concentrated on the whispering palms.

"I don't understand why Rhonda died," Margery said. "Did Craig really kill her to get her job at the hotel?"

"He killed her because he thought she was going to split with the cash," Helen said. "He found a plane ticket Rhonda had bought for her mother and went ballistic. Craig thought she was running out on him with the money and he beat her to death. She loved that man and he killed her for no reason. You know what Craig told me? 'It worked out.' Because he got her job at the hotel."

"He really said that?" Peggy said.

"His exact words. He was cold. Then Craig joined the Full Moon's permanent floating treasure hunt. The whole staff goes home at night and thinks of new hiding places, then spends all day nosing around the hotel. I found Denise pulling up the potted plants by the roots, Sondra taking apart the air-conditioning vents, and Cheryl tearing up the rugs."

"Do you think Rhonda knew her boyfriend was the dead robber's accomplice?" Margery said.

"No," Phil and Helen said at the same time.

"The police found some cards with a fake name and architect's address in Craig's apartment," Phil said.

"Good," Helen said. "Then he told me the truth." For some reason, Rhonda's innocence was important to her. "Craig said he posed as the son of the architect who designed the hotel. He fed Rhonda some story about needing to find the money because he had gambling debts. He gave her fake fifties and false promises of love. But Rhonda couldn't find the money fast enough. Craig was paranoid that she was going to run. He killed her."

"Why didn't Craig just rent room 323 after his partner got shot?" Peggy said. "That would have been the easiest way to search the hotel."

"He needed to get into the work areas and the other guest rooms," Helen said. "A guest couldn't do that. A maid's job was the ideal way to search. He was obsessed with that money. Everyone at the hotel is."

"It's only a hundred thousand dollars," Peggy said. "That's not a lot of money these days."

Peggy had been taking too many stolen limo rides, Helen thought. "It is if you work for a living," she said. "It would take a Full Moon employee seven years to make that much money. Seven years of picking up dirty towels and used condoms, cleaning toilets and hauling soiled sheets. No wonder the staff went crazy looking for it."

"Well, it's over. You caught the killer. Congratulations," Margery said. She raised her wineglass in a salute. Peggy joined her. Phil hoisted his beer. But Helen didn't lift her glass.

"I'm sorry," she said.

"For what?" Margery said.

"I don't know," Helen said.

CHAPTER 29

. . . .

"Get your rear in gear, Helen. I need you back at work." Sybil's voice swirled out of the phone like cigarette smoke.

Helen squinted at the clock in her darkened bedroom. What time was it? Eight o'clock. In the morning or at night? She wasn't sure anymore. "Work?" she said stupidly.

"Yeah. You've heard of it," Sybil said. "At the Full Moon, remember? You've been off three days on my dime. Vacation's over."

Helen heard Sybil sucking on a cigarette and nearly choked on the imaginary smoke. "I thought everybody canceled their reservations."

"I ran a couple of ads in the papers up north advertising two nights for the price of one—plus an AARP discount," Sybil said. "Those AARPsters aren't afraid of a bargain. They're the kind of trade we want. Nice and quiet. No drugs except Lipitor and Viagra. The hotel is filling up again. I need you to work today."

"Now?" Could she face that lake of blood?

"The blood's gone," Sybil said, as if she read Helen's thoughts. "I hired a crime scene service to clean it up. I couldn't ask any of you to do that. I had them remove the blood in the bathroom in 322 while they were at it.

But you'll have to clean up the fingerprint powder. I couldn't afford the whole room."

Helen almost choked with laughter. Trust Sybil to pinch pennies any way she could. Then she remembered Craig asking who would clean that room, and her laughter died.

"Will there be a memorial service for Craig?" Helen asked.

"Who wants to remember a double killer?" Sybil said. "His body will be shipped home to his mother in Minnesota when they finish the autopsy. Good riddance. After what he did to poor little Rhonda, I'd like to bury him in a Dumpster."

Helen's shoulder hurt, her head ached, and she'd been popping aspirins like after-dinner mints.

"I know you're probably still hurting after the way that jackass beat you up, but we need you," Sybil said. "We're shorthanded. I've got a line on a nice widow who wants to clean, but she can't start till next week. You can work with Cheryl. She'll do the heavy stuff. All you'll have to do is dust and vacuum. She'll even lift your vacuum off the cart."

Thumbs sat on the bed, watching Helen with calculating eyes. The cat woke her up at six this morning, demanding breakfast. At least he'd let her fall back asleep after she staggered out to the kitchen and fed him. Any minute now he'd start the lunchtime campaign. She was tired of hanging around the house looking at the cat. He was probably tired of her.

"I'll do it," Helen said.

"Good, see you in half an hour."

Helen threw on some clothes, happy to be out of the apartment. The morning was fresh and clean. Flowers were blooming and the sun was shining. It was good to be alive. She walked into the side door at the Full Moon, the way she did every morning. She threw it open without thinking, then stopped dead. Her feet froze on the threshold.

Craig had died running for this door in his desperate rush to freedom. He'd been shot down five feet away. At least, she thought it was five feet. Maybe it was four. She studied the carpet, but couldn't see any sign of his death. The lake of blood had vanished.

Helen took one tentative step into the hotel, then another. Then she walked boldly down the hall. Somewhere she crossed the spot where he died. She heard applause and saw Denise and Cheryl cheering her on.

"You did it," Denise said.

"Took me a full five minutes to step into that hall," Cheryl said. "But I didn't cry—not after what Craig did to Rhonda."

"OK, ladies, we've spent enough time chatting," Denise said. "We have work to do. I need you both to start in 322."

Helen and Cheryl groaned.

"I know, I know, but we're full up tonight—that's the good news—and we need that room back in service."

Upstairs, Helen examined 322's bathroom tile with a professional eye. She didn't see any of Dean's blood in the white grout. She wondered how the crime scene cleaners did it.

"The cleaners did a nice job in the bathroom," Helen said.

"I'd have paid them myself to clean this room," Cheryl said. "Look at this mess."

The room looked like it was covered with coal dust. Black fingerprint powder was on every surface. *All you have to do is dust,* Helen thought. Sybil suckered me again. Dusting this mess will take all morning. Vacuuming it will take all afternoon.

"I'll start making the bed," Cheryl said. "At least I won't have to strip it. Looks like the cops took the sheets and the spread. You feel well enough to dust?"

Helen's shoulder was stiff and sore when she started,

but after half an hour she felt better. No, she felt good. Maybe stretching was what she needed. "This finger-print powder is worse than cigarette ash," she said. "And look at this. Every picture and lamp shade in the room is crooked."

"The cops knocked the mattress off-kilter, too," Cheryl said. "Can you help me put it back or should I call Denise?"

"I can do it," Helen said. She grabbed the back end of the massive queen-size box spring and dragged it forward, then dropped it in surprise. Under the box spring was a huge, empty square of carpet. She'd always thought the box spring was bolted to the bed, or the pedestal was solid wood. Not so. The pedestal was an open wooden frame, and the mattress and box spring sat on top of it, unsecured.

"Hey," Helen said. "You can move that mattress and get inside the pedestal." She looked inside the pedestal frame. It was like a box without a top.

"You can, but who'd want to?" Cheryl said. "These mattresses are heavy." She gave the box spring a mighty shove and it overshot the pedestal at the front end. Helen looked down into another boxed section of carpet and saw . . . a blue nylon gym bag. The bag looked oddly lumpy, like it was stuffed with bricks.

"Somebody left their gym bag here," Helen said.

"Nobody in their right mind would leave it there," Cheryl said. "That bag was stashed."

"Maybe it belonged to the dead guy, Dean," Helen said. "Let me see if there's any ID inside."

She unzipped the bag. No ID. But she'd recognize those dead presidents anywhere. The bag was stuffed with more money than she'd ever seen, all neatly banded. Helen stared at it, frozen with shock.

Cheryl recovered first. "The robbery stash," she said reverently. "We looked everywhere for it, but we never thought to look inside the bed pedestals."

"Maybe that money belonged to the murdered guy," Helen said.

"Skip? He'd never have a cheap nylon gym bag. He always had leather luggage."

"Skip?" Helen said. She forgot the gym bag.

Cheryl went white as unbaked biscuits. Why did she look so guilty? Helen wondered. Then she knew. Dean's murder suddenly made sense. Craig had been telling the truth: He didn't kill the man in 322.

"Skip was Dean's name when you knew him years ago, wasn't it?" Helen said.

"No," Cheryl said, but her answer was a plea.

"Yes," Helen said. "Angel is a Christmas baby. She was conceived in March. Let me guess: Skip was down here on spring break. You were the prettiest girl on the beach and he was a handsome stranger. You fell in love with him and you got pregnant. He refused to pay child support."

Two tears started down Cheryl's cheeks. Helen had her answer.

It was an old story. Spring break in Florida was a wild week of drunken revelry. But some paid a high price for the beach bacchanal. Beer-sozzled college kids broke their necks diving off hotel balconies into the pool. Students died from alcohol poisoning, boating accidents or DUI car crashes. They were robbed, beaten and hustled. They had unprotected sex. Angel was the aftermath of these rites of spring.

"Skip denied the baby was his," Helen prompted.

"He told me he lived in Chicago," Cheryl said, wiping her eyes. The tears kept coming. "He was in graduate school. He promised he'd keep in touch after spring break. He gave me his phone number. But when I called, it was a wrong number. I didn't know his real name. I felt so stupid. I'd spent a week with him, and I didn't know anything about him.

"Then I found out I was pregnant. I tried to trace him, but I didn't have any money to hire a private eye. I went to the hotel myself. The desk clerk said he couldn't give out the names of guests. I tried to bribe the kid. He said there was no way to track him down. Skip was one of six guys who'd crashed in a room. He didn't use his credit card. The hotel clerk recognized his picture, but had no idea who he was.

"Skip—what a joke. That's what he did. I never saw him again until he turned up at the Full Moon all these years later."

"You didn't recognize him, did you?" Helen said.

"Not at first. I couldn't believe my hot beach boy was that fat old businessman. Skip had lost his hair and gained fifty pounds. But it was more than that. He looked so serious, so pompous."

"What tipped you off?"

"He looked vaguely familiar in that photograph. Remember, that's what I said. The Scotch bottle by the bed stirred up my memory. Skip drank Johnnie Walker Black when most kids were still chugging Coors. He made a big deal about buying the best. But the Phi Beta Kappa key finally did it. I used to tease him about that. He was so proud of it. He even wore it on his bathrobe when we made love. He still wore it after all these years. That key unlocked my memory. Ironic, wasn't it?"

Helen remembered the scene. Cheryl had dropped the spray bottle when Helen mentioned that key. The maid had dithered about being a klutz. But she was shocked, not clumsy.

"That's when I took a good look at the picture on his desk," Cheryl said. "I recognized those mean little eyes. I knew it was him. I should have seen the resemblance sooner.

"I looked at the two children in that photo and thought I'd explode. Those kids had everything, while I was buying clothes for Angel at garage sales. I was furious. I wanted justice. Dean was going to pay child support for Angel or his wife would find out exactly what kind of man she'd married. My Angel deserves a decent life."

"So you confronted Dean in his room," Helen guessed.

"I hid in the hall bathroom until all the maids were gone. I'd already called my mom and said I had to work late. I asked her to watch Angel. She bitched about it, and that had me on edge. I waited till Sondra was busy checking in a long line of customers. Then I used my passkey card on Skip's room."

Cheryl wasn't crying now. Her voice was steady. "I walked in on him in the shower. He'd been drinking, and that made him slow and stupid. He recognized me. I guess I haven't changed as much as I thought. He wasn't scared. He was"—she hunted for the right word—"contemptuous. He thought he was so far above me. He was standing on a bath mat wrapped in a skinny hotel towel, but he acted like he was the king of the world, and I was some peasant.

"I told him we had a child. He knew it. He knew it and he never said anything. He let me struggle alone all these years. He said he couldn't be sure the baby was really his."

"The oldest deadbeat-dad excuse in the world," Helen said.

"He was my first," Cheryl said. "Am I a fool or what?"

"How did Skip find out you were pregnant?" Helen said.

"The hotel clerk. The one who wouldn't help me. He called the guy who'd rented the room at spring break, and that guy called Skip to warn him. Men stick together. Skip said I was trying to blackmail him into paying child support for some other man's kid. He told everyone I was a money-grubbing slut, and then he went on with his life. He never came back to Fort Lauderdale. Skip said he hated Florida."

"So how'd he wind up at the Full Moon?" Helen said.

"He had to attend that business conference here. He

had no choice. His boss ordered it. Skip—Dean I guess he is now—thought it was safe to come to Florida after all these years. The hotel where he'd spent spring break had been torn down."

"He didn't know you worked here?"

"Of course not. He'd forgotten all about me until I turned up in his room. I showed him the photo of our child and said, 'How could you abandon our Angel?'

"He looked at her picture, grunted, and said, 'What's wrong with it?' It! He called our child *it*.

"I said, 'Her name is Angel and she has Down syndrome.'

"He said, 'She's a retard? You want my money for a retard? That's not my fault. That's your stupid cracker genes.'

"I was so mad, I picked up the first thing I could lay my hands on. It was the Scotch bottle he'd brought into the bathroom. I swung it as hard as I could and hit him in his lying face. The next thing I knew, the bathroom was covered in blood, glass and Scotch, and he was on the floor. He was dead. I didn't care."

Helen saw the boiling anger in Cheryl's eyes. She was still furious at the insult to her child. Cheryl's arms were roped with muscle from years of making beds, moving furniture and hauling heavy trash bags. She could easily kill an overweight, out-of-shape man.

"What did you do then?" Helen asked.

"I'd been wearing my cleaning gloves, so my fingerprints weren't on the bottle. It wouldn't have mattered if they were. I was the maid. I packed up the big pieces and buried them in the Dumpster, just in case. I checked the room to make sure I didn't leave anything behind, like my photo of Angel. Then I put out the privacy sign and shut the door.

"Nobody saw me. I was invisible, even with bloodstains on my smock. I threw it away, along with my clothes and the shoes. Nobody missed the smock. Nobody cleaned the room the next day. The Dumpster was emptied the next morning, and the bloody clothes and bottle pieces were buried in a landfill. It was two more days before Skip was found."

"The cops think Craig killed him," Helen said.

"Yes," Cheryl said. She stripped off her gloves. She wasn't crying now. Her voice was quiet, matter-of-fact. "I guess you'll be calling the police."

"Who will take care of Angel if you go to prison?" Helen said.

"My mother," Cheryl said. "She doesn't like my little girl, but she'll do it out of duty."

Angel would live on cold charity, because her mother had lashed out in a moment of rage.

Helen remembered the day she'd caught her husband with Sandy. Her hot red anger had overflowed like lava, and she'd started swinging that crowbar. If she'd connected with her ex-husband's head instead of his SUV, she wouldn't have stopped until she'd beaten the scumbag to death. And she'd had less provocation than Cheryl.

"I deserve to go to jail," Cheryl said. "He had a family."

But they would be well provided for, Helen thought. Skip—or Dean—would have had plenty of insurance. Men like him always did. If Cheryl went to prison, Dean would still be dead and Helen would have created a new orphan. The lake of blood would grow deeper. She would drown in it for sure.

"I'm not calling the police," Helen said.

She picked up the gym bag. It was so heavy, it wrenched her back. "I think there's a hundred thousand dollars here. Take the money. Wait a month, then give Sybil notice, quit your job, and leave town. Go to Ohio."

"You're not going to turn me in?" Cheryl said.

"A jury of women would never convict you," Helen said.

"What about the company it was stolen from?"

Cheryl sounded slightly dazed. "The money belongs to them."

"The telemarketers? They're out of business," Helen said.

"Don't you want any?" Cheryl said.

"That would be stealing," Helen said.

CHAPTER 30

································

Helen did not get justice when she divorced Rob. But she knew how to give it.

Her judgment on Cheryl was just. The abandoned mother had already served seven years of hard labor. Working as a hotel maid was the hardest physical labor Helen had ever done. Add the burdens of caring for a child, dealing with a mean mother, and scrounging for money, and Cheryl had shouldered more than her share of punishment. It was time to set her free from her prison. The robbery money would give Cheryl and Angel the life they deserved.

Helen felt no guilt for covering up the murder of Dean Stamples. The police had told his family that Craig was the killer. They would have closure (how she hated that cheap word). Pinning Dean's murder on Craig wouldn't ruin an innocent man's reputation. Craig had committed plenty of crimes.

With Craig as the killer, the family would never suffer through a murder trial. Dean Stamples would stay the picture-perfect daddy, killed in a senseless crime. His wife and children would not find out that he was a heartless seducer who'd abandoned a pregnant woman.

Helen wondered if his wife already knew Dean's

cruelty. Men like Dean didn't get kinder and gentler as they aged. Maybe she saw her husband's death as a release.

The sun was low in the sky when Helen left work. At the far corner of the lot she was transfixed by a strangely beautiful sight. Three large green iguanas and half a dozen doves were sitting together on the warm asphalt. The iguanas were the brilliant color of a new leaf. Their saw-toothed heads and scaly backs were magnificently grotesque. The largest was nearly four feet long. The gray doves were softly pretty. Beauty and ugliness existed side by side in South Florida.

If Helen believed in signs, she could take this as a blessing on her plan for Cheryl. Helen didn't. Believe, that is. But as she walked home from the Full Moon, she felt at peace for the first time since she'd looked into the lake of blood. She would find Phil as soon as she got home. She'd dress up and they'd go out and celebrate. She'd been moping alone in her room too long. Of course, she couldn't tell Phil why she was celebrating. He thought too much like a cop to understand. But he'd be happy that her mood had finally lightened.

When she got back to the Coronado, Margery had already started celebrating. She met Helen at the gate and handed her a chilled flute of champagne. "Cheers," she said. "You're a free woman."

"What happened?" Helen said.

"Marcella is going to marry your ex-husband on her yacht, the *Brandy Alexander*. The wedding's at sunset tonight."

Helen spilled her drink on the sidewalk. "Ohmigod. That's less than an hour away. We have to do something. We can't let Rob marry the Black Widow."

"Why not? You're divorced. Why should you care?" Margery said.

"I'm not a murderer," Helen said.

"You won't be killing him," Margery said.

The way she said it, Helen wasn't sure if she meant Rob was in no danger—or she was absolving Helen from blame when Marcella killed him.

"What do you know about this Marcella?" Helen said. "Tell me the truth."

"She's someone I've known forever," Margery said. "We were in the secretarial pool together when we were very young. I was already married when I met her. She married the company owner and hit it big. We keep in touch, maybe because we still remember what we used to be and no one else does. We have dinner when she's in town between husbands."

"I heard she was beautiful," Helen said.

"When she was young, she was a knockout," Margery said. "I was cute, but she had the real thing. She looked like Annabella Sciorra, only sexier."

"Tony Soprano's dead girlfriend?"

"Among other roles. The first time, Marcella married for money and got it. She spent the rest of her life trying to marry for love."

"Will she get it?" Helen asked.

"No, she only finds soul mates—other people like herself. When she's disappointed, she moves on to another man."

"After she murders the man she married," Helen said. "She's a self-made widow."

"You can't prove that," Margery said. "Her husbands died from accidents or natural causes."

"But they're all dead. Rob will be number six," Helen said. "He'll die, too."

"Not if he really loves her," Margery said. "If it's true love, he'll live happily ever after."

"He never loved anyone," Helen said. She was surprised by the bitterness in her voice.

"He never loved you," Margery said. "That's not the same thing. This is Rob's last chance to catch a rich wife. Don't you see his potbelly, his thinning hair, his thickening features? His looks are going. He's been cute all his life, but the teddy bear is going to turn into a gargoyle real soon, unless he gets a major infusion of money for a makeover. He won't even be attractive to a woman Marcella's age much longer. Rob can't support himself, not the way he likes to live. Let him try to have the life he wants. Let him go."

But Helen couldn't. She'd wanted to kill Rob. In her daydreams she stabbed, shot and strangled him a thousand times. But she couldn't send him off to be murdered in cold blood. He'd been a lousy husband, but he didn't deserve the death penalty for adultery. She had to warn him. It was a question of justice.

"I have to go to the port," Helen said. "You told me her yacht was there."

"Find your own way," Margery said. "I'm not driving you. I won't help you screw up your life."

"Phil will help me," Helen said.

"Don't count on it," Margery said. "Anyway, he's not home. He and Peggy are picking up something for me at Home Depot."

"You deliberately sent them away," Helen said.

Margery said nothing.

Helen didn't have time to argue. She grabbed her purse and ran for the bus stop on Las Olas. She'd missed the five-thirty bus. The next one wasn't for another forty minutes, if it was on time. A cab. She could take a cab. She checked her purse. She had three dollars and twenty-one cents. She'd lose valuable time walking back to her apartment for her money. Calling a cab would take more time. Port Everglades was what—two, maybe three miles? She started running.

By the time Helen reached Federal Highway, she knew she should have waited for the bus. She was hot and sweaty. Her shoulder ached and her head throbbed. She had to go into the tunnel under the river, and it was dark and thick with exhaust fumes. Cars honked and darted around one another, ignoring the STAY IN YOUR LANE signs. She was coughing and drenched with sweat when she climbed out of the steep—or what passed for steep in flat Florida—tunnel. She ran faster.

Davie. She was at Davie Boulevard, eager to cross the street. Every nerve seemed to burn and crackle under her skin. But the red light lasted an aeon. Entire species went extinct, stars died and mountains pushed up out of the sea while she waited for the light to change.

Finally, it was green. Run! she told herself. Faster! She tried not to think about Rob and all the ways he'd cheated and humiliated her. She didn't want to remember the other women's perfume on his shirts, the lipsticked cigarettes in his SUV ashtray, the single gold earring she'd found wedged in the seat. An earring that did not belong to her.

She tried not to remember the good times, either, the long nights in their four-poster bed. Rob had always been an enthusiastic lover, at least until the end. She remembered the night they were married, when he'd given her a full-body kiss, starting with—

She pulled herself out of the past. Where was she?

At some big intersection. A sub shop was on one corner, a Denny's on another, and a Burger King squatted on a third. She could be at any city intersection in America.

Wait! There was the street sign. It was Southeast Seventeenth Street. The port was down here. All she had to do was turn left.

Again, the red light refused to change. She tapped her foot impatiently. She caught a glimpse of herself in the window of a turning car. She looked like a crazy woman with her wild hair and damp, bedraggled clothes. How was she going to convince Rob he was with the Black Widow? Marcella would be cool, calm and insanely rich. Her ex would never listen to Helen. He'd never listened to her even when they'd been married.

I'll worry about that later. First, I have to find him.

Helen ran past pizza places, burger joints and chicken shacks. By the time she hit Miami Road, the shops and restaurants were richer. The stoplights were kinder, too. They turned a friendly green when she reached the corner. Now she was running past gourmet delis and yacht outfitters. Even the supermarket had an ornamental fountain, like a park. A bus stop bench said, INJURED ON A SEA CRUISE? CALL 1-800-SEASICK.

Yep, she was definitely approaching the port. There it was, the entrance to Port Everglades, where the giant cruise ships docked. Traffic was backed up for nearly half a mile, an impatient line of cars and trucks. Helen skimmed past the lumbering, rumbling machines spewing exhaust. Now she was glad she was on foot. She was swift. She was sure. She was going to make it. Then she got to the guard kiosk and skidded to a stop.

"May I see your identification, ma'am?"

"My identification?" she repeated, panting, trying to catch her breath.

"Your driver's license or passport. I need a picture ID."

Helen didn't have one. She didn't cash checks, use a credit card or an ATM machine. She didn't carry her fake driver's license unless she was actually driving. It was at home in a drawer.

"It's—" Helen said, and stopped. She wanted to tell the guard, "It's a matter of life and death." But she could see his face clouding. She was a disheveled, hysterical-sounding woman with no identification. She would seem crazy—or worse, threatening—if she made a scene.

Helen gave up. She knew it was hopeless. "It's at home. I forgot it. I'll go get it."

The guard turned away from the silly woman to confront a honking truck.

Helen felt hot, scared and furious. This is all your fault, Rob, she thought as she ran back to Seventeenth Street. If you hadn't betrayed me and tried to take all my money . . . If I wasn't on the run from you . . . I would have a car and a driver's license. And you wouldn't be marrying your killer.

Then Helen saw one more chance to save her ex-husband. The megayachts were parked—no, docked, they docked boats, didn't they?— near the Seventeenth Street Causeway. Maybe Helen could get Rob's attention from the monster drawbridge. She started running again.

The great sweep of the causeway loomed before her, a concrete mountain.

Once again she underestimated the distance. Fifteen minutes later she reached the bridge, gasping for breath. She clung to the railing and looked down over the edge at the wide port. All she saw were cruise ships.

Damn! The big yachts must be in the marinas on the other side. Helen darted through the screaming, honking bridge traffic and narrowly missed getting sideswiped by a scooter. "Are you nuts, lady?" the rider screamed.

"Yes!" Helen shouted.

When she got to the middle of the causeway, she saw it was actually two spans, with a gap in between. She'd have to go back down to the bottom and climb up the other side.

There was nothing to do but run. At last Helen was across the wide, white lanes. Her clothes were soaked with sweat and she was gasping like a beached fish. She clutched the railing and looked over the side of the bridge.

Marcella's yacht was there. The *Brandy Alexander* was almost as big as a cruise ship, and a lot better looking. It was sleek white with black glass. The decks were draped with garlands of flowers and white ribbons.

Helen stared at the yacht. There was too much space between the dock and the water. No, wait. The ship was moving away from the dock. It was leaving Port Everglades. It was going to sail under the bridge and be gone forever.

She could see a man and a woman on board, dressed in white and toasting each other with champagne.

"Rob!" Helen screamed. "Rob! Come back! Stop!"

She shouted and waved and called Rob's name, but he only saw the woman in white.

The yacht was sailing under the bridge. They were far below her, but Helen could see her ex-husband wore an ice-cream suit, a white tie and a white rose in his lapel. Margery was right. He did have a potbelly and he was developing a small bald spot. His new bride had unnaturally dark hair, bright makeup and a formfitting white lace suit.

"Rob!" Helen shrieked, and her throat felt like it would burst.

Rob toasted his new bride and looked into Marcella's eyes. He would never see Helen again.

"Rob!" Helen cried once more, but now her voice was a useless croak. She had screamed herself hoarse. Rob hadn't heard her.

She ran down to the end of the bridge and over to the other side, more slowly this time, knowing she could never stop him now. She watched the yacht disappear into the pink glow of the sunset. Then the dark ocean swallowed it.

She knew she was watching her ex-husband go to his death. She knew she couldn't stop him. She'd tried to save him. She really had. Whatever happened to Rob, Helen had a clear conscience.

She wondered if Margery had arranged that, too.

EPILOGUE
....

"**M**issouri Man Killed in Boating Accident near St. Thomas."

Helen dropped her morning coffee when she saw the headline in the newspaper, and the milky brown liquid splashed across the Coronado pool deck.

She'd been getting up early to read the paper before work. For three weeks she had checked every drowning, heart attack and boating accident in the Caribbean, trying to reassure herself that Rob was safe. Helen kept seeing her ex sail into the sunset with his serial-killer wife, oblivious to her warnings.

Helen had never felt so hopeless, or so useless. She didn't even tell Phil that Rob had married Marcella. She didn't know how he would react.

Helen read the headline again, in case she'd made a mistake. Her hands were shaking so badly the newspaper crackled. Rob was dead. She knew it. She didn't have to read the rest of the story. The Black Widow had struck less than a month after her sixth marriage. Rob hadn't lasted as long as the dim-witted bodybuilder.

How did Marcella get away with murder this time? Helen didn't want to know. Yes, she did. The answer was right in front of her. She forced herself to read the story. It was such a small tragedy, only three paragraphs.

"A 26-year-old Joplin, Mo., man drowned when his sailboat collided with a speedboat," the story began.

Helen stopped reading. It wasn't Rob. Some other man had died. Nobody would mistake Rob for a twenty-six-year-old, even if Marcella bought him the best trainer and tailor in the Caribbean. Besides, Rob was from St. Louis.

She sank back in her chaise and closed her eyes, dizzy with relief.

"The son of a bitch is safe," Margery said. "Some other poor slob died in the Virgin Islands. Too bad."

Her landlady materialized by the pool like a purple-clad genie.

"Because a man died—or because Rob didn't?" Helen's voice sounded harsher than she intended. Things had been cool between her and Margery since Helen's frantic dash to the port on the night of Rob's wedding.

"Rob is the right name for that man," Margery said. "He stole your common sense. When are you going to quit checking for news of his death? Has it ever occurred to you that it might not make the papers? Maybe Marcella will push him overboard some night and sail on."

"The crew would talk," Helen said.

"Marcella can buy a lot of silence," Margery said. "Of course, the couple could live happily ever after. You couldn't stand that, could you? What are you really looking for in that newspaper? Which would upset you more: knowing Rob was dead—or alive?"

Helen slammed down the paper and glared at her landlady. Margery had a smug smile and a lit cigarette. Helen wanted to slap that smile off her face. She was tired of Margery's know-it-all attitude. She wished her landlady would wear some other color besides purple. The woman looked like a walking bruise.

"Margery the fixer," Helen said. "You wrap up lives in neat little packages and hand them back as gifts. You even fixed my guilt, in case Rob got himself murdered.

Did it ever occur to you that I didn't want your present? I can take care of my own life, thank you."

"Must be scary now that your ex-husband is gone." Margery took a long draw on her cigarette. "Twice gone. He's remarried and out of the country. Changes everything, doesn't it? Now you'll have to think about what to do with that silver-haired hunk next door. Are you going to marry him, or let some smarter woman run off with him? He won't stay on the shelf forever, you know."

Margery sat down on the edge of Helen's chaise. Helen flapped her hands and waved away the cigarette smoke. She was in no mood for a lecture with carcinogenic side effects.

Margery ignored her. "What about the rest of your life, Helen? Are you going to get yourself a decent job? Buy a phone and quit borrowing mine? Get a bank account and run up credit card debt like a normal American? You can even get a driver's license and own a car. This is your chance to join the grown-up world, Helen. Rob's gone for good. It's over."

"No, it's not," Helen said. "Rob is harder to kill than a sewer rat. He'll be back."

"A rat and a black widow spider. I'll put my money on the spider," Margery said. "And, yes, I arranged the whole thing. So sue me. I saw a chance for you to quit wasting your life. Don't bother thanking me."

"For what?" Helen said defiantly. But deep inside, Helen was glad Rob was gone. Her life had been blighted by her fear of discovery and his relentless greed. Before she went on the run in South Florida, she'd had to live in self-inflicted blindness. She'd worked so hard not to see Rob's infidelities. Now Helen was tired. But she was also angry. The anger won.

"I'm supposed to thank you for making me run across town like a half-wit? I should thank you for letting me shriek my lungs out on that bridge? Sure, I'll thank you—when we can ice-skate on Las Olas in August."

"Have you finished screaming like a fishwife?" Margery said. "You never answered my question. When you read that paper, are you hoping Rob is dead or alive?"

Helen remembered her heart-pounding fear when she saw the news story. "I want him alive. So I can kill him myself."

"You had your chance and blew it," Margery said.

"I did, didn't I?" Helen said. The absurdity finally hit her. A giggle escaped her. Then she started laughing. Margery joined her. They laughed so hard they woke up Phil. He stepped out of his apartment wearing only his jeans, a sight that struck Helen silent. A bare-chested Phil was no laughing matter. He looked like a sun god with his silver hair and bronze skin, only not so frightening. The friendly sun god next door.

"Tell me again you're sorry Rob is gone," Margery said under her breath.

"What's so funny, you two?" Phil said.

"We were celebrating," Helen said. "Rob is married."

"To the Black Widow? Couldn't happen to a nicer guy," Phil said.

"You aren't worried he'll die?" Helen said.

"We're all going to die," Phil said. "I can't think of a pair that deserves to live together more."

"But you were upset when you saw him with Marcella," Helen said.

"I was surprised. Now that I've had time to think it over, I've decided it's better she marry Rob than some innocent."

"Awwwk!" Pete said, and Peggy floated over to the pool area with her green sidekick. The loss of Glenn and her money had given her a remote, ethereal air. She looked like a princess in a tower.

"What did I miss?" Peggy said.

"There's a story on page 4A you ought to see," Margery said.

"It's on 7A," Helen corrected.

"Not that one. The turnpike story. Read it out loud,

Helen. Top left-hand corner. I'll clean up that spilled coffee before it stains the concrete."

"The headline says, 'Fort Lauderdale Residents Arrested in Turnpike Phone Scam.' " Helen's voice trailed off as she looked at the lumpy woman frowning in the mug shot. "Holy cow, it's Arlene. I didn't recognize her without her big earrings and fake smile."

Phil and Peggy crowded in closer for a look at the paper.

"The cops probably confiscated the earrings as lethal weapons," Phil said.

"Of course she's frowning. She's got nothing to smile about," Margery said, as she threw a bucket of water over Helen's spilled coffee. "You're supposed to keep reading."

"It says here that Arlene the shoulder surfer and her accomplice—"

"That's Glenn," Peggy said. "That's him in the other photo. I never realized his eyes were so small. You were right, Helen. Those two were in it together."

"Looks like they're facing federal charges together, too," Helen said.

"I wonder if I can get my twenty thousand dollars back," Peggy said.

"Don't bet on it," Margery said.

Peggy would never see Glenn or his money again. But the pair would get ten years in a federal prison.

"That was your doing, wasn't it?" Helen said to Margery one morning, when the headlines announced Arlene and Glenn's prison sentence.

Margery shrugged so hard she nearly sent her grape off-the-shoulder blouse tobogganing down her chest. "Maybe. I did give the authorities Arlene's car make and license plate number, plus a little information about her lobby hobby."

"Any chance Peggy will get her money back?" Helen said.

"No. Glenn's attorney claims that his client has no money, but I don't think that lawyer does charity cases. I suspect Peggy's money went for Glenn's defense. Not that it did him any good."

"Poor Peggy," Helen said.

"Oh, she'll have another man soon enough," Margery said. "But she deserves a better one. Maybe this time she'll spend her money on lottery tickets."

"But she always loses," Helen said.

"Only thirty dollars a week," Margery said. "That's a lot less than twenty thousand."

The Full Moon survived Craig's death. Once the killer was dead, tourists seemed to think the hotel was safe. Sybil's two-for-one deal killed any lingering doubts.

Even when Sybil stopped the two-for-one coupons, the hotel stayed filled. The cranky hotel owner was really sorry when Cheryl gave two weeks' notice. She needed the hardworking maid.

Helen cleaned rooms with Cheryl for four days before she got up the nerve to discuss the question she could ask no one else: "Why was the money stashed in room 322? I thought the robber stayed in 323."

"He did," Cheryl said. "I think I know what happened. When we clean, we put the rooms of the people who have checked out 'on the latch.' We leave the door open with the safety latch out so we can run in and out without unlocking the door every time. There are no guests' belongings to steal in an empty room.

"I think the robber saw the cops pull into the lot and knew he had to run for it. He couldn't run fast with that heavy bag. He had to stash the hundred thousand dollars someplace quick, and his room would be searched for sure. I'm guessing room 322 was on the latch, and he hid the money under the box spring. Nobody thought to search there, because the mattress pedestal looks solid. I'm sure he planned to send his accomplice back for the cash, except he got killed."

It made sense. And it set off a strange chain reaction. Craig courted Rhonda to get information about the hotel. After that, Helen couldn't count all the ifs ... If Rhonda hadn't been murdered. If Cheryl hadn't worked the third floor that day. If Helen hadn't noticed the Phi Beta Kappa key on Dean's robe, would Cheryl have recognized her old lover?

Helen tried not to think about that. At least some good came out of Dean's death. He'd abandoned his pregnant lover long ago. Now his death provided the money she needed for a better life.

Helen was relieved when Cheryl's good-bye party finally rolled around. She helped decorate the hotel's breakfast room with balloons and streamers. Angel came to the party in a blue dress with a lace collar. Her dark hair was like silk. Angel solemnly shook hands with her mother's coworkers and carefully ate a piece of Denise's double-chocolate cake. She didn't want icing on her party dress.

She watched her mother open the presents—sets of luggage for Cheryl and Angel, including a Barbie suitcase on pink wheels. Angel's eyes shone when she saw that. She gripped the handle and never let go of it for the rest of the party.

Cheryl opened her gag gift, a huge can of whipped cream, to snickers and jokes that bored Angel. The little girl started counting the Cheerios in the Plexiglas cereal bin.

"How many did you count?" Helen asked her.

Angel pointed to the sloping top row. "Do you think that counts as one row? Or does it turn into two when it goes downhill? Where would you stop?"

"Here," Helen said, pointing to a spot halfway down the cereal hill.

"Me, too. But it's confusing. I'm not good at math."

"Lots of people aren't," Helen said.

"I try. It's important to try. I try to have friends, too. But I didn't get invited to Sarah's party last Saturday.

Everyone else went, and I had a new dress. My mom says I'll have friends at my new school."

Helen swallowed the lump in her throat. "Yes, you will," she said, "and you won't even have to try."

Cheryl came over then, looking almost as pretty as her daughter. When she wasn't wearing the shapeless hotel smock, she had a trim figure.

"You've lost weight," Helen said.

"Twenty-five pounds," Cheryl said. "Though you'd never guess it the way I'm shoving cake in my mouth." She hugged Helen good-bye. "Thank you," she whispered.

"Keep in touch," Helen said. She always said that at good-bye parties, but she never expected to hear from Cheryl again.

Helen was wrong. Two weeks later, she got a postcard from Ohio. It said, *Having a wonderful time. Saw our first snowfall. Our Angel made snow angels.* It was unsigned, but Helen knew who'd sent it.

The postcard should have left Helen happy. Instead, she felt oddly restless. She prowled the Coronado grounds late at night, trying to figure out what was wrong. The moon cast silver shadows on the lawn and the palms whispered sweet promises. Helen had every reason to be content, but she wasn't.

On the third night, Phil slipped out of his room and joined her aimless wandering. "Where are you going?" he said in a low voice. Sound carried at night around the Coronado pool.

"In circles," Helen said.

"Literally or figuratively?"

"Yes," Helen said. "I don't know what I want to be when I grow up."

"Why grow up?" Phil said. "You don't have to. Let's run away."

"Where?" Helen said.

"Anywhere you want. I don't start another job for four days. Where would you like to go: New York, Las Vegas, San Francisco, the Caribbean?"

"Not the Caribbean," Helen said.

"Oh, right. How about the Keys? I know a secluded little hotel. I could get us a room. Throw your swimsuit in a bag and we'll go."

"Sybil is shorthanded. I'd be fired."

"And that job would be a big loss?" Phil asked.

"No," Helen said. "I'm sick of working in a hotel. I want to throw my towels on someone else's floor. I want another person to make my bed. I want room service and an ocean view."

"It's three in the morning. If we leave now, we can have breakfast on the hotel patio. It overlooks the water. Leave Margery a note so she'll feed the cat."

"She hates cats," Helen said.

"She'll make an exception for Thumbs. Come on, Helen." Phil held out his hand.

Should she stay or should she go? Helen knew if she refused, she'd be accepting a new life of drudgery.

Man or mop? It was no contest. "To hell with the job," she said. "Let Sybil fire me."

It was eight o'clock when they pulled into the little hotel on the Gulf side of the Keys. The sun was bright in a china blue sky. Purple hammocks with deep pillows swayed between the palm trees. The water was a stunning turquoise.

Phil unlocked the door to a suite overlooking the water. "It's all ours. Nothing to do for four days."

"Nothing?" she said.

"Nothing we can say on a postcard to Mom." He grinned wickedly. "What do you think of the room?"

Helen looked at the white wicker four-poster bed draped with mosquito netting, the charming rocker with the looping arms, and the seashell mirror. The walls were the same turquoise as the water.

"It's very clean," Helen said.

Phil wrapped his arms around her and began kissing her neck. "Is that all you can say about this room—it's clean?"

"I love four-poster beds. The rocker is very cool. The wicker chaise looks big enough for two."

"We can test that," Phil said.

"The view is stunning," Helen said.

"That's more like it. Now you sound like a hotel guest, not a hotel maid. Shall we see if the bed is as good as it looks?" Phil said.

"Love to," Helen said. "But first, let me remove that spread."

Read on for a sneak peek at the next
Dead-End Job Mystery, by Agatha and
Anthony Award–winning author
Elaine Viets. . . .

CLUBBED TO DEATH

Available now from Obsidian

"**D**o you know who I am?" The woman's high-pitched whine sliced through Helen Hawthorne's phone like a power saw cutting metal.

Yes, ma'am, Helen thought. You are another rude rich person.

"I am Olivia Reginald. I am a Superior Club member. I spend thousands at this country club."

Everyone spends money here, Helen thought. That's how they get in. "How may I help you, Mrs. Reginald?" she said.

The power-saw whine went up a notch. "I'm sitting by the pool waiting for you to call. I left a message at eleven o'clock. It took you half an hour to call back."

"I'm sorry, Mrs. Reginald, but we've had a busy morning."

"My husband is *in* the pool but I can't go *in* until I arrange a guest pass for my sister. Laura is staying at our home while we're on vacation. How can I enjoy myself when I have to wait by the phone?"

I'm sitting in a stuffy office on a fabulous January day in South Florida, Helen thought. How can I enjoy myself when I have to deal with you?

"I'll fax the paperwork right now," Helen said.

"I am on vacation. I am not sitting by a fax machine. Just give Laura the guest pass. I said it was OK."

"I can't," Helen said. "I need your written approval. It's for your protection. When you give someone a guest pass, she can charge thousands of dollars to your account. It will take two minutes to fax the paperwork to your hotel."

"Well, hurry up. I'm wasting my vacation on the phone."

Helen fought the urge to say something straight out of high school: "My heart bleeds purple peanut butter."

Instead, she summoned heroic willpower and the memory of her new credit-card bill and said, "Yes, ma'am."

"Do you know who I am?" should be the Superior Club's new motto, she thought. In the old days, the members would have never asked that question. Everyone knew the Prince of Wales, the Queen of Romania, and Scott and Zelda Fitzgerald. For the club's gently bred socialites, the question would have been unthinkable. A lady didn't want to be known outside her circle. The painted mistresses of the robber barons were politely infamous, but always discreet.

The new members were a different breed. They'd invaded the historic Superior Club like a swarm of termites, and they were just as destructive. Helen prayed the balky fax-copier machine was working, or she'd have to listen to Mrs. Reginald's power whine again.

Helen never made it to the copy machine. She was stopped by another club member before she got down the hall. This one looked like he'd escaped from the Early Man display at the natural history museum and hijacked a suit. His forehead was so low it seemed to collapse on his thick eyebrows. Make that eye*brow*. The man had only one, and it was fat and furry. Helen was sure his back and chest were covered with a thick pelt.

The surprise was his hands, which he must have

swiped from a higher primate. They were long and slender and only slightly hairy around the knuckles.

The creature spoke with an educated accent.

"I'm a doctor," the caveman said. "This is an emergency. I need to speak to the department supervisor."

"I'm sorry, she's out to lunch," Helen said. In more ways than one, she thought. "Solange will be back in about two hours. How may I assist you?"

"You can't." His eyes narrowed to feral slits. Helen wondered if he had a stone ax up his sleeve. "I need someone important and I need him now."

The doctor's simian face was hard, but not from exercise or responsibility. This hardness came from too much cocaine, too much money or both. It stripped the softness from the personality, leaving only the nasty "gimme" part. Helen had seen many versions of the doctor at the Superior Club, although none quite so hairy.

He was right. She couldn't help him. She was only a clerk in customer care—a polite name for the country club's complaint department. The other staffers didn't even look up when the doctor screamed at Helen. They'd heard these tantrums before.

"How much longer are you going to keep me waiting?" The doctor's soft, smooth fingers drummed the marble countertop. His brownish hair bristled with rage. "Didn't you hear me? I said this was an emergency."

Maybe someone really was dying, Helen thought. He was a doctor, after all. "Let me find Kitty, our manager. May I have your member number, please?"

"What's that got to do with anything?" the doctor said.

"I can assist you faster, sir."

"I'm a doctor," he corrected her, as if he expected her to bow down and worship him.

Helen dropped Mrs. Reginald's paperwork on her desk and sat at her computer. She looked expectantly at the caveman, her hands hovering over the keys. He capitulated. "My Superior Club number is eight-eight-six-two."

Helen typed in the number and saw the confidential profile.

Doctor Rodelle "Roddy" Dell, breast augmentation specialist, married to Irene "Demi" Dell. Status: Paid in full. See comments on behavior.

A boob doctor. So what was the big hurry? Someone needed an emergency C cup? Of course, there was that young woman at the fitness center who'd picked up too heavy a weight and busted the stitches on her new implants. She had to go to the emergency room. Imagine the embarrassment when you bust your boobs, Helen thought.

"Are you going to stare at the computer all day?" the doctor demanded.

Helen picked up the phone and called Kitty. "Dr. Rodelle Dell is here, and he has an emergency. His member number is eight-eight-six-two."

Helen heard the clack of Kitty's keyboard as she looked up the account. "Oh, no. Roddy the Rod. Is he foaming at the mouth?"

"That would be correct," Helen said. "He says it's an emergency."

"He's too important to have anything else," Kitty said. "Bring him to my office, please. And stay. I need a witness with Dr. Dell."

"This way, doctor," Helen said. She noticed little hairs trapped in the gold and steel links of his TAG Heuer watch. He looked like a well-dressed Cro-Magnon.

And what do I look like, in my navy uniform with the gold Superior Club crest on the chest? Helen thought. A nobody. An eleven-fifty-an-hour clerk. The sad part is, this is more money than I've made in years.

Helen knocked on the door to Kitty's comfortably

cluttered office. She could hardly see her Kewpie-doll boss over the vase of yellow roses, the piles of paper and framed photos of her children. A teddy bear in pearls and a pink dress slouched next to her computer. The only empty space was where the photo of her almost-ex-husband once stood.

"Please sit down, doctor." Kitty indicated a leather wing chair that shrieked "country club." Usually, Kitty's soft voice and big brown eyes disarmed the angriest club member.

The doctor paced in front of her desk, too agitated to sit. Helen stayed in the office doorway, but he didn't notice her.

"I have an emergency," he said. "I need my bill."

"The monthly statements will be mailed this afternoon," Kitty said. She checked the computer. "Yours will go to your home in Golden Palms."

"That's the emergency, damn it. I can't have my wife see that bill."

"Is there a problem, sir?" Kitty said.

He was too upset to correct her about his proper title. "I treated a friend—a young woman—to a day at the Superior Club. She's one of my office staff. Strictly business. It helps her perform better."

Doing what? Helen wondered.

"She needed to relax," the doctor babbled. "Job stress. We had breakfast in the Superior Room before I went to the office. Then she used the pool, the fitness club, had some lunch and bought a few things in the gift shop. The total came to three thousand dollars. I let her put the charges on my club account. My wife, Demi, will completely misunderstand the situation when she sees those charges."

The doctor was sweating, though it wasn't warm in the office. Helen was sure Demi would understand perfectly. That philandering cheapskate. As a club member, the doctor got a 15 percent discount on meals, goods and services if he used his club card. That could be the most expensive four hundred and fifty dollars the doctor ever saved.

"What would you like me to do?" Kitty's dark hair curled innocently around her smooth forehead. Her lips were soft and pink. Only her determined chin gave a clue to her real strength.

"I'd like you to give me the damned bill right now so Demi doesn't see it," the doctor said.

"I'm sorry," Kitty said. "I can't do that. Your wife is a member of this club. I cannot deny her access to her own account, which she shares with you. Club rules require me to send the statement to your billing address. But I can give you a copy now if you wish."

The doctor's fist crashed down on Kitty's desk. The teddy bear jumped and the children's pictures rattled. "I don't want a copy. I want the bill. I'm entitled. I make all the money."

"But it's also her account as long as you two are married," Kitty said.

"That's just it," the doctor said. "She'll give the bill to her lawyer."

"If I were you, doctor, I'd be home tomorrow when your mail arrives. Then I'd explain those charges to your wife. Have a nice day. Helen, please show the doctor out."

Helen had no idea how Kitty managed to defeat him with her soft words, but the doctor realized he was dismissed. He pushed past Helen and slouched out of the office.

The two women waited until he slammed the mahogany door to customer care. "He is a brilliant boob doctor," Kitty said. "But rumor has it the only way he can cop a good feel is through his specialty. Otherwise, he has to give the ladies lavish gifts."

"But why bring his mistress to the club?" Helen asked. "He knew he was going to get caught."

"That's part of the thrill," Kitty said. "You've only

been here a week, sweetpea. You'll see a lot more emergencies like this one. Some idiot brings his bimbo to the club and then tries to cover up his mistake. Do these guys really think their wives won't find out? Demi plays golf and tennis here. One of her friends is bound to spot her husband with another woman."

"If I knew the name of his wife's lawyer, I'd fax the bill to him," Helen said.

"I know Demi," Kitty said. "She's no fool. She won't divorce the doctor during his peak earning years. Besides, he still cares enough to try to cover up. My guess is she'll get another little gift from Harry Winston. When she's finally had enough, Demi will cash in her diamonds for a good divorce lawyer."

Helen saw Kitty staring at the empty spot where her almost-ex-husband's photo used to be. She still loved him. Helen had no idea what caused the split. A single tear slid down Kitty's cheek.

Helen silently shut the door to the office and went back to her desk to unearth Mrs. Reginald's guest pass paperwork. The woman was still languishing by the pool. She'd call back any minute and assault Helen's ears with that power-saw whine.

Jessica, at the next desk, was on the phone with a club member, making placating noises without making promises. It was an art form Helen had yet to master.

"Yes," Jessica said in her hypnotic voice. "Yes, I do understand."

It's her acting training, Helen thought. Jessica sounded so sincere.

She had remarkably pale skin for someone who lived year-round in South Florida, and long straight blond hair that was either natural or a first-rate dye job. Helen really envied Jessica her bones. She had razor-sharp cheekbones, a strong chin and a thin elegant nose.

Jessica's aristocratic face had earned her small, choice parts in the New York theater, but she made her real money selling champagne and pricey chocolates in TV ads. Four years ago, Jessica and her husband, Allan, moved to Florida. Their luck ran out about the same time as her acting career went on hiatus, and she took a job at the club. Fifty was a tough age for an actress. Jessica liked to say, "My greatest role is pretending to like the members at the Superior Club."

Helen heard her finish another bravura phone performance. "Oh, I'm so glad you're feeling better," Jessica said, and hung up.

Helen wanted to applaud.

"I saw the doctor slam out of here," Jessica said. "What was that all about? Was it really life and death?"

"Yes. His death. The doctor's wife will kill him when she gets this month's statement," Helen said. "He's been fooling around with some bimbo at the club."

"They can't even come up with an original sin," Jessica said.

"You actresses," Helen said. "Always complaining about the script."

Jessica laughed. "I'm not much of an actress these days."

"You're resting," Helen said. "Isn't that the phrase?"

"If I get any more rested, I'll be dead."

"If I don't get Mrs. Reginald her guest pass, I'm dead," Helen said.

The Superior Club was like a stage set, Helen thought. The imposing pink stucco buildings were designed by Elliott Endicott, Addison Mizner's greatest rival, in 1925. Critics called Endicott's semi-Spanish architecture derivative. Helen thought it looked like it came from a Gloria Swanson movie. But that was OK. Gloria was once a club member, too. She must have felt right at home with the lobby's thronelike chairs, massive wrought-iron chandeliers and twisted candelabra.

Behind this imposing front was a warren of battered storage rooms and dark passages that reminded Helen of backstage at the theater. They were used by the staff.

But it was the club members who provided the drama. Too bad Jessica was right. The stories were old and trite, and it was easy to guess the endings.

Helen picked her way down the narrow, scruffy back hall of the customer care office to where the fax-copier machine growled and groaned in a former coat closet. The noises reassured her. The beast was working. Mrs. Reginald could receive her forms, sign them, fax them back and then go soak her head.

Helen's office was part of the stage set. She sat at one of five original desks designed by Elliott Endicott, coffin-size mahogany affairs carved with parrots and egrets. Endicott loved parrots and used to have them fly freely around the indoor garden in the lobby, until members complained the ill-mannered birds ruined their clothes and hair.

The drawers stuck on her antique desk and one leg tilted inward. The matching chair, with its original parrot-print fabric, was fabulously uncomfortable. But the view from Helen's window made up for it. She could see the yacht club basin and the seagoing mansions. Today, the place looked like a boat show. Yachts the size of cruise ships were docking. Hunky young crew members in tight white uniforms were scrubbing decks and reaching for ropes.

"What's going on?" Helen said. "Where'd all the yachts come from?"

"It's the party tonight," Jessica said, as if that should explain everything. "Oh, I forgot. You're new. Every year Cordelia van Rebarr, of the Boston van Rebarrs, has a yacht party. She invites some amazing entertainer to perform at a private party for one hundred of her closest—and richest—friends. This year it's Eric Clapton."

"The real Eric Clapton? Not an impersonator? How can she afford him? The man sells out stadiums."

"The man himself," Jessica said. "Some people have money. Cordy is rich. She hires the major names for her parties the way you'd get a DJ."

"Ohmigod. Imagine listening to Eric Clapton at a private party."

"You won't have to," Jessica said. "Customer care helps out at the party. That's why you're working late tonight. We all work on party night. We'll get to hear Clapton. It makes up for what we have to listen to during the day.

"It's the social event of the season. Cordy's guests arrive by private plane or helicopter. About twenty come by yacht. That's twenty yachts at fifty dollars per foot per day. And none of the guests stay on their boats. They all take rooms at the yacht club for another thousand a day."

Jessica broke off and said, "Look at that one. It's huge, even for this crowd. Must be over a hundred feet long."

The flashy white yacht's dark windows gave it a sinister look, like a drug dealer in a white suit and sunglasses. A very successful dealer, Helen thought. The yacht had a helicopter and a swimming pool.

Then she saw its name.

"The *Brandy Alexander*," Helen said. She didn't even realize she'd said the name out loud.

"Now there's a real-life mystery," Jessica said. "Anyone who says there are no good roles for older women doesn't know this story. That yacht is owned by a merry widow somewhere south of sixty. She's had five—or is it six?—husbands die on her. Her first one, the rich old one, died of a heart attack in his eighties. His death may have been natural. After that, she married one young stud after another. Rumor says they played around on her, and shortly after she found out, they died. Sometimes it was a boating accident, or a problem with a dive tank, or a fatal case of food poisoning. She's never been charged with murder, but she's notorious. I can't remember her name, but she's a club member."

"Her name is Marcella," Helen said. "The Black Widow."

"You know about her?" Jessica said. "She's married again. I wonder how long this one has to live."

"His name is Rob," Helen said. Her voice seemed to come from far away. "I tried to stop the wedding, but he wouldn't listen."

"Really. How do you know him?"

"He's my ex-husband," Helen said.

Dead-End Job series from national bestseller

ELAINE VIETS

Shop till You Drop
Murder Between the Covers
Dying to Call You
Just Murdered
Murder Unleashed
Murder with Reservations
Clubbed to Death
Killer Cuts
Half-Price Homicide

"Wickedly funny." —*Miami Herald*

"Clever." —Marilyn Stasio,
The New York Times Book Review

LOOK FOR THE BOOKS BY
ELAINE VIETS
in the Josie Marcus, Mystery Shopper series

Dying in Style
Josie Marcus's report about Danessa Celedine's exclusive store is less than stellar, and it may cost the fashion diva fifty million dollars. But her financial future becomes moot when she's found strangled with one of her own snakeskin belts—and Josie is accused of the crime.

High Heels Are Murder
Soon after being hired to mystery-shop a shoe store, Josie finds herself immersed in St. Louis's seedy underbelly. Caught up in a web of crime, Josie hopes that she won't end up murdered in Manolos...

Accessory to Murder
Someone has killed a hot young designer of Italian silk scarves, and the police suspect the husband of Josie's best friend. Josie tries to find some clues—because now there's a lot more than a scarf at stake, even if it's to die for...

Murder with All the Trimmings
Josie Marcus is assigned to anonymously rate year-round Christmas shops—easy enough, she thinks, until she learns that shoppers at one store are finding a deadly ingredient in their holiday cake. Josie must get to the bottom of it all before someone else becomes a Christmas spirit.

The Fashion Hound Murders
Josie Marcus has been hired to check out a pet store's involvement with puppy mills. When the employee who clued her into the mills' existence shows up dead, Josie realizes that sinking her teeth into this case could mean getting bitten back...

Available wherever books are sold or at penguin.com

Penguin Group (USA) Online

What will you be reading tomorrow?

Tom Clancy, Patricia Cornwell, W.E.B. Griffin,
Nora Roberts, William Gibson, Robin Cook,
Brian Jacques, Catherine Coulter, Stephen King,
Dean Koontz, Ken Follett, Clive Cussler,
Eric Jerome Dickey, John Sandford,
Terry McMillan, Sue Monk Kidd, Amy Tan,
J. R. Ward, Laurell K. Hamilton,
Charlaine Harris, Christine Feehan...

You'

*Read exc
find tour schedu
and*

Subscribe to Pen
and get a
at exciting new t
long before everyone else does.

PENGUIN GROUP (USA)
us.penguingroup.com

Also by Elaine Viets

Dead-End Job Mystery Series

Shop Till You Drop
Murder Between the Covers
Dying to Call You
Just Murdered
Murder Unleashed
Clubbed to Death

Josie Marcus, Mystery Shopper Series

Dying in Style
High Heels Are Murder
Accessory to Murder